MONTREAL NOIR

EDITED BY
JOHN McFETRIDGE & JACQUES FILIPPI

AKASHIC
BOOKS

BROOKLYN, NEW YORK, USA
BALLYDEHOB, CO. CORK, IRELAND

Published by Akashic Books
©2017 Akashic Books

Series concept by Tim McLoughlin and Johnny Temple
Montreal map by Sohrab Habibion

ISBN: 978-1-61775-345-9
Library of Congress Control Number: 2017936118

All rights reserved
First printing

Printed in Canada

Akashic Books
Brooklyn, New York, USA
Ballydehob, Co. Cork, Ireland
Twitter: @AkashicBooks
Facebook: AkashicBooks
E-mail: info@akashicbooks.com
Website: www.akashicbooks.com

ALSO IN THE AKASHIC NOIR SERIES

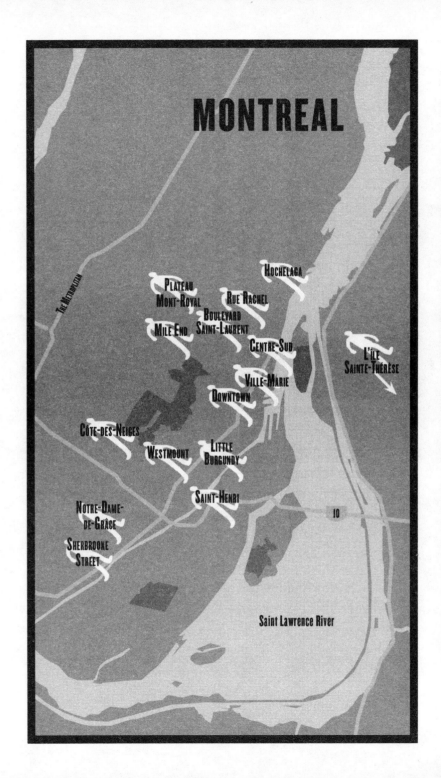

TABLE OF CONTENTS

PART III: ON THE EDGE

INTRODUCTION
A Beautiful Mess

Montreal is an island, both literally and figuratively. It took us longer to put this anthology together than we'd hoped, but that didn't surprise us much. Montreal is one of the oldest cities in North America and seems to be in a constant state of flux, changing its personality every few decades. Today, the city has its own language: Franglais (or Frenglish). Maybe the first word spoken in that language was *noir*.

Noir is Montreal.

It's unsettling, it's subversive, it's palpable, but it's never obvious. Noir is in the shadows. Montreal's long history is dominated by cultures coming together, almost. And cultures coming apart, almost. But always continuing.

When Frenchman Jacques Cartier reached the island of Montreal in 1535, he was met by the inhabitants of the village of Hochelaga, the Saint Lawrence Iroquoians. Yet when Samuel de Champlain arrived seventy years later, the village was gone. Champlain established a fur trading post, which grew slowly, and in 1725, walls were built to fortify the French village.

After the Seven Years' War in 1763, French colonies in North America became British but kept the French civil laws, the seigneurial system, Catholicism, and the French language. Immigration opened up to more than just Roman Catholics and by 1830 Montreal was more Anglophone than Francophone. The city remained that way into the next century, when many people began moving from rural Quebec for jobs in Montreal factories, bringing back the Francophone majority. The first major exodus from Quebec came between 1840 and 1930, when about 900,000 French Canadians left for work in New England (including the ancestors of Jack Kerouac and *Peyton Place* author Marie Grace DeRepentigny, who published as Grace Metalious).

You may be wondering what any of this has to do with the short stories in this volume, but history is everywhere in Montreal. And everything.

Canada claims to be a mosaic of people, as opposed to America's melting pot. In Canada, we don't strive to melt into one identity, we are a mosaic of many identities. Yeah, that's the polite and positive spin we put on the struggle that people have gone through to maintain their own identities, and Montreal is ground zero for that struggle.

Montreal has its own identity. Multicultural, urban, industrial—it's not like the rest of Quebec. For a long time it was the biggest city in Canada, the financial and cultural center, but it was never much like the rest of the country. Only forty miles from the US border, Montreal has always been a popular destination for Americans, though it's definitely nothing like America.

In fact, in 1775, Montreal was the first place occupied by American forces who thought they would be welcomed as liberators. The idea was that French Canadians would join Americans against the British, but as always, Montreal was complicated and unpredictable and things didn't go according to plan. The Americans left in 1776.

In the late 1800s, an Irishman and ex–British soldier named Charles McKiernan, known to all as Joe Beef, ran a canteen that refused service to no one. "No matter who he is, whether English, French, Irish, Negro, Indian, or what religion he belongs to," he told a reporter. In an advertisement, Beef bragged: *He cares not for Pope, Priest, Parson, or King William of the Boyne; all Joe wants is the Coin.* Today, Joe Beef is the name of a trendy restaurant.

In the early twentieth century, Montreal was already a busy port and known as an open city, though it really took off during the American Prohibition in the 1920s. As a popular song of the time said:

> *There'll be no more orange phosphate, you can bet your Ingersoll,*
> *We'll make whoop-whoop-whoopdie night and day,*
> *There'll be photographs of breweries all around our bedroom walls,*
> *Goodbye, Broadway, hello, Montreal . . .*

We have no idea what *your Ingersoll* might be, or why you'd want to bet it, but there was no prohibition in Montreal. There was, however, an Amtrak train from New York several times a day.

During World War II, Montreal was an industrial center, as the Lachine Canal, lined with factories, churned out materials for the war effort. The city was also the place where more than a million raw recruits from Ontario and Western Canada changed trains on their way to Halifax, where they would ship out to European battlefields. Most of these men had at least a few days to enjoy Montreal's nightlife, which was still booming.

After the war, the rest of the province of Quebec, which had always been much more conservative than Montreal, elected a premier whose era became known as *La Grande Noirceur.* The Great Darkness. The Noir. And Montreal was officially "cleaned up." Really, the crime was just pushed back into the shadows.

The postwar boom sent the suburbs spreading out in every direction. New expressways were built, tunnels were forged for a metro system, new bridges were constructed to link the south and north shores to the city, and an island was established in the Saint Lawrence River. The world was invited to experience the island for Expo 67, the World's Fair.

At that time we had something called the *Révolution tranquille*, the Quiet Revolution, which included over two hundred bombs, two political kidnappings (one ending in murder), civil liberties being suspended, and the army being called out into the streets. So it wasn't really all that quiet. But eventually the violence passed, the army left, and Montreal went back to being Montreal.

Back to the noir.

There is a story that the idea for the Pink Floyd song "Another Brick in the Wall" came to Roger Waters during a concert in Montreal. He felt the desire to build a wall between himself and an audience that made too much noise during the quiet parts of the concert—the concert in front of 80,000 people in the cavernous Olympic Stadium. If it's true, it's the only time anyone ever thought of putting up a wall in Montreal. Two referendums on separating Quebec from the rest of Canada have been held, but for all the talk of the "two solitudes" (a term popularized by Hugh MacLennan's 1945 novel of the same name that suggested a lack of connection between Anglophone and Francophone communities), there was never any physical separation inside Montreal. No walls or fences were ever erected. The idea would have been seen as idiotic by everyone in the city, far too obvious. This isn't Berlin or Belfast or Johannesburg or Jerusalem—this is Montreal. Birthplace of Leonard Cohen, Saul Bellow, Michel Tremblay, Maurice Richard, Mordecai Richler, and Oscar Peterson; the setting for great works by Gabrielle Roy, Mavis Gallant, J.D. Salinger, Dany Laferrière, Brian Moore, and many more.

And now, *Montreal Noir*.

Perhaps it's fitting that a collection that brings so many of Montreal's cultures together is noir. Much of Montreal's literary tradition was defined by the two solitudes and most of the works delved deeply into single neighborhoods. Gabrielle Roy's *The Tin Flute* (*Bonheur d'occasion*) in Saint-Henri, Mordecai Richler's *The Apprenticeship of Duddy Kravitz* in Mile End, Michel Tremblay's great plays set on the Plateau, and Yves Beauchemin's *The Alley Cat* (*Le Matou*) reveal some stark differences from before and after the Quiet Revolution. Even the pulp novels of the 1950s written by David Montrose and Al Palmer were set in Montreal. Palmer's *Montreal Confidential* did for the city what the original did for New York City, taking place almost entirely in Westmount and the western half of downtown. Trevanian (Rodney Whitaker) brought an outsider's eye with *The Main* and was one of the first to blend the two solitudes into a single story.

This collection, with voices of both French and English writers, visits many neighborhoods and combines them into something that is, if not totally coherent, at least as coherent as the beautiful mess that is Montreal. Patrick Senécal and Tess Fragoulis take us downtown, where three major universities mix business with shopping. Michel Basilières and Howard Shrier show us how much The Main has changed from the 1950s to today. And how little.

Along the Lachine Canal, Catherine McKenzie takes us through Saint-Henri, Robert Pobi continues to Little Burgundy, and Samuel Archibald reaches the old port and Centre-Sud. On the other side of downtown, Ian Truman's gritty, grimy Hochelaga seems far from the gay village of Geneviève Lefebvre's Ville-Marie, even if it is right next door. Arjun Baju explores the dreamlike Mile End that may not even be real.

The residential neighborhoods surrounding Mount Royal, the Plateau, and Côte-des-Neiges are brought into focus by Johanne Seymour, Martin Michaud, and Melissa Yi.

Montreal is an island, and Peter Kirby walks us to the very edges; Brad Smith escorts us to the Montérégie, off the island but still in the shadows.

Each neighborhood is different and, of course, each Montrealer (Montrealais) is different, making up the pieces of the mosaic of our city. Some are bright and shiny, others are dark and somber, but all have a shadow in the noir.

2017 marks Montreal's 375th birthday and we're pleased to add this collection to the literary life of an amazing city.

John McFetridge & Jacques Filippi
Montreal, Quebec
August 2017

PART I

CONCRETE JUNGLE

RUSH HOUR

BY PATRICK SENÉCAL

Downtown

Translated from French by Katie Shireen Assef

"Slight congestion on South Shore exits. Traffic is flowing smoothly on Jacques-Cartier. Décarie northbound is experiencing delays; there's a broken-down car on the 640. North Shore bridges are all clear."

"Thank you, Hugues. It's 3:35. And now, we turn to the new bill that has just been—"

Hugues takes off his headset, props it on the center console, and turns onto Notre-Dame East, still a clear drive for now. Between the front seats, the two-way radio that communicates with Transport Québec and the highway patrol is silent: a good omen. While he's listening to a traffic update on another station, one of the two cell phones mounted on the dashboard rings. He activates the speaker.

"Traffic, bonjour!"

"Hey, Hugues! How about this weather, eh?"

"Well, it's spring, Diane. Time to get out your golf bag!"

He'd recognized the voice immediately, as he always does with his regulars. This particular resident of Laval has called him every day for the past seven years. Others have been communicating with him since he started this beat sixteen years ago.

"Can hardly wait! Say, Hugues, I'm on Acadie northbound, and it's starting to back up something awful."

Hugues grabs his notepad and jots down a few symbols only he can decipher.

"Already! The 15 must be jammed then."

"Well, screw it. I think I'll stop off at Rockland Centre and wait for it to pass—"

"Diane, no! You'll go on another shopping spree!"

She chuckles softly and they chat for a while, about everything but traffic, then she tells him she'll call again later. Hugues has no idea what Diane looks like, and the same goes for most of his regulars. He likes these odd, distant friendships that develop over the years with people he'll probably never meet, the familiarity that grows between disembodied voices. It's his favorite part of the job, and it's what he'll miss most when he retires. He's only fifty-three, so it'll be awhile, but that doesn't mean he'll get to stay on the road. At most stations, the "car office" has been replaced by a conventional one, full of screens and telephones. Hugues may be the top traffic reporter in Montreal, but he knows that his bosses are keen on this change. Doing this job from an office would be beyond depressing.

He shakes off the thought, takes a call from another regular, makes notes, listens to an update on another station. After ten minutes, still on Notre-Dame East, he answers a call on one of the two hands-free phones.

"Traffic!"

"How *is* the traffic, Hugues? Not too stressful, I hope?" It's an unfamiliar male voice. Probably a first-timer, or someone who hasn't called in a long while.

"Oh, no! It's normal for a Thursday afternoon."

"No shit. You have no clue what stress is, Hugues."

Hugues stops at a red light. An arrogant jerk calling in to

take jabs at his job? He's had two or three of those in sixteen years. The main thing is not to egg him on by getting angry.

"And you—you know what it is, I suppose?"

"Oh, yes. I know."

"And what is it that you do, sir?"

"For the moment, I'm unemployed, and I might be for a long time. But everyone knows my story, Hugues, even you."

"Really? You're a star, then? Well, good luck to you, and good—"

"I used to work in traffic, but a much more complex kind than your little road-bound racket. You didn't want to admit that last year. You belittled my job on the air to make yourself look good."

Hugues frowns. Notre-Dame is starting to jam, so he turns onto Avenue Haig. "What the—what are you talking about?"

"Come on, Hugues, try harder."

The reporter glances down at his dash screen: *Unknown Number.* Of course. "Listen, I'm hanging up now. I have other things to—"

"You're on Haig, then? Perfect, pull over," the man says.

Hugues feels his jaw drop. He looks in the rearview mirror; no one seems to be following him. "But how do you know—"

"I advise you to pull over *now.*"

Hugues wonders if he has finally come across someone a bit more sinister than the average crank caller. He comes to a full stop at the side of the road, ignoring the ringing of his other cell phone. "All right then, who are you?" he asks.

"Try harder, I told you. I gave you plenty of clues."

Hugues clicks his tongue in irritation. He doesn't remember bad-mouthing any reporter a year ago. And what other kind of traffic is this guy talking about? And suddenly, he understands. "Létourneau," Hugues sighs.

"At least you have the decency to remember my name."

It would be difficult to forget—the story had made head lines around the world. Philippe Létourneau, a forty-something Quebecer who worked as an air-traffic controller in New York, had committed a disastrous error by allowing a plane to land on a runway where another aircraft was already parked. The crash had been horrific, causing nearly a hundred deaths.

On the morning after this tragedy, in the middle of the first traffic report of the day, the program host had said to Hugues, on the air, that it was a good thing his job wasn't as complicated and stressful as air traffic.

"Well, sure," Hugues had replied, "but both jobs demand a lot of responsibility, mine as much as his. I have to antici-pate everything that happens on these roads, or drivers'll be furious with me. Sadly, I think this Létourneau lacked profes-sionalism and failed to manage the stress of his job. It's terrible for him, I know, but there's no messing around in this line of work."

What had made him go on like that? Pride? The need to tout the importance of his profession? A little of both, perhaps. Even his bosses had reprimanded him after the pro-gram. Behind the steering wheel, Hugues now smooths back his graying hair, nervous. "Monsieur Létourneau, what I said was ridiculous."

"That's an understatement, Hugues. You make a mistake, people are unhappy. I make a mistake, people die."

"Listen—"

"It's been a year since I came back to Quebec and I still can't find work. Post-traumatic stress it seems. Funny, I have a feeling the condition doesn't affect road traffic reporters."

"Look, I'll apologize on the air if you want."

"No, no, Hugues. I think that for you to truly understand

what an asshole you were, you'll have to live through what I lived through."

Perplexed, Hugues can think of nothing to say.

After a long silence, the ex-controller says in a neutral voice, "I've planted a bomb in downtown Montreal."

Hugues blinks, then raises his voice in anger: "Okay, listen, I understand that you're upset, but that's no reason to make such a sick joke! Even if I know you're lying, I'll have to alert the police, it'll be a shitstorm downtown and—"

"Look to the east."

"What?"

"Look to the east, Hugues. You won't be sorry."

Disconcerted, Hugues turns his head toward an empty lot that stretches out for a good kilometer.

"You're looking? Perfect. Five, four, three . . ." Létourneau whispers.

"But what are you—"

". . . two, one, zero."

For a few seconds, Hugues sees nothing. Then he makes out the plumes of smoke rising several kilometers to the east; a small cloud, pitch black and ominous. Quickly, his exasperation is overtaken by a fear that crawls right up his throat. He turns his pale face toward the cell phone, as if he can see the man on the other end of the line. "What have you done?!! What the—"

"Calm down, Hugues, that wasn't the bomb I was telling you about. This one was much smaller, planted in an abandoned building. I set it off from a distance, so I couldn't see if there were any people nearby, but I'd be surprised if there were."

Hugues moistens his lips, his eyes still fixed on the phone. "I don't believe you."

"Listen to your two-way."

Hugues stares at the black box. After a few seconds of silence, an anxious voice comes on: "Alert, explosion on Rue Jean-Grou, at Pointe aux Trembles. Police are sending a team over right now. There appears to be no victims, but we are awaiting confirmation."

"Do I have your attention now, Hugues?" asks Létourneau.

Hugues squints at the smoke in the distance, breathing faster. His second cell phone rings again. He ignores it.

"Hugues, do I have your attention?"

"Yes."

"Perfect. Get back on the road. Head downtown. If you take another direction, I'll know and I'll set off the bomb."

His hands trembling, Hugues shifts up a gear and accelerates toward Rue Sherbrooke. Dry-mouthed, he manages to ask: "You . . . you've become a terrorist?"

The ex-controller lets out a laugh, at once bitter and amused. "Come on, Hugues. On the Internet, anyone can learn to make a bomb."

"So, what do you want?"

"I've planted a bomb on a street downtown and it'll do much more damage than the one you just saw, especially in the middle of rush hour. It's programmed to go off automatically, but I can set it off whenever I want. So if you call the police, if I see a few too many cops or squad guys hanging around downtown, I set it off. Ditto if I hear you make any hints about a bomb or try to warn people on the air. Is that clear?"

"Why are you warning me?"

"I told you, I want you to live through what I lived through. For you to understand that your so-called stress is nothing compared to what I—"

"You're insane!"

"Call the psychiatrist I've been seeing for the past six months and tell him he botched his diagnosis," responds Létourneau.

"Your plan makes no sense! You're the one who'll set off the bomb. I won't feel what you felt. I won't be responsible."

"If you manage to find it in time."

"What?"

"You're the most popular traffic reporter in the city, Hugues, make the most of it. But to be clear, I won't have you announcing on the air that there's a bomb on this or that street, no, no. That'd be too simple, too amateurish. And it'd just create panic. You've got to behave like a professional . . . manage the stress, understand? So, if you find where it's hidden, you'll say on the air that the street is backed up, or under construction, it doesn't matter, whatever you want, and you'll tell people to take a different route, like you normally do. If you can do that, you'll prove that you can manage the same kind of stress I had to deal with, and I'll deactivate the bomb."

Hugues stays silent for a moment, astounded. He keeps driving on Sherbrooke, then crosses Papineau, now heavily jammed, approaching downtown. "You're insane!" he blurts out again.

"You're repeating yourself, Hugues. I know, it goes along with your job, but still . . ."

"How am I supposed to guess where your fucking bomb is?"

"It's a year ago today since the accident, Hugues. I want the story to play out all over again, same time, same place, but through—"

"The same place? But it was in New York!" Hugues shrieks.

"Oh, please, Hugues, you've never heard of symbolism?"

"Wh . . . what?"

"By the way, don't worry. I synchronized the timer with your station's clock, so we all have the same time down to the second. And I know you give four traffic updates per hour: at three minutes past the hour, then eighteen, thirty-three, and forty-eight. It's 3:44, you've got four minutes before your next update."

"I won't find shit in four minutes!"

"In that case, pray the bomb won't go off before the next one, at 4:03."

Hugues feels his body shaking. "You're screwing with me! You're just trying to scare me to death!"

"After what you've seen over at Pointe-aux-Trembles, do you really want to take that risk?"

The reporter massages his forehead as he crosses Rue Saint-Denis.

"Stay downtown, don't drive anywhere else until it's all over," Létourneau says. "If you go too far in another direction, I'll know."

"You . . . you installed a tracking device under my vehicle, is that it?" Hugues asks with a quiver in his voice.

"Very good, Hugues. And if you try to remove it: *boom!* I'll call you later."

"Wait—"

But the lunatic hangs up. For a few seconds, Hugues hardly notices the heavy traffic around him. *This is a bad joke,* he thinks. *It has to be.* Yet the voice that comes on the radio quickly shatters this illusion.

"Confirmation: a device has exploded on Rue Jean-Grou. One wounded. Police on-site. The area will be closed off for the rest of the day."

Hugues starts to turn his head when a ringing invades his eardrums; it takes him a moment to realize it's his console signal, alerting him that he'll go on the air in less than two minutes. The cars inching forward along Sherbrooke come back into his peripheral vision, just as one of his cell phones rings.

"Tr . . . traffic, bonjour."

"Hugues! It's Paul! Hey, it's not looking good on Papineau Bridge, lemme tell you."

Hugues's hand flutters as he takes his pad and jots down the notes from this regular who's been calling him for ten years, not really seeing what he's writing.

"Okay, Paul, thanks . . ."

"You don't seem too cheery, Hugues."

"No, it's just . . . I've got a cold. Thanks, Paul." He disconnects, slips his headset on, and the voice of the on-air host fills his left ear. *Don't say anything about a bomb, or danger. Stay professional.* A wave of nausea makes him grimace as he waits for his cue.

"Now, the traffic update with Hugues Nadeau."

For a second that lasts an eternity, the reporter is incapable of making a sound.

"Hugues?" the host calls out.

"Yes, Valérie. Traffic is getting heavier downtown. Papineau Bridge is gridlocked. The broken-down vehicle on the 640 has been removed, but the jam has already formed . . ." He goes on like this for thirty seconds, managing to keep his voice natural, only a little stiff-sounding, though he wants to scream his lungs out with every word. Afterward, Valérie asks him if he has any updates on the explosion at Pointe-aux-Trembles. Hugues licks his lips several times. "Ah, well . . . nothing too serious it seems, but the area around Jean-Grou is closed, so drivers should avoid it."

"Thank you, Hugues. Now, we turn to some new film releases . . ."

Hugues removes his headset and turns onto Union, a small avenue, almost empty. There, he parks close to the curb, opens the passenger-side door, and vomits on the asphalt. He sinks down into his seat and takes several deep breaths. Panic washes over him, but he has to stay calm and lucid, he simply has no choice. *Think. Hard and fast.* If the bomb is timed to go off before the next traffic update, it's all over.

He voice-dials a number on one of the two cell phones and Muriel, a fact checker for the program, answers. "Muriel, I need you to find me some information on the plane crash that happened in New York last year."

"Why? You want to talk about it on the air?"

"It's . . . it's been a year today and I might want to fit in a reference to it, yes. Perhaps mention the exact time of the accident."

"What? Why? I might not have time, Hugues, we're in the middle of a show, you know how it is."

"Just do what you can, okay?"

He hangs up, shaking his head. He's an idiot to count on Muriel, she's clearly much too busy. He takes out his personal cell phone, connects to the Internet, and brings up the Google home page. Shit, he was never good with the keypad, his thumbs are too slow. And his next update is in twelve minutes.

Finally, he finds an article that appeared in *La Presse* last year, the day after the accident, and starts reading: *TWO DELTA AIRPLANES CRASH IN NEW YORK. Yesterday, at 4:25 p.m., Philippe Létourneau, an air-traffic controller at John F. Kennedy Airport, changed the course of this city's history . . .*

He stops reading: 4:25! The bomb will go off in thirty-one minutes! That leaves him two more traffic updates. He breathes a little easier. But now he has to find the spot. The bomb obviously can't be in New York, so where? Trudeau Airport? It has to be there. But not in the building itself, no. Létourneau said he'd planted it on a street. What's the name of that road that leads to the airport? That narrow road that everyone's complained about for years?

He grabs his personal cell phone again and brings up Google Maps, indifferent to the ringing of another phone. He zooms in as close as possible on the area surrounding the airport and scans the road names in panic.

There are two possible routes. He knows that one is more commonly used than the other, but which? On the map, even in satellite mode, it's not clear. He brings his face up close to the phone, blinks several times . . . Yes, that's the one. Boulevard Roméo-Vachon. Now, what's the alternative route? He grabs his notepad, his eyes darting from screen to paper, and writes, crosses out, rewrites.

One of the hand-free cell phones rings and Hugues glances at it in exasperation. He reads *Unknown Number* on the dash screen. Létourneau? He connects. "Yes?"

"Are you sweating yet, Hugues? I'll bet your idea of stress is already *quite a bit* different," Létourneau taunts through the speaker.

"I figured it out! I found the time and place! It's at—"

"Tell it to your listeners, Hugues, not to me. And I see you've been parked for almost ten minutes. Get driving."

"I had to look up—"

"Act like a pro and drive!" Létourneau yells.

Realizing that the slightest annoyance could cause this lunatic to set off the bomb, Hugues hurries to get back on the road. His hands are so damp that he has to wipe them on his pants before gripping the steering wheel.

The voice on the other end of the line softens. "Perfect. Now stay downtown."

"Can't you tell me if I—"

But Létourneau has already hung up. Hugues bangs his fist on the dashboard and curses. He rubs his left eye, then glances at the clock. 3.59. On the air in four minutes.

A cell phone rings. *Goddamn these drivers and their traffic tips!* Yet if he doesn't keep doing his job as usual, he'll deliver a half-assed update. And Létourneau had ordered him to stay professional to the end. *Manage the stress!* He lets out a joyless laugh and activates the phone.

"Hey, Hugues, I didn't stop at Rockland Centre after all!"

It's Diane again. Hugues tries to make his voice sound normal. "That so, Diane?"

"Pffft, no, I've been spending too much money lately anyway! You know, last week I bought my little . . ."

He barely listens, his head buzzing, as he answers in monosyllables. Finally, Diane tells him that the 15 is now backed up from the 440; he thanks her and disconnects.

Turning west on René Lévesque to join the long line of bumper-to-bumper cars, he takes another call from a regular who cracks a few jokes with him. And Hugues laughs too, a laugh that tears at his chest and makes his lips twitch as he scribbles in his notepad, his vision blurring.

At 4:02, he puts on his headset. A minute later, Valérie's voice fills his ears: "Well, Hugues, the traffic's getting heavier, I imagine?"

Don't go to the airport! Don't take Boulevard Roméo-Vachon, there's a bomb! Obviously, he says none of these things. He clears his throat and in his normal voice . . . *professional* . . . he starts his update: "Yes, Valérie, it's pretty slow all around. I've just been told that Roméo-Vachon is closed—the boulevard that leads to Trudeau Airport. I don't know why, but it's closed. I suggest taking Jacques-de-Lesseps—but via Chemin de la Côte-de-Liesse, not Autoroute Côte-de-Liesse."

"So, if you don't want to miss your flight, take Autoroute Côte-de-Liesse to Jacques-de-Lesseps—"

"No, no, no! Not the autoroute, the chemin!" Hugues cuts in impatiently. "Take Chemin de la Côte-de-Liesse, or you'll end up on Roméo-Vachon!" He blurts out these last sentences a bit too passionately, and the host stammers a disconcerted, "Right, thanks."

Turning north on Atwater, Hugues grinds his teeth. Goddamnit, he has to stay calm. He continues his update in a smooth voice, summing up the situation on the other main roads of Montreal. "And don't forget," he concludes, "for those heading to the airport, avoid Roméo-Vachon."

"Thank you, Hugues. Now for the weather, with . . ."

Covered in sweat beneath his spring jacket, Hugues takes off his headset and sighs as if a hundred kilos had just been lifted off his shoulders. *I did it! I figured it out!* He'd solved Létourneau's little puzzle, hadn't he? As he drives past the old Forum, one of the cell phones rings: *Unknown Number.* He answers, feverish.

"You did that like a pro, Hugues," Létourneau says, a note of amusement in his voice.

"So I guessed right, then? I told people to take a different route. Now you'll deactivate the bomb?"

"If you're right, yes."

"Well, am I right or not?" Hugues asks testily.

"You'll know when the bomb is supposed to go off. If it doesn't, you were right. Otherwise . . ."

"But . . . but why can't you just tell me now?"

"So that you can experience stress, Hugues. Real stress. To the very end."

The lunatic hangs up again and the reporter stares at the cell phone, then grabs it and hurls it to the back of the car. He regrets it immediately. *Shit, that's the Bell Mobility phone!* Létourneau probably has a phone on the same plan and won't be able to contact him if his is broken. Hugues pulls over, reaches back to grab the cell phone, and checks—it still works. Reassured, he sets it on its stand and slowly smooths back his hair, letting out a sigh that quickly turns into a gasp. He straightens up—if he stays parked too long, Létourneau won't be happy. He gets back on the road and heads east on Sherbrooke. He feels ridiculous driving in circles like this, but does he have a choice?

He starts to wonder: *Could I have guessed wrong?* Hiding the bomb on a street near the airport seems to fall right in line with Létourneau's logic, with his desire to be as faithful as possible to last year's events . . .

A cell phone rings. Grudgingly, he answers. It's a woman named Juliette who reports in an almost giddy voice that she's calling for the first time. She starts telling him about her daily commute and Hugues is about to cut her off when she mentions that there's a broken-down car in the Lafontaine Tunnel. Hugues thanks her, disconnects. He could call the cops and warn them of a bomb near the airport, couldn't he? Létourneau told him that if he saw too many cops downtown, he'd set it off, which means that the lunatic must be downtown, not at the airport. So he wouldn't be able to see the cops arriving there . . . He stops at a red light at the corner of Guy, frowning. This thought reminds him suddenly of the exact words Létourneau had used: he'd planted a bomb not just on any street in Montreal, but on a street *downtown*—he'd said that very clearly.

Hugues screams again, pounding his fists on the steering

wheel. How could he have been so stupid to forget this detail? Besides, Roméo-Vachon isn't big enough for an explosion to cause as many deaths as the crash. He has to start over from square one.

A cell phone rings, the indifference of its tone unbearable. The name of a regular comes up on the dash screen. "Fuck you!" Hugues spits in the direction of the phone.

He turns on Mackay, furiously massaging his right temple. He thinks through the details of last year's tragedy and tries desperately to make connections with the present, with Montreal. At least he got the time right: 4:25. That leaves him seventeen minutes, and ten minutes before his next update. He'll never make it in time. He stops at a stop sign and squeezes his eyes shut, concentrating with all his strength. *The two planes crashed in New York . . . There's no Rue New York in Montreal, so it can't be that . . . What, then?*

Startled by the sound of several car horns blaring behind him, he accelerates and turns east onto Sainte-Catherine. The traffic is dense, he can drive slowly and think. But his goddamn cell phone rings again and to save face from his blunder on the air, he has to answer.

"Hey, Hugues, where'd you get that info about the airport?"

It's Denis, a traffic reporter from another station, the only other one who still works from his car. Denis tells him he had no problem on Roméo-Vachon and that Hugues's last update caused total chaos on Jacques-de-Lasseps. Hugues mumbles that he'd obviously gotten a bad tip.

"Huh. Well, it happens!" Denis says. "Hey, pretty nice out, isn't it? Soon we'll be seeing all the ladies strolling around down—"

"Sorry, Denis, I've got to go." He hangs up, but his other cell phone rings.

A caller gives him an update on Champlain. When it rings again a minute later, he ignores it; he can't think if he's constantly being interrupted. He turns onto Union, sweat running down his face. Less than four minutes before his next update. And it'll be the last one before 4:25! It's not possible. It's just not possible!

He starts to moan involuntarily, racking his memory as he drives on autopilot, not registering when he turns west onto René-Lévesque, barely seeing the road or the cars in front of him. *Crash in New York . . . Two airplanes . . . What airline was it, again? He'd read it earlier . . . Delta, yes . . . Shit, there's no Rue Delta in Montreal.*

But there is Hôtel Delta—downtown.

The buzzing in his brain stops all of a sudden. *Could the bomb be planted there?* Létourneau said it was on a street. *Where is the hotel, exactly? On Avenue du Président-Kennedy . . . and the airport in New York was John F. Kennedy Airport!*

This revelation arrives with such intensity that for a moment he sees nothing but a blinding white light. A shock brings him back to reality, propelling him forward with such force that his nose collides violently with the steering wheel. Dazed, he realizes he's hit the car in front of him. The driver leaps out of his Lexus, curses, marches up to Hugues's vehicle, and starts kicking the passenger door.

Hugues jumps out to calm the guy who, seeing the reporter's bloody nose, stops kicking, but remains furious.

"Jesus Christ, learn to drive!" the guy says as he eyes the logo on Hugues's car. "And you're a traffic reporter? Bravo, genius!"

Hugues apologizes, says that the damage seems minor, and manages to remain polite even if he wants to tell the guy to fuck off; but the latter insists they call the police. Other drivers pass by slowly and cast jeering looks at the two of them.

With shaky hands, Hugues holds out the station's business card to the man. "Call them, they'll . . . It's one of the largest radio stations in Montreal, they'll take care of it!"

The guy stares at him skeptically and, grumbling, finally agrees to leave.

Hugues hurries back to his car, gets behind the wheel, starts driving again, checks the time: 4:20! He missed his 4:18 update! All because of that fucking imbecile.

A cell phone rings. He answers, sure that it's Létourneau.

Damnit, it's Diane. "Well, Hugues, I should have stopped at Rockland after all, my girlfriend just called to tell me there was a sale on—"

He disconnects, cursing. Then he dials a number and the voice of his program director comes on.

"Where'd you go, Hugues?"

"Technical problem, but I'm back! You can put me on the air now."

"That's okay. We can put you back on at 4:33," the director says.

"No! Listen, Simon, it's a circus downtown, I have to . . . I have to go on!"

"Come on, it can wait."

The reporter glances at the clock on his dashboard: 4:21 p.m. Four minutes before the explosion. "No, it can't! I need to go on right away!"

"Hugues, listen, you—"

"Simon, it's the first time I've ever asked you this and I swear it'll be the last, come on, just put me on the air!"

Simon sighs, baffled. "Okay, in thirty seconds, after Gaétan's sports brief."

Hugues disconnects, puts on his headset, wipes the blood flowing from his nose, stops at a red light. Chest heaving, he stares at the clock as if looking into the eyes of a dangerous beast. 1.23.

Valérie's voice finally comes on: "And now, back to our friend Hugues with his traffic update—"

"I've just been informed that Avenue du Président-Kennedy is closed near Hôtel Delta! Completely closed!" the reporter interrupts in a jumpy voice. "I suggest taking Maisonneuve, via City Councillors or de Bleury. It'll be much faster! Okay? Is that clear? Président-Kennedy closed near Delta!"

"Very well, thanks, Hugues . . . And for the rest of the traffic?"

"Eh? Ah, well . . . let me . . ." He grabs his notepad, disoriented, and turns north on Peel. "It's . . . There's still heavy traffic on the 15 and the 640; Lafontaine Tunnel is backed up from Anjou; for the other South Shore bridges, expect half-hour delays, except for Victoria, which isn't too bad for now."

Valérie thanks him again and he tosses his headset onto the passenger seat. He parks on the side of the road and keeps his eyes on the clock, his heartbeat pulsating in his head like a death knell. 4:24 p.m. . . . *My God, please tell me I didn't guess wrong, I beg you* . . . 4:25! He holds his breath.

Hugues hears nothing but the reassuring hum of traffic. No explosion, no loud or unusual sounds. He turns his head in the direction of Président-Kennedy, at least a kilometer away: no black cloud on the horizon. He keeps studying the sky for a moment, then looks back at the clock: 4:26 p.m.

He starts to chuckle, a nervous, ambiguous chuckle, punctuated by convulsive sobs.

A cell phone rings: *Unknown Number*. Hugues switches the speaker on.

"You were late with your update," says Létourneau.

Hugues wants to tell him he can shove his bomb up his ass, but he knows that the lunatic could reactivate it. "I did it! It's 4:27 and the bomb hasn't gone off!" he crows.

"When people realize that Avenue du Président-Kennedy wasn't closed, they won't be happy . . . You'll lose your luster, my poor Hugues." Létourneau laughs. "I was sure you'd tell them to take Maisonneuve via City Councellors or de Bleury. I've been listening to you for a year, Hugues, I can predict every piece of advice you give."

"I figured it out, damnit, that's all that matters!"

A long silence, then Létourneau calmly murmurs, "Drive to Rue Sherbrooke, just east of Saint-Marc. I think it'll interest you."

Hugues winces. "Why? You . . . you aren't gonna cheat me, are you?"

"I don't cheat, Hugues. Come on, hurry." And he hangs up.

Hugues hesitates, then gets back on the road, torn between curiosity and anguish. While he drives toward Sherbrooke, three different calls come in, but reading the regulars' names on the dash screen, he doesn't answer. He turns right on Sherbrooke and weaves through the slow traffic; confused, angry, and intrigued, all at the same time. *Does Létourneau want to meet him? To convince him not to warn the cops? Is he really that insane?* His cell phone rings: *Unknown Number. It must be him.* "Traffic?" he says.

"You're on your way?"

"I just crossed Lambert-Closse, I'll be there in a minute. What do you want, Létourneau?"

"The point was for you to live through every stage of what I experienced."

"And I did, so?"

"No, you didn't. You didn't feel guilt. I did, Hugues. I sent more than a hundred people to their death."

"Goddamnit, Létourneau! The *deal* was I had to guess where you hid the bomb!"

"Yes, that *was* the deal."

Hugues passes Saint-Marc when out of nowhere a pedestrian steps off the sidewalk and plants himself in the middle of the street, in front of the vehicle. Hugues slams on the brakes, but the stranger, who must be around forty, long-haired and shabbily dressed, doesn't move. A cell phone against his ear, the stranger stares at the reporter with an unsettling intensity. In a second, Hugues realizes who it is and a shiver runs through him. He calls out in a voice both victorious and enraged, "I did what you asked me to do, Létourneau! Admit it!"

The man smiles, then moves his lips close to his phone. Hugues hears Létourneau's voice in his ear: "Well, if you say you succeeded, then it's all over." As he says this, the ex-controller takes a pistol out from under his belt, points the barrel to his temple, and pulls the trigger. Hugues's scream is muffled by the sound of the explosion.

Cars stop in the middle of the street and cries of shock erupt. While a crowd gathers around the body, Hugues remains frozen, gripping the steering wheel. He gets out of his vehicle slowly, but stays close to it. The crowd blocks his view of Létourneau's body. Almost all the cars on the street have stopped, and curious bystanders arrive from all sides: Sherbrooke is in total chaos.

You didn't feel guilt. I did, Hugues. I sent more than a hundred people to their death.

Is that why he killed himself? To make Hugues feel responsible? Well, his plan failed. All the reporter feels is a great sadness. And yet, he can't help but sense another meaning behind Létourneau's words, though he doesn't know what.

His console alarm tells him he'll be on the air again soon. Shaken, he gets back in the car and puts his headset on. Then, at 4:33, he starts the update in his normal, professional voice, but a bit more restrained than usual: "Valérie, a terrible event has just taken place on Sherbrooke, at the corner of Saint-Marc—a man has killed himself, in the middle of the street." The host exclaims in surprise while Hugues continues: "Obviously the street will be closed for a while. Since the Collège de Montréal campus is just north of Sherbrooke, drivers will have to take a detour to the south. Those heading east on Sherbrooke can take Lincoln to Guy, those heading west can take Maisonneuve."

He gives two or three directions for the other bridges, then disconnects. He rubs his eyes and lets out a long sigh, his body drained of strength, more tired than he's ever been.

Policemen start to appear from all over, and one of them approaches Hugues's vehicle. He gets out again, introduces himself, and rambles off the whole story in a minute. Stunned, the officer listens, then says he'll send a team to Delta immediately to remove the bomb, even if it is deactivated.

"You stay here, all right?" the cop shouts as he walks away. "We'll have to question you further on this whole affair."

Hugues sits back behind the steering wheel, his eyes closed, indifferent to the chaos that reigns on the street. A cell phone rings. He wants to ignore it, but he glances at the dash screen and sees that it's Muriel, the fact checker. He answers.

"Sorry it took me so long to find what you asked for, Hugues, but like I told you, I'm swamped."

"That's okay, Muriel." Hugues sighs weakly, closing his eyes again. "I don't need it anymore."

"You sure? I have all the information right here: the controller was named Létourneau, the crash took place at 4:40 . . ."

Hugues opens his eyes. "You mean 4:25."

"Eh! No, no. Oh, I understand: 4:25 was when Létourneau told the pilot he could land on the runway."

Hugues sits up straight. Then he remembers the beginning of the article he'd read earlier: *Yesterday, at 4:25 p.m., Philippe Létourneau, an air-traffic controller at John F. Kennedy Airport, changed the course of this city's history . . .* Shit, if only he'd read the rest of the article, he would've realized that it was Létourneau's call, and not the crash, that had changed the course of history. The accident had happened fifteen minutes later. Hugues checks the time: 4:38. Panic threatens to overwhelm him again, but he forces himself to stay calm: even if he got the time wrong, he still found the right spot. Létourneau must have deactivated the bomb before killing himself. He'd promised him he wouldn't cheat, after all. But why hadn't he told him he'd guessed correctly? Hugues starts sweating again.

"What else did you find?" he asks Muriel.

"Well, both planes belonged to Delta Air Lines, the one on the runway had arrived from Miami twenty minutes before, and the other was coming from Lincoln, Nebraska."

The word *Lincoln* echoes in the reporter's mind. He'd said the name of this street on the air a few minutes ago . . . And what had Létourneau told him earlier? *I've been listening to you for a year, Hugues, I can predict every piece of advice you give . . .*

In his last update, he'd told drivers to take Lincoln. Suddenly he understands: Létourneau hadn't wanted him to feel responsible for his suicide, but for something much worse. The reporter swallows the scream that rises in his throat and spits into the cell phone: "Tell Valérie to put me back on the air, right away!"

"Oh come on, not again! You pulled this on us earlier and it wasn't even urgent!"

"Damnit, Muriel, it's . . ." But what's the point? Létourneau is dead, he can't deactivate the bomb. He'd killed himself before the reporter could deliver his last update, the one that would've warned people of the explosion. He'd killed himself because Hugues was sure he'd succeeded.

If you say you succeeded, then it's all over.

He lets out a gasp so disturbing that Muriel starts to ask, "Hugues, are you . . ."

The sound of the explosion is distant, but loud enough to drown out the voice of the fact checker. Hugues's cell phone slips out of his hand and flies to the back of the vehicle; the earth shakes for a moment as he watches the hysteria rising around him. And he sees, from two hundred meters away, the immense black cloud rising and spreading across the sky, all the way to Rue Sherbrooke, toward him, filling his nostrils, invading his soul, where it will remain for as long as he lives.

SUCH A PRETTY LITTLE GIRL

BY GENEVIÈVE LEFEBVRE
Ville-Marie

Translated from French by Katie Shireen Assef

The Girl

The kid had been easy.

The heavy door of the former convent creaked open at dusk. Amid the swarm of novice ballerinas rushing down the stone steps, the little one emerged, bareheaded, coat unbuttoned, into the biting February wind.

Beautiful like her mother, she was. Vain like her mother too. A doll who would rather freeze to death than pull a stocking cap over her silky blond bun. How stupid they were, little girls, always wanting to please, to entertain, begging to be *watched*. Didn't they know they were headed for a massacre? That in a few short years they'd end up on the scrap heap?

The blond child scanned the crowd of silicone-breasted mothers and exhausted Filipina nannies, and seeing the hand that waved at her, she ran cheerfully toward it. All that was left was to pluck her like a little spring crocus.

"Marisa's not coming to get me today?"

No, not Marisa. Marisa had been neutralized with vermouth and a handful of sleeping pills—and *out* went the nanny. It had sufficed to let the pills dissolve in the bottle she nipped at all day; Marisa had slumped in her chair like a wheel of Camembert left out in the heat. When she woke up—*if* she woke up—she'd be out of a job. Too bad. What mattered was to get everything done before the parents reported the girl's disappearance.

"Marisa's busy with your brother."

An incredulous look from the girl. "My brother's at his friend's house."

"Your *brother* threw one of his tantrums. Marisa had to go pick him up."

Impromptu lies were always the best.

"What a moron," the kid retorted, jumping at the chance to insult the brat who plagued her seven-year-old existence. She had a viper's tongue, which she got from her father. She knew how to smile in your face and stab you in the back. Cute as she was, her shitty genetic baggage was showing.

The door of the SUV slid open and the kid held out her arms, letting herself be pulled in, already comforted by the warm breath of the machine. Ten minutes later she was asleep, her frail body wiped out by the same cocktail as her nanny. When she woke up the next morning, it would be easy to distract her until the plan was fully executed. A plan whose success hinged on one simple fact: there was no escape route.

Géraldine

Géraldine Mukasonga wakes in the freezing dawn to the sound of her phone ringing. A moment later, David Catelli's voice is in her ear.

"Gérald, it's Dave. I'm coming to get you. We have a body."

No *hello* or *how are you*—David didn't bother with niceties. They'd catch up later, in the Dodge, if there was time between the briefing and the crime scene.

Géraldine takes a shower and dabs her neck with a few

drops of a Serge Lutens perfume, which she wears as a courtesy to offset the smell of death. She pulls a merino wool sweater on over her head, enveloping her soft skin in a cocoon of warmth. She fastens her duty belt around her waist, reassured by the weight of the Glock against her hip, and turns on the alarm system that now protects only her bed, coffeemaker, and books. Her apartment has been bare since the breakup, as unsettling as a blank page when no words will come.

Anne-Sophie had left with all she could fit into her truck, everything down to the bottle opener. Nothing remained of their untimely love affair, only an unfortunate truth: Géraldine's promotion to sergeant detective had gotten the better of their relationship. It wasn't just men who struggled with a woman's independence.

Géraldine rushes down the stairs and climbs into David's Dodge Caravan with a quick grunt of relief, as if coming home at the end of an exhausting workday. Putting the van in gear, David casts a sidelong glance at her.

"That bad?" she asks.

"That bad."

He doesn't ask her about the breakup. Not yet. For the thousandth time, David tries to tell himself that he's used to her beauty, to the glow of her skin, the delicate curve of her neck, the fluidity of her movements. But when Géraldine smiles at him, he wants to die.

"What do we have on our hands this morning?"

"A body full of bullets, found in a restaurant parking lot on Rue Ontario."

"Who called it in?"

"A couple of swimmers training at the pool nearby, stopped at the Palace for lunch."

"The Palace?"

"It's the name of the restaurant."

Géraldine glances at her watch. The truck's dirty windows block out the already weak light of dawn struggling through clouds.

"Hell of a time for a swim," she says.

Yes, Géraldine, people are crazy. They wear swimsuits in the dead of winter, and they have passionate feelings for inaccessible, forbidden women. If one day I had nothing left to lose and I stopped being afraid of hurting innocent people, I'd tell you what I feel when I see the light reflected in your dark-brown eyes. That would be a day of darkness, a day of despair.

David steps on the accelerator, defying the traffic light that changes to burnt orange.

Krazynski

It's barely daylight and the first one, that dirty pig, has already been wiped off the map, executed point-blank in a parking lot. Who'd have thought that revenge could be so easy?

Raymonde Krazynski puts up more of a fight. As soon as the barrel of the gun presses into her soft, fat belly, she starts running at an astonishing speed for a bowlegged Ukrainian journalist. Her breath is ragged from emphysema, and she flails about like a shrew, screaming and stumbling over an orange tabby cat. Krazynski tries to crawl away, desperately grasping at the latch of the glass door that opens into the garden. She wants to live.

It's odd: someone who's assassinated so many people through her journalistic slandering has such a sudden and scared impulse to survive.

"Yes, but they were words! Just words!" cries Krazynski. "You can't compare, please, I beg you, I was only doing my job—"

The bullets shatter her skull and cardiac muscle—one can't call what she had a heart. Behind Krazynski the glass door splinters into a thousand fragments. It's pretty, all that red and gray on the snow. How delicate death is, in the end. On the paved curb of the cul-de-sac, the tabby cat watches as if waiting to be alone with its mistress's corpse, to better devour her.

Him

The snow crackles beneath Géraldine's red Converse. Her coat is unbuttoned, her lovely head covered with a fur chapka hat; she faces the cold like an enemy from whom one must hide any sign of fear.

Géraldine and David duck beneath the yellow-and-black tape, weaving their way through a cluster of forensic technicians. Above the workers' heads are clouds of gray mist rising like Native American smoke signals. The body is near the restaurant's side entrance, between a dumpster, cement wall, and a mountain of hardened snow plowed to the edge of the parking lot. The sky is the same hazy pink as the froth on the lips of the corpse, drowning in its own blood.

The first thought that comes to Géraldine's mind is the crime scene's vulnerability. The killer had to act in a matter of seconds or risk being caught.

"A professional," David says.

"Or not," Géraldine mutters.

The corpse is laid out stiff on a slab of ice wearing an un-buttoned Armani blazer. The blood blooms over a lavender polo with its logo of a jockey in midswing. And then David sees what Géraldine is looking at now: the pants, unzipped, reveal boxers stained a deep red, suggesting a violence too intimate to be anything other than the work of a professional killer.

"Guys are still wearing Ralph Lauren, then?"

David nods. "Not so much in this part of the city."

Rue Ontario is Montreal's epicenter of misery, a street that lacks even the audacity to be a bit ethnic or colorful, qualities that would at least put a multicultural sheen over its dejection. Rue Ontario has remained filthy and white after all these years, pallid as an old candle stump left in an abandoned church.

Dr. Attila Mihalka approaches Géraldine and David, rubbing his hands together, beaming, icicles hanging from his long mustache. In theory, the forensic doctor is retired, but since his replacement is a wimp always teetering on the edge of burnout, the old Hungarian is back on the job, and he's never been in such a good mood.

Géraldine points at the corpse's bloody boxers and asks: "Am I dreaming, Doc Attila, or was he . . . ?"

"Castrated? You're not dreaming, my dear. Three bullets point-blank from a hunting rifle, and a beautiful castration—*shlang*. No mercy. Reminds me of Budapest in '58, except there they hung us by our feet."

"Castrated," repeats Géraldine, dazed.

The old Hungarian nods enthusiastically.

"Did you find the . . . you know. His *thing?*" asks David.

"The pièce de résistance is missing, but I can tell you one thing: whoever did this wasn't messing around. You can see the serration of the blade in the flesh, like on a deer. If I end my career on this case, I'll be happy."

Any minute and the old Hungarian will be jumping up and down, thinks David, who feels the toast he had for breakfast rising up his throat. Géraldine's husky voice brings him out of his nausea.

"Pre- or postmortem castration?"

"Probably right after he was shot. It must have been agonizing because, you see, there was a lot of blood. It's very vascular, a man's . . ."

Géraldine turns toward David. "What do you think it means?"

David shakes his head, his face alarmingly pale. "I think it'll help us find out who the victim is."

"What do we know apart from his bad taste in clothes?" asks Géraldine.

"Nothing. No papers, no car keys, no cell phone. His pockets were empty; all that's left is his money."

Géraldine raises a delicate eyebrow. "How much?"

"One thousand in hundred-dollar bills."

Géraldine kneels down and leans over the waxy face, its mouth open in a final gasp before death. *Here's a man who believed that everything was owed to him,* she thinks, *even life.* Then she looks up at David. "And what do you make of that?" she asks, pointing to the tattered bills.

"I think he came here to buy someone's silence. I think that when you wear suits like his, a thousand bucks is nothing, but for the murderer it's a fortune. I think it wasn't the first silence he'd bought, and I think—no, I'm sure—that this guy had no respect for the person he came here to see."

Géraldine nods in agreement. She likes it when she can detect a rare tremble of anger in David's voice. In the Nyamata massacres that had taken her entire family, the gentle ones had been the first to die. It's not good for a man to be incapable of anger.

"Say, lovebirds, may I?" Attila's voice brings them back to reality. The wind is glacial, and the doctor wants to leave with his castrated corpse.

Géraldine stands up, extending a leather-gloved hand to David. "Where are the swimmers?"

Attila the Hungarian strokes his mustache, and points his chin toward the Palace. "Eating."

Clearly, some people never lose their appetite, David thinks, hurrying at Géraldine's red-sneakered heels.

The Swimmers

Spreading thick layers of butter onto their toast, bursting egg yolks with ferocious stabs of their forks, planting their knives in the flesh of sausages as if a man hadn't just been murdered and castrated in the adjacent parking lot, they eat. They're carnivores, assassins, ogres. Five girls and three boys, sedated by chlorine, high on endorphins and caffeine.

I really must learn to swim, Géraldine thinks, impressed by their energy.

"You're the ones who found the body?" asks David.

"It was Pat," says a small blond girl, pointing to a man whose sweater hugs every muscle of his sculpted body.

Géraldine pulls up a chair and sits down at the end of the table. "Would you like to tell me about it?"

In a swift gesture, the man soaks up the last traces of his egg yolk with a piece of bread. Behind him, giant jars of skinned peppers recall the killing in the parking lot. "I'm always the first one out of the pool. I was getting ready to put my bag in my car when I saw the body."

Géraldine looks up at him, trying to read his face. Its lines are clean and sharp, as if sketched in chalk. The man takes advantage of the pause to swallow his mouthful of egg-soaked bread and wash it down with a gulp of coffee. There's nothing calm about him. "Did you touch him?"

"Yes. I felt for a pulse. I'm a first responder. I didn't touch anywhere else. I got up and called 911. Your men arrived seven minutes and twenty-two seconds later."

Seven minutes, twenty-two seconds. "Are you always so precise with your timekeeping, monsieur?"

The serious-faced man lets a thin smile curve his lips. "Pat Visconti, I'm a bus driver, I have a schedule to follow, I'm always on time."

"He's an ironman," adds one of the girls. "Pat has a stopwatch built in his ass."

Pat and his internal stopwatch grate on Géraldine's nerves. She catches David looking at her, attentive as always. Sometimes it occurs to her that they're too intimate, prisoners of a Kevlar cocoon that no one else can access. If they weren't protected by the fact that he's married to an adorable woman and she's plagued by a traumatic past, they'd be dumb enough to sabotage their alloy of steel and titanium with a love affair.

Concentrate on the victim, Géraldine.

"Can we get someone on the identification of the victim?"

Géraldine feels someone touch her sleeve. A perfume of bleach and artificial musk invades her nostrils. And then a voice, gravelly from smoking: "I know him."

Cynthia

It's been thirty-two years since Cynthia started waitressing at the Palace. Her hair has gone from platinum blond to flamenco black to auburn. This morning, Cynthia is a redhead. She says her fox's mane gives her courage. She needs it today.

She's never spoken of what she saw. It was so long ago, and the humiliation still stings when she thinks about it today. But now the man is dead, and a woman is willing to listen to her. And so, seated in a corner booth, meticulously tearing apart a paper napkin, Cynthia tells her story.

She was twenty-three years old, raising a child by herself and working two shifts per day, serving up massive amounts of trans fats to already obese customers. One day a man sat down in her section, joined by a dark-haired, freckled little girl. The man was well known, preceded by his reputation and influence—all of Quebec watched *Family Life* on Thursday nights. He was the head honcho behind the popular sitcom that featured rambunctious cherub-faced children and parents overwhelmed by adulthood.

Everyone knew the *Family Life* producer had grown up in poverty, had started from nothing, and had made it to the top through flair and determination. *Family Life* was the childhood he'd always wanted—it offered an innocent and candid vision of adolescence and spurned the resignation of adult life. *You have to believe in your dreams,* the man often repeated in interviews. His success was proof of it.

The young waitress had never seen the darling little brunette before, but the child must have been full of promise for such an important man to want to take her to lunch. He'd ordered crêpes for the girl. For himself, eggs and bacon, but no butter on his toast.

"If I want to have a chance with you, my dear Cynthia, I've got to watch my figure," he teased her. Cynthia had blushed, she remembers, and hurried back with fresh coffee to top off his cup. He always left a big tip, and showed sincere interest in her; he flirted by acting as if he had no chance with her, when they both knew he had every chance in the world. Some mornings, Cynthia would forget that he was married with children, and daydream that they fell in love. All the other waitresses, jealous of the tips and attention from the famous man, would mock her adoration of him. All except Diane. But Diane was old, Diane was bitter.

And then one morning, when Cynthia had forgotten to give him his confiture, she'd turned around and seen the

man's hand, a manicured hand, anchored by a fat gold sig-
net ring, on the frail shoulder of the child. An ogre's hand,
a bear's paw, so fat, so heavy, so implacable, resting there on
its fragile prey, that all the blood in Cynthia's heart turned to
lead. *A paternal hand, that's all,* the young waitress had tried
to convince herself. *He's married, he has children, that's all, no
more, it can't be that, this is the man who's had every success and
still comes to eat at the Palace, in my section, the famous man who
hasn't forgotten his roots, it's me, me he's making a play for, not
her, a little girl . . .*

The man raised his head, he met Cynthia's eyes for a moment, and his expression transformed, terrifying. It didn't last
long, only a few seconds, and the charming smile returned. He
left a more generous tip than usual, and when she saw that extra bill, Cynthia knew. She'd seen correctly, and he was paying
her to feign blindness.

"He never came back to the Palace," Cynthia now tells
Géraldine, her eyes lowered, all the shame in the world on
her tired shoulders. "It's funny, you never would have thought
he'd come back just to . . ." She pauses and looks into her lap.
"Never mind."

To be shot down like a dog. Cynthia doesn't say the words,
and yet Géraldine hears them very clearly.

"His name is Paul," says Cynthia. "Paul Normand."

Valérie

The first thing you notice about her is her cleavage, accentu-
ated by a Donna Karan cashmere yoga top and the smattering
of freckles covering her chest. Her face has been lifted and re-
modeled, cheeks tightened, lips plumped, wrinkles removed.
But the cleavage doesn't lie. Paul Normand's wife has over-
indulged in the sun, her husband's credit cards, and laziness.

Above her balloon-like breasts are a thousand brown spots; even Valérie can't cover up her aging skin.

Her eyes, periwinkle blue, are like her life: vacant. The number you have dialed is not in service, and all the namastes in the world can't slow the march of time, nor the ravages of a life so carelessly lived.

Even with her senses dulled by white wine, even anaesthetized by all the chemicals that are supposed to make her less anxious, less depressive, but that really just allow her to bear her own passivity, Valérie must have seen something. You don't spend three decades of your life with a pedophile and not once see him place his hand on the thin shoulder of a little girl in need of love and attention. Little girls in need of love and attention: there had been hundreds in his life. He'd devoured them like sweets, without a hint of remorse, right under the nose of his wife, who stood by and let him do it. Faced with the alternative—giving up the vacations he paid for in the Grenadines, and bringing charges that would make all those good times look like nothing but a constant stream of shit over the years—Valérie had never had an attack of conscience. She'd turned her head and swallowed more pink, yellow, and blue pills, enjoying the sun on the deck of the sailboat, forgetting everything in the turquoise waters of the Caribbean, a cocktail in hand.

And now she had the spots to show for it. All over her chest. Like the markings of a permanent shame.

With Valérie, there's no need for a weapon. It's enough to press down on her throat with both thumbs until she stops breathing. She barely resists, complicit even in her own murder.

Paul

Géraldine jots the name down in her notebook: *Paul Nor-*

mand. Beside her, David hunches over his smartphone, already scouring the web. He's shocked to discover the number of pages devoted to the impresario and his protégés.

"And the little girl, the dark-haired child, she has a name?" Géraldine asks the copper-haired waitress.

Cynthia stares at a couple in front of her and wonders how long they've been together. "I don't know. He always called her *sweetie*. You'd have to watch the credits at the end of the show, they always list the names . . . Seems to me it was a boy's name, a unisex name, Renée or Claude . . . Danielle perhaps?"

Michelle

She always knew the police would come and that it would be because of him. It was inevitable. That man couldn't be content with a single victim. You only had to watch him eat, a meticulous ogre sucking the honey from each cell of the honeycomb before tossing it aside, empty. Even when he wasn't hungry, Paul's appetite had gotten the better of him. Money, power, and little girls' asses: he was insatiable.

Michelle didn't have to know the names to be sure that there were others. She knew they existed. Somewhere in the nebula, they formed an army of phantom stars. One day, or perhaps one night, a thread would connect them, and their constellation would have a name. A constellation of ghosts.

Yes, Michelle always knew the police would come. There had been periods in her life when this certainty had retreated, a she-wolf frightened by the sound of the hunter's footsteps. But on very calm nights, holding her breath so as not to scare it away, Michelle could feel the fetid breath of certainty on her neck and, possessed by a sort of drunkenness, she had to fight the desire to get up in the middle of the night, drive to a police station, and report him.

Paul Normand raped me. I was ten years old. And his greatest crime, the most disgusting, the most repulsive—much worse than his rancid cock—was that every time he made me believe I was lucky to be chosen among all the others.

It would be a relief to spit out his name, like when she sticks her fingers down her throat to make herself vomit. But once she'd emptied her stomach of all that bitterness, she would have to face the world and pay the consequences.

All those who had never had their neck squeezed so tightly that black and yellow marks were left there for days—those who had never had their throat brutalized by the pounding of a cock that thrusts by force—who'd been spared from the soundtrack of a man panting and groaning as he came—*they* would feel entitled to judge her, to condemn her.

Opportunist, liar, bitch, mercenary, careerist, calculating, prof-iteer, mytho-, nympho-, parano-, schizo-, manipulating, pathetic, sad, narcissistic, crazy, aggressive.

At best, she would be deemed *fragile.* But this was the worst epithet in her line of work, where one could recover far more easily from accusations of nymphomania than of a fragility that would worry any investor.

And so, Michelle had hoped that someone else would get up in the middle of the night, go into a police station, and beat the shit out of the silence, pounding it over and over again, right in the stomach. A single report would be enough for others to come out of the woodwork, and soon there would be a veritable stampede.

Be patient.

She always knew the police would come. She didn't think it would happen today, in the middle of rehearsal with her troupe, the last run-through before their big show in Vegas. But she never thought she would make it there either, her name on the marquee of the Barroco: *Directed by Michelle Sullivan.*

When her assistant leans close and whispers that two in-vestigators want to speak with her, Michelle feels a wave of heat come over her and the familiar shudder of disgust travel down to the small of her back.

Paul

The police advance toward her, excusing themselves to the acrobats and dancers who move back to clear a path. *How handsome they are,* Michelle muses. *He, a milky-white Pierrot; she, an ebony Colombine.* She can't resist the urge to magnify images, to dramatize them. It's stronger than she is.

The black woman holds out a dry, warm hand. "Géral-dine Mukasonga, major crimes. And this is my partner, Da-vid Catelli, also major crimes." The woman pronounces the word *crimes* in a voice like burnt caramel, rough beneath the sweetness. "We'd like to ask you a few questions about Paul Normand."

"What has he done?"

Pierrot and Colombine exchange a look. *They communi-cate well,* Michelle thinks. *It's fluid, they have no need for words.* Acrobats are like that, aware of the slightest quivering in their partner's body. Their life depends on it.

"He's dead," says Pierrot. "We found his body in the park-ing lot of a restaurant on Rue Ontario. A witness told us about you."

Paul is dead, Michelle thinks. She never imagined he could die before he'd paid for what he'd done. He won't have to go to prison, he won't be shamed, publicly humiliated. It's not fair. "Who told you about me?"

"A waitress at a restaurant. She remembered you as a

child," Géraldine says. "You were on a TV show he produced, and he brought you there for lunch."

Family Life: bitter sperm and fake maple syrup. Michelle had never eaten crêpes again, and she'd never owned a television.

"Mademoiselle Sullivan, your first reaction when we mentioned Paul Normand's name was to ask us what he'd done."

"You said you were from major crimes," Michelle replies, holding Colombine's gaze for a long moment. "Should I have thought otherwise?"

"Paul Normand was murdered. Three bullets in the chest. Most likely from a hunting rifle."

Michelle closes her eyes, to better imagine the scene. The images are magnificent—the dirty snow, the pink dawn, the expression on Paul's face as he turns around to meet his assassin—filmed in forty-eight frames per second, so she can truly savor the giant's surprise as he realizes his feet are made of clay and nothing will save him.

"He was mutilated as well."

"I beg your pardon?"

"Castrated, if you prefer."

Michelle starts laughing. At first it's an incongruous sound that escapes her throat—ruined from years of making herself vomit—then her laugh becomes a clear cascade, liberated from the fat hand of Paul. *Castrated, the son of a bitch.* In the immense rehearsal hall, in front of her troupe, her assistant, the technicians, and the two police officers, her wild laughter echoes as if there were ten, a hundred, a thousand people laughing. She couldn't have imagined the scene if she'd tried.

"Would you like to tell us about it?" asks David.

Michelle's gaze comes to rest on Olga, scouted at a gymnastics club in Komsomolskoye, whose graceful child's body coils and uncoils in meters of shimmering red silk, defying the implacable laws of gravity to catch the light of the projectors. Her little Olga, so proud of being able to support her family of five in Chechnya. *With me, she's safe, Michelle thinks. With me, the only risk she runs is a mortal fall. That's better than living with the snarling snout of a bear in your face every day, better than a shitty role on a shitty TV show, better than being humiliated by a despot in search of toys to break. Now I'm the one in power. I'm at the top, and yet I didn't become a despot. Paul Normand raped me, but he didn't break me.*

"No," she finally says, stunned to hear herself pronounce such a powerful word.

"Your testimony would be confidential," David reassures her.

The black woman, for her part, says nothing, but her phenomenal eyes take everything in. *Vigilance*, thinks Michelle. *She knows. We come from the same country, she and I, one that demands vigilance at every moment.*

"You know how many women are directing shows like the one I'm preparing for in Vegas? *Zero*. I'm the only one. If I talk to you, if I tell you my story and it goes public, everything I've managed to do in my life, all my struggles, all my accomplishments, everything that's mine will be taken away from me again, and I'll go back to being precisely what I don't want to be."

"What's that?"

"A victim." And Michelle turns her back on Colombine and Pierrot.

Géraldine and David watch Michelle walk away.

Anorexic, David thinks, his eyes fixed on the jutting collarbone exposed by the low neckline of one of those Breton striped sweaters French actresses wear.

So graceful, thinks Géraldine, *like a Modigliani model who survived the war in a crumbling attic.* She turns to David. "She told us enough to know where to look."

He shakes his head. They'll have to go through all the credits of all the shows produced by Paul Normand, a laborious task that will slow them down. "It would've been simpler with a deposition," he says.

"For us, yes. Not for her."

The door opens onto the biting February cold. The wind has risen, blowing flurries of snow everywhere. David wonders if he'll dare to ask the question that's gnawing at him before they get back to the car and are overtaken by the demands of the investigation.

"Do you understand that, Gérald?"

"Understand what? Be clear, David."

"Choosing to stay silent, you understand that?"

"Yes."

"You don't think there's an obligation to report?"

"No."

He starts the Dodge's motor, turning the heat to maximum.

"There are worse things than not reporting," adds Géraldine. "You can report and have the world turn its back on you."

The windshield wipers struggle to clear the snow from the glass.

It's true that when you think about the fact that a million men, women, and children were hacked to pieces with machetes over three months, and that no one came to help, it can really do a number on your desire to speak out.

While they wait for the vehicle to warm up, David checks his phone one last time, hoping to find a clue in the dense jungle of web pages dedicated to Paul Normand. A quick scan tells him the entertainment industry has just held a ceremony in homage to him, that he's working on new and ambitious projects, that his daughter Stéphanie is his greatest pride, that he poses shamelessly with his grandchildren: like here, playing hockey, or here, next to a Christmas tree. The only off note: one of his ex-protégés, who'd left the fold, had been savaged in a vitriolic newspaper article. A failed comeback for the ex–child star turned has-been who'd never really *been* at all.

"It's sickening how much has been written about him," David says. "I mean, this guy produced quiz shows with B-list actors, cheap copies of successful variety shows, and some dumb soap operas, but to read the articles, you'd think he has a great body of work. I mean, really, he's not Picasso!"

"You know, David, if Picasso were alive today, he'd be the star of a reality TV show about hotshot art collectors outbidding each other for his work."

David shrugs. "Okay, smart-ass."

Géraldine's silvery laugh fills the cabin of the truck. For an instant, David tells himself he wouldn't mind being treated like an idiot for the rest of his days if it meant he could hear that laugh. He shifts into first, just as Géraldine's phone rings.

"Mukasonga," she answers.

From the way she goes silent, concentrating with an intensity he's never seen in anyone else, David knows it's important.

"Amber Alert for a seven-year-old girl, Raphaëlle Boisclair . . . the granddaughter of Paul Normand."

David stares straight ahead at the road, obscured by blowing snow.

Stéphanie & Vincent

The gate closes behind them, prisonlike. A monstrous house, bloated with money and ostentation. On the lawn that has clearly been landscaped by a designer, snow covers the trees, shrubs, and a fountain modeled after the Trevi Fountain. David whistles faintly, impressed. His wife probably wouldn't like the house, but confusedly, he thinks it's what is expected of a man: that he provide a nest—the grandest of nests, the coziest, the safest—to the mother of his children.

"I guess that's why I'm not in a relationship anymore," says Géraldine, gesturing at the manor. "If I had to live here, I'd die."

"You think we should tell them about Paul Normand?"

"Yes. But we won't."

David nods. He doesn't question Géraldine's decision, and he knows she'd do the same for him. They're smart enough to know not to get in the way of intuition by prematurely questioning it.

And then, a shockingly good-looking couple appears in the doorway. He looks like the product of a focus group for women who are bored in their marriages, while she, athletic and glowing, could be taken for a Norwegian ski champion. Géraldine feels a sudden pang—Stéphanie Normand looks too much like Anne-Sophie. Both she and her husband are red-eyed, their bodies stiff with anguish, a vague expression of disbelief on their faces. Their nest, majestic as it may be, hasn't protected their daughter.

In the vast white kitchen, Stéphanie and Vincent do their best to answer questions. They were in Quebec City for Stéphanie's class reunion at the private boarding school where she'd spent her adolescence. Marisa has worked for them since Raphaëlle was born; they'd never seen her drink before. They've had no contact from the kidnappers, not a word, not even a warning to not contact the police. And so they'd filed a report. Terrified at the thought that their little girl could be in danger—worried that the news outlets will get wind of the story—incapable of imagining that Raphaëlle might be suffering, they take turns speaking: her first, then him, to have the last word. Each time, Vincent tacks a phrase onto his wife's statement, as if to assert his authority. *Something isn't right with them*, David thinks. *He's not happy.*

"Was there something we should have done, besides calling you?" asks Stéphanie.

"No, no, you did the right thing," David says.

"It was my first instinct to contact you," adds Vincent. "Steph didn't want to, she was afraid of the media attention, that it would make things worse."

The way Stéphanie's face tenses is subtle, but it escapes neither David nor Géraldine.

"She's seven years old," Stéphanie keeps repeating, her voice hoarse with worry. "Seven! I can't even imagine someone would want to harm her."

Plenty of people are lining up to harm children, Géraldine thinks. *Your father harmed them constantly. And you, his daughter, what do you know of his crimes?*

A look from David brings her out of her trance. He knows what his partner is thinking, he knows all too well, but unlike her, he still believes in the presumption of innocence.

"Do you know anyone who might hold a grudge against you?"

They shake their heads in unison. Vincent shrugs. "Everyone loves my wife. Even people who don't like her at first end up loving her."

"And you," asks Géraldine, "does everyone love you?"

"Me? I'm not important enough for anyone to hate."

No, Vincent is not happy.

"And your father, Mademoiselle Normand, could someone have reason to come after your daughter because of him?"

It's David who asks the question. Géraldine admires his composure and his grace. No trace of accusation in his question, only a concern that inspires trust. He's good, David. Before them, Stéphanie is silent, placing her hand in her husband's. To buy time. *She knows*, thinks Géraldine. *She knows who her father is.*

"My father has led an impressive career for nearly forty years. He started from nothing, he's a self-made man, and he succeeds in all he does. There will always be jealous people, people who try to blame others for their own failures."

The girl who failed her comeback, David says to himself, his investigative instinct on maximum alert. The one who was destroyed by the critic everyone fears. He takes his time before asking the question, very calm. "Are you thinking of someone in particular?"

Stéphanie turns toward her husband. As if she were seeking approval she doesn't need. "I don't want to speak ill of anyone."

But you will anyway, Géraldine thinks, waiting for the rest, in perfect complicity with David.

"Raphaëlle's life is at stake, Steph," her husband says, insistent. He takes a deep breath, finally seizing the occasion to play the lead role.

He has no clue that it's exactly what his wife wants, think Géraldine and David, neither of them buying her act. For the cruel words to come from his own lips, so as not to taint hers, full and pure.

"A poor girl my father-in-law employed when she was young. A limited talent, you could say that, I think. But she was cute, and she was in *Family Life* for a while. And then . . . she let herself go, she became . . . enormous, and so he was forced to get rid of her."

Get rid of her. Like she's a mangy dog.

"She tried to make a comeback, and when she realized that she had no talent, no charisma, nothing, she started making up stories and telling lies."

"What sort of lies?"

"That it was my father-in-law's fault she hadn't made it. That he took her out of school to make her work, that he exploited her, stole her childhood."

"Took her out of school?"

"Yes, but her parents agreed to it. And it's not like she was on her way to becoming a neurosurgeon," says Stéphanie, contempt in her voice.

"Nothing's easier than blaming your mentor when the truth is that you just aren't talented enough."

David nods. "You think she could resent him enough to kidnap your daughter?"

Tears flow, unstoppable, snotty tears, down Stéphanie's polished cheeks, a torrent that the barrier of her thin hands fails to contain, even with her husband's arm around her shoulder.

"I don't know, I really don't know. I don't understand how anyone could want to hurt my little girl. She's an innocent child. Please find Raphaëlle, find my daughter."

Her

The day has been long. And tiring. Since the kidnapping this morning, she's barely slept. She has an ache in her shoulder, bruised by the recoil of the rifle, a pain in her knee, which she bumped in the chase with the journalist, and a headache from driving all day. And then there's the blood that's seeped into her clothes; its fetid odor has nauseated her, kept her from eating, and she feels weak. Or else it's the cancer that has spread beyond her lungs. Perhaps it's lodged in her bones already, she doesn't know. When the doctor told her both lungs were affected, that it was already quite advanced, she said, *No, no scan,* she didn't want to know, what good would it do? She said no chemo either, and she stood up from that cursed chair, very straight, electrified by a vigor she'd never felt in her life. It puzzles her now to think that she came into being on the day she was sentenced to death.

She'd left the rifle in her truck, emptying the remaining bullets, and parked in the alley behind the house on Rue Butternut, in the nondescript enclave of Saint-Henri. The lock on the wooden garage door is still there, intact. *Perfect.* Roger is still inside. In what state? She doesn't know, and she doesn't give a damn. Last night, she brought him into the shed with a forty-ounce bottle of vodka, and before the poor idiot realized what was happening to him, the wooden door had closed him in, padlocked. She knows he didn't find the strength to break down the flimsy partition that would've allowed him to escape. She knows he chose liquor. It was what he'd always done, even if it meant selling his own daughter.

She presses her ear against the door. Silence. She imagines Roger curled up in the arms of his great love, vodka, and realizes that in spite of her lungs, gangrenous from the tumors, she can finally breathe. They're all dead. The father who was supposed to protect her daughter; the one who watched her husband rape children and did nothing; that bitch of a journalist who had nothing better to do than blame the victims; and him, finally him, the heavy-handed ogre who chased little girls and destroyed them, one after another.

As for Paul's daughter—the one whose elite private-school education had been paid for by the work of kids he'd taken out of school to make the machine turn faster—she must know

now, deep in her gut, what it meant to fear the worst for your child.

Justice has been served.

She enters the house by the back door. The smell of vegetable soup impregnates the walls, the wind comes in through the joints in the aluminum windows, and the paint is chipping, discolored by time and tobacco. Nothing has changed since that first day when Paul Normand, stinking of cologne and money, came in to make them an offer that would change their lives.

She sets the keys to the truck on the kitchen table. The sound of the television drifts down from upstairs. Canned laughter. A cheerful little tune she can tell from a thousand others: the theme song of *Family Life*. She hears footsteps coming up the walk, and turns to see two silhouettes looming in the doorframe. A man and a woman. *Police.*

Claudine is not afraid. She's held back for so long, been silent and ashamed for so many years. She wraps a shawl around her shoulders and goes to let them in. They're young, good-looking, especially the woman, who raises her head, hearing the sound of the television and a child's laugh from upstairs. She exchanges a brief look of relief with her colleague.

"Madame Claudine Lachance?"

"Yes. Come in, come in, it's freezing."

She closes the door behind them, heads toward the kitchen, busies herself putting on the kettle.

"I only have bagged tea. Do you take it with sugar? Milk?"

"Neither," they respond in unison. *Like me*, thinks Claudine, strangely comforted by the idea that she has something in common with the officers who have come to arrest her. The man pulls out a chair and sits down, laying his pencil and papers out neatly on the kitchen table. He looks like a boy who's just come home from school. She tells him so; he smiles.

"I like my things in order," he says, clicking his pen open.

The woman, for her part, remains standing. Her long, delicate fingers graze the cookbooks, the glass poodle figurine, the photo of a girl with big brown eyes in a white porcelain frame.

The kettle whistles just as footsteps begin to descend the worm-eaten staircase. The light steps of a child first, in ballet shoes. Then others, heavier, in Phentex slippers.

David turns around at the same time as Géraldine. Before them is the small blond head of Raphaëlle, laughing, alive. And behind her, obese and dull-eyed, an overgrown child hidden behind layers of flesh and medicated lethargy, broken.

Like every time she looks at her daughter, her little Victoria, Claudine wants to die. Her daughter who was so delicate, so sensitive, and whom she hadn't defended, hadn't protected, her daughter whom she'd left in the hands of Paul Normand because she was afraid of him, afraid of Roger, afraid of standing up to all the men who told her what to do, who told her to stay silent.

"All my life I was afraid," says Claudine, to no one in particular. "I don't even know what I was afraid of. Of seeing the world as it was, I think, of not being strong enough to face reality. I was guilty, like everyone else; I went along with it because he paid us, because he dazzled us, because he was from our world and knew how to talk to us, because I believed it would lift us out of our misery, because my daughter wanted so much to be chosen to act on that show. My God how she wanted . . . We were always telling her she had to believe in her dreams. Cursed, shitty dreams."

Stunned by the violence of these last words, Raphaëlle clings to Victoria's fat leg as the woman strokes her hair, puts a vagabond barrette carefully back in place. Géraldine sets the photo down, between portraits of a faded Jehane Benoit and a dashing Ricardo. Of the lovely little doe-eyed brunette in the white porcelain frame, nothing remains. Not the faintest glimmer in her eyes. Everything has been ravaged, lost. A shipwreck.

"I was a bad mother. But today I paid my dues. Yes, I killed him. And then I killed his wife, the journalist, and my husband. I killed them all, and my turn will come. I'm not afraid anymore." Claudine smiles at David and Géraldine, straightening her thin shoulders proudly. This small, frail, nondescript woman of sixty, whom everyone pushed aside without a thought, was capable of the worst.

David turns toward Géraldine and detects no sign of distress on her smooth face. He's not surprised. He sometimes wonders if his partner didn't leave her soul behind in the massacre at Nyamata.

"When I'm on the inside, and too weak to say it, you'll tell the journalists."

"What's that, Madame Lachance?" Géraldine asks in a calm voice.

"You'll tell them that my daughter, my Victoria, was a pretty little girl, such a pretty little girl."

THREE TSHAKAPESH DREAMS

BY SAMUEL ARCHIBALD

Centre-Sud

Translated from French by Donald Winkler

Yeah, I remember the story, even if I don't get to tell it very often.

It happened after the war. They found the kid in the Frontenac Library bathroom with a needle sticking out of his arm. It was no surprise he'd been shooting up. Ontario Street's known for its poets, whores, and druggies. Simon was all three. He often peddled his ass to pay for his dope, then when he got straight for a while, he gave poetry readings. Sometimes, like on that day, he went to the library and left his dogs tied to a bicycle rack at the door while he picked up books by Carole David or Patrice Desbiens. No one knew how long he'd been dead. No one knew what to do with his dogs. The medics brought out the body, with help from the Montreal police. They kept the dogs at the pound for a bit, in separate cages. There wasn't much chance of them being adopted. They were two pit bulls full of fleas and with shitty pedigrees. After a week, the vet came to give them the needle too.

That's how families bite the dust in the Centre-Sud.

In those days, no one knew the Indian was a cop.

It was Brisebois, his contact at the provincial police, who called him at home to tell him Simon was dead. The Indian asked if they were going to do an autopsy. Brisebois said everyone could see it was an overdose, but the Indian just laughed. Later, the Indian would tell me: "Simon may have had his faults, but he knew how to shoot up."

When you say *the war* around here, you don't mean Iraq or Afghanistan. You mean the Great Quebec Biker War. You had to be in Montreal at the end of the 1990s to understand: Maurice "Mom" Boucher thinking he's Joseph Stalin, the independents against the Hells Angels, about 160 dead, nearly 200 attempted murders, and bombs exploding all over the place. People stopped going out. It wasn't Montreal anymore; it was Belfast. When the government and the police got fed up, they threw everyone inside.

The Indian was too young to play a role in the 2001 deployment, he was still in Nicolet. His superiors posted him in Montreal afterward, undercover, so he could keep an eye on things in the city. He did little jobs around the neighborhood, like peddling stolen goods and driving taxis for escorts. He lived just below us, in Dan Quesnel's triplex on Larivière Street. It was just by Saint-Eusèbe Church and the McDonald's cigarette factory, where in spring and summer the dried tobacco smells so much like cinnamon buns that it's been twenty years since I've eaten one of those damned buns.

The Indian made Brisebois promise to at least check out the stash they'd found in Simon's pockets.

Brisebois called him back the next day to tell him they'd found coke and a bag of almost-pure heroin.

The Indian went to an AA meeting on Wednesday. People were used to seeing him there; being an alcoholic was part of his cover. He picked up a donut and listened as people spilled their guts until the cigarette break. Then he went to ask Keven Savoie if he knew where to find Kim. The guy told him that Kim barely came around anymore, but he could find her on Mondays and Thursdays at Walter Stewart Park. She played in a lesbian softball league.

He caught up with Kim the next night, after her game. She played shortstop, really good hands. Kim was Simon's oldest friend, but since she'd stopped using, she hadn't seen him much. After getting herself clean, Kim started working for Stella, a sex workers organization. She handed out condoms and guidance to the girls in that part of town.

Kim and the Indian sobbed in each other's arms for ten minutes. Kim couldn't tell him a lot, but she had the same thought that he did: there was something fishy about Simon dying from a heroin overdose. Smack, for him, was a rich kid's drug, and he mainly shot coke. Besides, where would he have gotten pure heroin with half the country's criminals behind bars?

In those days, the Indian called himself Dave Tshakapesh.

He'd taken the name in memory of his grandfather, who had been a bush pilot for Hydro-Québec and for outfitters in the north. He'd married a Robertson from Pointe-Bleue and spent most of his life with the Innu, the Atikamekw, and the Cree. He knew lots of stories, which he'd told Dave years ago, when he was just a kid. Stories about Carcajou, the Wendigo, and especially Tshakapesh, the boy who succeeds in everything he undertakes.

Tshakapesh was born prematurely, when the black bear devoured his father and his mother. It was his sister who found him, rolled into a ball in the uterus that had been ripped from his mother's body. Tshakapesh's sister brought the little creature back to camp, where he wormed his way out of the womb all by himself. Then he stood up and asked his sister to go and get his bow and arrows so that he could avenge his parents. Dave loved that idea: a baby born ready for war.

When Simon died, Dave knew something terrible was going to happen. He'd dreamed that a giant bear was marching through the Centre-Sud, holding onto the big L-shaped tower of the Quebec police, the building all the kids on Ontario Street see when they look to the sky, the building everyone still calls by its old name: the Parthenais Prison.

The following afternoon, Dave went to see Big Derek.

You don't see Big Derek around here much anymore, but back then, he was kind of a celebrity. He trained for strongman competitions, and he had his picture in the paper along with Hugo Girard. In the crime world, he was known as the doorman at Sex Mania, the strip club at the corner of Ontario and Bercy. He was a pimp. He dealt dope to the strippers and collected debts for the Ontario Street loan sharks. People got really good at digging out money when Derek came to the door. He appeared to weigh three hundred pounds, he had tattoos up and down his arms, and he could pull a fire truck with his jaws. That fucker had muscles in places good Christians don't even have skin.

Derek lived in an old house that had been spared demolition when its working-class neighborhood was torn down. He'd bought it from a retired schoolteacher and immediately took down her crucifix and sacred hearts, replacing them with laminated *Scarface* and porn star posters. Mixing a Jack and Coke, he asked: "Did you go to the funeral?"

Dave said no.

Derek hadn't gone either. At that point, the Indian had no intention of telling Derek he didn't think Simon had done himself in. All he wanted to do was scout the territory and let Derek get smashed, so he would relax and tell too many stories. With his cocktail recipe, that wouldn't take long. Derek made his Jack and Cokes Centre-Sud style: four ounces of Jack Daniel's, slightly less Coca-Cola, and two lines of coke on the side. His cocaine left a strong taste of burnt rubber at the bottom of your throat, and it loosened the tongue.

Derek talked to him for hours about the balance of power in Centre-Sud. On his nights off, he watched porn with the TV muted while sweeping the police frequencies with his scanner. He was the archivist for a kingdom of bums that went from Davidson to Saint-Denis Street, between Sherbrooke Street and the river.

Before the Indian left, Derek said: "I always knew he'd come to a bad end. I hate the fucking bikers, but they're right about one thing: you should never do the dope you're selling."

Derek sniffed a line here and there, but you'd never find him in the bathroom with a needle sticking out of his arm. Still, he had no business preaching to anybody. His vice was pussy and everyone knew it. He screwed the girls at Sex Mania, he screwed the escorts he chauffeured, he even screwed the twenty-dollar whores strung out on crack who no sane guy would touch with rubber gloves. He was always up for a new hustle or some crazy deal, because he spent more on hookers than what the hookers brought in.

Yes, Derek and the kid knew each other.

The summer before, some gangbangers from Saint-Michel robbed several freight trains and turned up at the Indian's place with a box of samples. Fencing stolen goods was Dave's number-one cover. These guys had emptied all the crates from a railcar stalled under the Rachel Street overpass. Not knowing what they were getting, they'd stolen twenty-five cases of luxury dildos—silicone brands that looked like old iMacs. Orange, pink, red, and mauve. Anal plugs, high-class battery-powered vibrators, clit ticklers—the works. Dave had a network for selling cigarettes and booze. Clothes too. He sold douchebag suits to the wannabe mobsters in Saint-Léonard, and ghetto getups to the wiggers in Hochelaga. But for dildos, Dave needed a whole other network. Simon and Derek were his best salesmen, each in his own department. Derek sold the toys to strippers, and Simon dealt here, there, and everywhere in the Gay Village. After that, Dave, Derek, and Simon kept on working together; they even went for a beer from time to time to honor the summer they'd rained down dildos on the town.

Dave got home that night thinking about all he'd learned, which wasn't much. But he did learn one thing: according to Derek, Edmond-Louis Gingras was the interim drug boss in Hochelaga and the Centre-Sud. Gingras was an old hand who worked mainly with whores, for the Italians. He'd married into the Mafia—one of Rizzuto's nieces. The Italians chose a perfect puppet to hold the fort while waiting for negotiations in prison to cough up the real boss. Derek believed that the power was going to Gingras's head: "You'd think he wants to keep the job forever. Seems he's even been doing a house-cleaning in the neighborhood, checking out people who've been talking to the police. There's a girl and a guy who've disappeared. When I heard about Simon, I even thought he might be a rat. But then I thought, no. Simon would never have snitched to the cops."

That night Dave went to bed with a heavy heart.

Simon would never have talked to the police—neither

would Derek—but they talked to him every day without knowing who he really was. The Indian followed his own strict rule: never ask someone for anything if you can make him do it without knowing it. He got information out of people by making them think he was their friend. He always told himself he was protecting them, but now he wasn't so sure.

During the night he had another dream.

He dreamed he was Tshakapesh fighting the black bear. He had no knives and could only use his fists against the fearsome animal that was twice as tall as he was. It had a shark's mouth, and its thick oily fur smelled of piss. He woke up in a sweat, reaching for his Glock. He remembered that his gun was at the station. He came knocking on the window of my room upstairs; he did that sometimes. He asked me if I knew anything about Edmond-Louis Gingras. I said yes, but I added that no one around here called him by that name. Because of his big fat ass and his big teats and the hair sticking out of his shirt collar, everyone called him Teddy Bear.

That was when Dave Tshakapesh realized that he, too, had someone to avenge.

After that, Dave got on Gingras's case.

The job was almost too easy. Teddy Bear needed people. The provincial police had dismantled the Rock Machine in the fall of 2000, and in the spring of 2001 they'd moved on to the Hells. On March 26 alone they'd arrested twelve people, and not just guys who emptied ashtrays. Dons, deadbeats, crooked lawyers. A hell of a catch.

It's not often you can say this, but at the beginning of the 2000s there was a shortage of criminals in Montreal. The Indian was a bright guy, everyone knew that, so he got work pretty quickly. He didn't have much trouble convincing his bosses to keep the pressure on. With the war freshly won, the cops knew perfectly well that crime was like nature: it abhors a vacuum. They didn't want a new despot rearing his head to reign over the empire's ruins. It took Dave one week to sell the idea of laying hands on Teddy Bear. Then he spent the summer cadging more and more jobs from Teddy Bear's men, while supplying Brisebois with information at the same time. The police moved in after him and took photos of Teddy Bear's dope stash, cash, and bungalows on the North Shore, where his guys had hydroponic grow ops.

One night, Teddy Bear asked to see the Indian alone.

Dave didn't tip off his boss at the provincial police. He was afraid they'd want him to wear a wire. He went to have a beer with Teddy Bear in an Ontario Street bar. They took a booth at the back, and Dave figured out that the bar was probably owned by Teddy Bear when he saw him get up and draw two drafts without asking for anyone's okay. He made his little bank-manager speech to Dave: he very much appreciated his work; he wondered if Dave was ready to get more involved.

Dave asked him what he was thinking of, and Teddy Bear told him he was having a problem with someone—his *friend*, Big Derek.

Big Derek had been playing the pimp behind his back for years. Now he was dealing too. Dave asked Teddy Bear if he was looking for a temporary or a permanent solution. Teddy Bear said permanent. That would set a good example, and they'd be able to place bets on how many shitheads it would take to shoulder that son of a bitch's coffin.

Dave pushed his luck a bit. He looked Teddy Bear straight in the eye and asked whether the kid's OD in the spring had been meant as a warning for Derek. Teddy Bear hesitated for five seconds before answering: "Yes, but he's a slow learner."

When Dave's bosses found out he'd been asked to kill someone, they were royally pissed off, since he hadn't recorded the conversation. Then they got used to the idea, and had a secret meeting on the other side of the city with their whole on-site team, Dave, and the government prosecutors. An undercover agent being asked to commit homicide—that was the breaking point. They looked at what they had, and one of the prosecutors said: "Go. We can nab them with what we've got."

Dave went home and watched baseball on TV, alone in his living room, while drinking a beer in Simon's honor. He went to bed late; he was keyed up, but his mind was at rest.

At two in the morning, he awoke in a sweat. He'd had exactly the same dream as when he'd spoken to Derek in June—he was fighting the black bear with his naked hands. Dave didn't like talking about his dreams much. They were very private for him. But he explained to me later that dreams don't tell the future or the past. They tell you how to behave, and whether you've behaved the right way. For him, it was as clear as spring water: he'd acted in accordance with his second dream, so he shouldn't have had to dream it all over again.

Unless the ancestors were trying to tell him that he'd made a mistake.

Something about Simon's story didn't hold water.

Dave got up and went to eat two eggs with bacon at Bercy's. He gave Kim a call to ask her if there was anything new. She'd heard nothing, but earlier in the week she'd talked to another social worker at Stella. This friend had an escort client who did heroin on and off. She was a girl from the neighborhood who put out for tourists in the Old Montreal hotels during the Grand Prix. Her pimp had slapped her around because she'd started shooting up between her fingers. She couldn't work anymore and was shit-scared of getting another beating, because she owed money to the guy who sold her the heroin. Dave asked Kim if she'd been able to get the name of the pusher.

"Don't tell anyone I said this, but it's Big Derek," she told him.

Dave put the story together piece by piece: a hundred times over, he saw the expression on Teddy Bear's face when he'd ask about Simon. Teddy Bear hadn't hesitated because he wasn't sure if he wanted to come clean, he hesitated because he had no idea what Dave was talking about. Teddy Bear didn't have Simon killed. The asshole was just showing off.

Big Derek had a source for smack, one of the independents. Who knew which one? The Chinese or the Arabs. He'd tried to bring Simon on board, but Simon had done himself in while testing the product. Instead of telling Dave the truth, Derek had sent him chasing after Teddy Bear. Derek had always hated Teddy Bear. It was dicey, but Derek was a gambler. He'd waited for the war to end before making his bundle, and he didn't want a new boss standing in his way.

It all made sense, but only if Derek knew Dave was with the police. But he was smart enough to have figured that out on his own. The only thing you couldn't know for sure was whether Derek had killed Simon by accident, passing him stuff that was too strong, or on purpose, to stop him from bringing Dave in on their plan to peddle the heroin.

The Indian was furious.

He spent the whole day brooding in his apartment, drinking O'Keefe's. Around four o'clock, he called me so I'd go buy some more at the corner store and come drink with him. It must have been a hundred degrees in that apartment. The Indian was downing the beer in his living room and sweating like a pig. When he wasn't talking to me, he kept repeating the same thing over and over, real low, between his teeth: "That fuck, that fat fuck, that fat fucking fuck."

I drank a couple with him. He ended up telling me the whole story and admitting, straight out, that he was a cop. He was drunk, so I asked him, "Are you sure it's a good idea, telling me that?"

He said his time around here was coming to an end anyway. He apologized in advance for the shit I'd be in, and I said: "Don't worry. I've known worse."

Around seven o'clock he told me: "I don't see any other solution. I'm gonna have to beat the shit out of Derek."

I asked him if he did judo or tae kwon do or something. He said no. He said it wasn't so hard to fight a guy bigger than you. You can't be intimidated; you have to wait for him to make a mistake. Tall guys and fat guys tend to put too much trust in their strength. Also, try not to hit them in the balls. The tall guys and the fat guys are used to people pulling that on them.

"So your plan is: don't be intimidated and don't kick him in the balls?" I asked.

I was skeptical. Derek was all fat and muscle, with skin as thick as walrus hide. I wasn't even sure he'd fall on his ass if you fired a twelve-gauge into his chest. I told myself that I'd spend the next few days getting all that stuff out of Dave's head, but when I asked when he intended to go and fight Derek, he eyed how much beer he had left in his bottle and said: "I'll finish this, and we'll go."

* * *

You would have thought it was a big neighborhood fair.

The Indian told whomever he met along the way that he was going to fight Big Derek. And they went to tell others, until almost a hundred people were gathered at dusk behind Sex Mania to watch the battle in the tobacco factory parking lot. It was up to me to go in and find Derek. I just told him, "Dave wants to talk to you outside."

When Derek came out, he saw the crowd and Dave in the middle of the circle, making his neck pop like Bruce Lee. "You kidding me, Dave? Go sober up at home, fucking Indian."

But Dave said he wouldn't budge without a fight. Derek laughed and moved into the circle. Things looked really bad. Face to face, Dave and Derek didn't seem to even belong to the same species. That must have struck Dave too, because the first thing he did was serve up a kick to Derek's balls. Derek dodged it, fast for a guy his size, then he delivered a right hook with all his strength to the side of Dave's head. Dave blinked and fell to the ground. I was sure he wouldn't get up.

"Had enough?" Derek taunted.

"Not enough, no, you piece of shit."

Dave got up and charged Derek again. He did that about ten times, fighting like crazy. Derek always ended up grabbing him and throwing him to the ground with a punch or a kick. The tenth time, he socked the Indian in the stomach, picked him up in his arms, and heaved him into the Polish butcher's dumpster. There was a long silence, and then we heard Dave scrambling around and cursing. Derek started back toward the door to the club, saying, "Everybody go home. The fight's over."

"No, it's not over," Dave declared, climbing out of the dumpster.

Derek didn't react and kept on walking. Dave took his key ring out of his pocket and threw a fastball to the back of his head. That put a big cut in Derek's hairy hide. When he turned around, you could see that the Indian had really managed to make him mad. I wasn't the only one who began to wonder how we could stop the fight or whether Dave was going to be killed.

Derek clobbered him one. Dave's cheek was swollen, and he was bleeding from his right ear. I was worried about internal bleeding too, because Derek kept on punching him in the gut and the ribs. Dave's skin had gone white, almost green.

Finally, Derek lifted him up and squeezed. A bear hug, like in wrestling. The Indian bellowed.

"Tell them what you are, Dave. Or I'll crush you."

"Go fuck yourself."

Derek squeezed some more. We heard Dave's spine crack.

"Tell them you're a cop."

Derek kept on squeezing. We thought he was going to break the Indian in two, but with all the blood and sweat, they were as greasy as a banana peel; Dave managed to slide his right arm out of the vise, and then raised his fist high in the air and slammed his elbow like a tomahawk into Derek's eye. We learned afterward that some bone fragments had gone right into his cornea. Derek let Dave go and fell to his knees, his hand on his eye. He was squealing like a pig. Dave went up to him, pushed Derek's hand out of the way, and threw a punch to his cheekbone as hard as he could. He said later it was like hitting cement, except the cement was hurting too. Dave struck three more blows and felt his joints give way, one after the other. He gave the fifth punch everything he had left in his fist and felt an electric jolt running up past his elbow to his shoulder. His hand was broken. Derek was swaying on his knees. The Indian stepped back five or six paces, then said in front of everybody: "Yeah, I'm a cop. And that makes *him* a fucking snitch."

There were two angles to his strategy that Dave hadn't told me about. First, he knew that the big guys and tall guys had a tendency to drag things out. Second, he always wore shoes that looked like plain city shoes, but they had steel toes. He took a run, five steps, and hammered Derek right under his jaw, like he was punting. We heard the jaw split along its length like a wooden splint. For about ten seconds, Derek tried to shut his mouth, sucking at the air like a fish. Then he fell back onto his bent knees. His legs were shaking. Dave came up to hit him again, but he held back. Derek was spewing a huge pink-and-red geyser into the air. It took five of us to turn him on his side, and if we hadn't had the idea, he'd have choked to death on his broken teeth.

By the time we'd done that, the Indian had disappeared.

The next day, people honored an old Centre-Sud tradition.

Early in the morning, they tossed twenty dozen eggs at the wall of Dan Quesnel's triplex. It was their way of marking the houses of those who'd talked to the police. Dave didn't even hear it. He was high as a kite from the painkillers he'd been given at the hospital. He'd been released during the night. They'd wrapped up his hand, put his face together a bit, and made him promise to come back right away if he started shitting or pissing blood.

It was the smell of rotten eggs cooking in the sun that woke him at about ten thirty. The smell, and the pain that had returned. He went out into the street. Monsieur Quesnel and I were trying to assess the damage. Dave apologized to the owner of the house and gave me three hundred dollars in twenties and fifties to rent a pressure hose and buy him a forty-ouncer of Johnnie Walker and a bag of ice. He watched me work all afternoon, sitting in a folding chair on the sidewalk, with his Scotch on one side of him and the pail of ice on the other. He soaked his hand—all messed up with staples, scabs, and stitches—in the cold water, and from time to time he dipped his fingers in his glass to collect some ice cubes. All afternoon we heard police sirens in the Centre-Sud. It was the guys from the provincial police and the Montreal police coming to arrest Teddy Bear and his boys. They'd had to move the operation up because of Dave's acting out, and they weren't too happy about that.

One day later the Indian left, and we never saw him again. Never saw Derek again either. When he got out of the hospital, he headed for the North Shore. We later heard that he had gotten himself arrested for forcing a thirteen-year-old girl into porn.

On that day before Dave left, I finished cleaning off the wall at six o'clock, and he gave me more money. He told me to go and buy hot dogs for us to eat in the stands of Walter Stewart Park. He wanted to see Kim play softball one last time. The heat had let up a little, and we felt good.

That night, for the first time, I decided to ask Dave if it bothered him that everyone called him *the Indian*. Did he find it racist or anything like that? Should we have called him something else?

"It's hard to answer, because where I come from, the word means two different things. If you say someone dead or gone is a *real Indian*, it means he's brave. Someone who knows how to live and honors the ancestors. My uncle Robertson once said of my grandfather that he was *almost an Indian*. That's the only time in my life I've heard that said about a white man, and I can't imagine a bigger compliment. On the other hand, if you say of someone, behind his back or to his face, that he's a *goddamn Indian* or a *fucking Indian,* it means he's a drunk, a fool, or a hothead, a guy you can't trust and who really doesn't know how to take care of his people."

So I asked him again: "Well, do you mind that?"

He grinned and said: "Nah. I'm good either way."

THE HAUNTED CRACK HOUSE

BY MICHEL BASILIÈRES

Boulevard Saint-Laurent

R yan the Rat—Academy Award winner and cousin to Mickey Mouse (or so he said)—was red-faced and waving his arms, spittle flying, defending his turf. He shouted. He swore. He threatened to call the cops. But the bigger, burlier, toothless, bald-headed panhandler grabbed Ryan's entire face with one fat hand and shoved him to the ground, beating him with a white cane.

In the slush, Ryan twisted and crawled away. The victor leaned on his glinting white cane and faced the door of the restaurant, smiling at the customers shuffling in and out of the cold. Puffs of steam escaped the open door, carrying the smell of smoked meat, french fries, and beer across Boulevard Saint-Laurent and into the bookstore.

I sat on a high stool behind a wooden counter, facing the display window. Every day I watched people line up, rain or shine, to eat at Schwartz's. Whether it was broiling in the summer or freezing in the winter, the restaurant's queue stretched for over an hour's wait. Even after midnight you had to share a table.

Ryan stood ten feet away from the interloper who had just beaten him, yelling still, but now looking for a gap in the traffic. Finding one, he made a break for it. He loped and staggered across the street, pulling himself up into the recessed entrance, and yanked hard on the handle. He stepped up across the threshold and jumped away as the ancient coiled springs slammed the wooden, glass-paneled door back to the frame. The bell rang.

"Hi, Ryan."

He was twitching, his wire-frame glasses askew, his tattered cotton coat open. "Jesus fucking Christ. That fucker beat me. Did you see that?"

"Yeah."

"Fuckin' took my spot. That was my spot. Suppertime, that's my spot."

"I thought you guys had a schedule."

"Yeah, we do. Now's my time. Fucker took my spot, how am I going to make my money now?" He made his way to the center of the bookstore, took off his coat, and sat on the couch. "Can I dry my coat on the heater?"

"Sure. Don't let it catch fire."

It was a dark evening in late November and no customers were in the store. I was pricing a box of paperbacks I'd bought earlier. Across the street, Fucker was nonchalantly panhandling. He seemed to be doing well. Panhandlers come and go, but in this neighborhood they are mostly fixtures. Guys like Ryan actually lived, grew up, and fell apart here. This guy with the cane was new.

"I don't recognize him," I said.

Ryan took off his toque, shook out his head, walked over, and stood in front of my counter.

"I don't know who he is, either. I told him we got a system here, and that he wasn't welcome in our territory."

"Gonna get your buddies together and talk some sense into him?" I asked. There were four or five of them, mostly spindly derelicts, but numbers count. And even though Cane Man—or Fucker—was big, Ryan's closest ally on the street,

Billy One-Eye, was a scrapper. I'd seen him hold off more than one cop at a time.

"I ain't seen anybody all day," Ryan said. "Can I use the bathroom?"

The toilet in the back room wasn't for customers, but we often let our friends use it. Ryan was wet with dirty slush. "Go ahead. Don't mess it up."

"No, I won't. I promise. Thanks."

A few customers wandered in, browsed the rickety shelves, glanced over the tables, asked for titles or authors, wandered out. Ryan's coat was still on the heater, but he hadn't come back.

I opened the door to the office, yelled his name. No answer. I went in, turned right between shelves stacked high with overstock, special items, books reserved for regulars, random stuff placed aside to be dealt with later. Around the corner, the bathroom door was open. Ryan was on the throne, pants around his ankles, head back like his neck was broken. Snoring.

I kicked his foot. "Ryan. Wake up, for fuck sake." I had to kick harder.

Eventually his head came forward, his eyes opened, and he saw me standing there. Confusion. Recognition. He cleared his phlegmy throat. "Sorry." He stood and pulled up his pants. I walked away.

Back at the counter, Ryan asked, "You got any paper I could use?" He was an artist, had been a famous animator. He really did have an Oscar. Or had.

I reached under the counter, pulled open the printer tray, and peeled out a few sheets.

"Any pencils?"

I shoved a dirty glass jar full of battered pens and pencils across the counter.

"Thanks." He sunk onto the couch and put pencil to paper. I finished pricing the books, set some of them out on the display table, shelved the rest in the new arrivals case. The phone rang, a regular came in and asked after the boss, a couple of arts students came and went, and Cane Man was still there, leaning hard on his cane, making a show of it, drumming up business. Snow fell, big flakes, slow and quiet, sucking up the noise of traffic.

Ryan looked over. "Ah, shit. What time is it?"

I glanced at the clock. "Ten."

"Shit. Ah, shit." He shoved his drawings aside, stood up, and paced back and forth. "Fuck."

"What is it?"

He hurried around the couch. "I'm late. I'm too late. Fuckin' hell."

"Late for what?"

"The mission. Closes at ten. Fuck. You gotta be there early to get a bed. Fuckity fuck."

Which meant Ryan had no place to sleep.

I took some twenties from the till, added up the day's receipts, shoved a wad of cash where the boss would find it, washed the floor, donned my coat, and locked the door. Ryan was sitting on the stoop, staring at Cane Man, who was still at his post across the street.

"I'll buy you a beer," I said.

He jerked his head up. "Really? Thanks, man. That's great." He stood up, stamped his feet, and got out of my way. We walked south a block under the orange streetlights. Snow came down heavy and silent. The street was a mess of shiny rivulets and tracks in the gray slush. It was almost midnight. Taxis drove north past us.

We went into Bar Saint-Laurent, really an empty retail space, no decor, shabby tables and wooden chairs. The kind of place you don't want to see in the light. I ordered a cheap pitcher of Boréale Rousse and poured glasses for the both of us.

Ryan grabbed his and drained it. His eyes shone, a deep satisfied breath gushed from him. He leaned forward and filled his glass again. There weren't many customers. Les Cowboys Fringants were thrashing from the speakers, a song about UQUAM girls on Rue Saint-Denis.

"Can I crash with you?" he asked.

"No." I was only willing to go so far. Ryan knew a lot of people, but he'd burned them all. His parents still lived out on the West Island, but they hadn't spoken to him for years, ever since the infamous mural incident.

In his youth Ryan wasn't so bad; as long as his alcohol and drug intake didn't get out of hand, and as long as someone made him take his meds, he was fine. But when he got a little money, when his short films began to be taught in film schools, he moved out on his own and unraveled. He got a huge commission on the strength of his Oscar and an offer to paint a giant mural of whatever he wanted on the lobby wall of the new the National Film Board building in Montreal. He had carte blanche and worked on the mural in secret until the unveiling. The mural's debut ceremony was posh, of course, with socialites, bankers, government ministers, and state-approved artists in attendance. They drew the curtain, and that was it. His career was over.

The scene depicted Ryan himself, masturbating to pictures of his mother.

His parents wouldn't take his calls after that. No one would. Over the years people tried to give him some help, work, a place to stay, money, but it always ended badly. For years he'd been in and out of hospitals, jails, flophouses, missions. Now he begged for spare change. For a few months in the summer, a carpenter on Duluth had been letting him sleep in his enclosed yard with the lumber. It wasn't indoors, but it gave him some safety and shelter from the wind and rain. But now it was too cold to sleep outside.

"I had a place to stay last week," he said.

"Yeah? What happened?"

He drank half the glass. "A guy offered me a place to crash if I knew where to score a rock."

"I thought you were off crack?"

"Yeah, yeah, I was," he said earnestly. "But shit, I needed a place to sleep. So I took him to my friend and he bought a few boulders and I went with him." He finished the glass. I poured.

"When we were high, he tried to give me a blow job." He shook his head, as if in disbelief, but it wobbled like he'd lost power over it.

"You take it?"

"Fuck no. I'm not a homo. But when I tried to leave, he beat me. I'm a little guy, I can't fight. He punched me every time I got off the couch. Then he tied me up."

"You serious?"

"Yeah. He got out ropes and fuckin' leather straps. Bondage, you know? He kept me there for days, he beat me and sexually abused me." Ryan went quiet, his head still trembling, his eyes on the table. He carefully brought the glass to his lips and sipped slowly. "Then he threw me out."

I was going to leave him with the pitcher when I finished my glass, but then Billy One-Eye came in. He saw us and came right over.

"Ryan, there you are. What're you doing here? Why didn't you come to the mission?"

"I got fucked up. It wasn't my fault."

Billy looked at the nearly empty pitcher on the table, and swallowed. His good eye made contact with mine. It was a question. I kicked out a free chair for him, raised my arm for the waitress. He sat and said, "I waited for you, saved you a cot beside me for as long as I could. When you didn't show up, I got worried. Came up here to see if you were still at Schwartz's or something. Thought you must be making a lot of money."

"Some fucker pushed me out."

"Big guy with a cane?"

"Yeah."

"He's still there. I asked if he'd seen you. He said no."

"Fuckin' liar," said Ryan. "He beat me up and took my spot."

I ordered another glass and another pitcher.

"Want to go talk to him?" Billy wasn't much taller than Ryan, but he was built solid. Big trunk, big arms and legs, round face. He still had both eyes, but one didn't work—it was enlarged, the iris milked over, bloodshot, leaky, like it was sore; the lid wouldn't close over it anymore. Billy was from up north, not soft-spoken exactly, but a kindhearted guy. Something in his voice was like a fairy godmother, no matter what he was saying. His thing was heroin.

The waitress came back with Billy's glass and the beer.

"Not now," said Ryan.

I had one more glass but it wasn't long before the second pitcher was near empty. Billy and Ryan were talking, but having two different conversations, both laughing, slurring words, asking me for cigarettes every minute or so. I didn't smoke.

I stayed too long; Max Ygoe came in, looked around, and saw us. He stomped his work boots over to the bar, took an upside-down glass from the sink, and slapped it on the table. He shook out of his raccoon coat and emptied the pitcher into his glass. Before setting it down, he craned around to the bar and waved it at the waitress. "Cheers, fellows," he said, and drained his glass.

"That's one you owe me," I said. I didn't like Max. He was a sculptor, chisels and stone, always covered in dust. A big guy, older, maybe sixty-five, strong, still a lot of muscle under slackening skin. He talked too much about whores in Rome after the war, and working with Irving Stone on that book about Michelangelo. Always a story about the cat houses, the black hair, and big tits. You could be introducing your grandmother to him, and she'd remind him of a hooker.

"You see that waitress?" She was coming over with the beer, and as she bent to put it on the table between us, Max pointed, almost grabbing her. "Look at those cans. Nice."

I handed her a twenty. "For the first two," I said, indicating the empty pitcher. She grabbed the empties and left. I filled my glass. I didn't want more beer, I just wanted back what Max took. I filled Ryan's and Billy's too.

"You shouldn't be buying beer for rummies," said Max, laughing.

Billy sipped. "Hey, fuck you."

Ryan lifted his glass and tried to smile. "Fellow artist."

"Working late?" I said.

He put his glass down, smacked his lips. "I sent off a commission today. For Portuguese Park on Rue Rachel. Got a new block of stone coming in tomorrow. A big one, need to make some room, get set up for the new project. I got thirsty." As if he'd reminded himself, he filled his glass again.

* * *

We walked back up the slope the way we'd came. I lived up near Mount Royal; Max's studio was right beside the bookstore. Billy and Ryan had nowhere to go, so they followed behind us, staggering, bumming smokes from people on the street.

With the beer in him, Max was convinced I was interested in listening to him talk about himself. He was going on about his new project and the big stone that was coming tomorrow.

Truthfully, no one cared about Max's work. He didn't have a dealer, no pieces in public galleries, and no one writing about him in the papers or art magazines. He made his living through public commissions, like the fountain for the park he'd just finished.

Max had been trying to change that all his life; he was about to start out on his latest attempt, "a big fucking piece," he was saying, trying to pierce me with his gaze. "A major piece. The only theme that matters—man. *Ecce homo*. Adam. He's going to be seven feet tall, emerging from the rock itself, dragging his cock into the world. Commanding. Frightening. Overpowering. Women and fags will cower before him. He will make my name."

"Nice," I said, but that's not what I was thinking.

"I'll get a fucking medal," Max went on. He noticed I wasn't looking at him. "Listen to me. There'll be a reception, dinner, and tuxedos. When the visual arts officer's standing at the podium introducing me, his wife will be under the table sucking me off."

Max and I stopped in front of the chain-link fence that enclosed the yard in front of his studio. It was above Berson's Monuments, a headstone maker that had been there since the twenties. One side the yard was stacked with marble and granite slabs waiting to be cut and engraved but most of the space was arranged with earth and grass and various mod-els of headstone set up so customers could get an idea of the effect. Under the yard's spotlight and the orange glow from the streetlights, the shadows were cast at odd angles and the headstones were all too close together. It was the perfect place for a sculptor—stone was always being delivered and Berson let him use the crane to load and unload his materials.

Across the top of the building, the original Hebrew sign was still visible. The language police tried once to get Berson to take it down, but they backed off quick when Mordecai Richler made fun of them in the *New York Times* for it.

Ryan and Billy had caught up to us, and now they noticed Cane Man was still across the street, trying his luck with the last few customers leaving Schwartz's.

Billy said, "C'mon, let's get him, there's four of us now." He pulled Ryan into the street with him. Ryan needed some convincing, but when the traffic that stopped for them became impatient and honked them out of the way, he went. Billy was already yelling at the guy with the cane.

"Shitheads," said Max.

"C'mon, let's go," I said.

"I'm not beating up a bum, for Christ's sake."

"We're not going to join the fight, Max. We're going to stop it." Eventually he followed me. When I made it across, Billy'd already got the guy's cane away from him and was whacking him. The guy had his hands up and his head bent away, but he was advancing on Billy. Ryan was doing nothing but yelling.

The guy saw me approach and stopped short, wondering. Max came up behind me. Cane Man, still fending off blows from Billy, looked him up and down, back to me, and said, "Eat shit, all of you."

Then he turned, ran up to the corner, and was gone.

"You forgot your cane!" Billy yelled. "Never seen a cripple run so good." He lifted the cane and cracked it in two across his knee.

Ryan was leaning back against a parked car. A waiter came out of Schwartz's and looked around. "No fighting here or we call the cops. Understand?"

"Yes sir," said Ryan. "No problem, sir." He started crying. The waiter went back inside.

"Ryan, what's wrong, buddy?" asked Billy.

"Nothing. Nothing more than usual. Fuckin' freezing, no money, no place to sleep. What are we gonna do, Billy?"

Billy had no answer.

Max said, "You guys come help me finish up. There's not much to do. You sweep my floor, you can sleep on it tonight."

"Really?" said Ryan. I was surprised too.

"But you leave tomorrow. It only locks from the outside. I'm coming back at ten thirty, I'll let you out then." He turned and crossed the street.

Billy yanked Ryan to his feet and they followed. I watched Max open the padlocked gate and secure it again after they entered. He led them between stacks of headstones, and then, for a moment, they disappeared. They came back into view climbing the outside wooden staircase to the balcony along the second floor, just under the Hebrew lettering. Max opened another padlock, an iron latch, pushed open the heavy wooden door, and went in. The door closed after them, and a dim light came on behind the murky windows.

I walked north up the hill. It was just after two in the morning and the snow had stopped, but it was white along the edges of the sidewalk.

* * *

The next day I watched a tractor trailer snake its way into Berson's narrow entrance, blocking the entire street. The winch pulled an enormous granite slab off the truck bed and it slowly slid across to the delivery door on the second floor. Max guided it by hand onto a pump truck. When the winch set it down, the balcony groaned and gave an inch. Max, Ryan, and Billy pushed the pump truck together. Max and Billy had their backs into it, but Ryan flitted around like a moth.

Thereafter, Ryan slept nights in the studio. He'd come and go through the lane in the back, hopping a fence, up the fire escape, and in through a window hidden in a crook between the buildings that Max left unlocked for him.

I wondered how long that would last.

It happened again, of course. I was locking up early a few weeks later. It was a Friday, in December now, and the first winter blizzard, although just beginning, had already dumped about two feet of snow in the past couple of hours. Many shops had closed before dinner, the plows were out, and traffic was a mess; no one had been in the bookstore since sundown.

Across the street, the only place of business that still had customers was Schwartz's, as usual, and there was Ryan, his shoulders piled in snow, arguing with Cane Man. I had to hop over drifts of snow up to my knees to cross the street. When I got there, a guy from Schwartz's had come out to join the shouting.

"There's always a fight with you," he complained to Cane Man. "Get lost and don't come back. You're not welcome here."

"It's a free country," he replied. "It's a public sidewalk. You can't stop me standing here."

"You can't stop me from calling the cops, either!" the waiter shouted.

"What for?"

The waiter took his notebook from his back pocket. "Not paying for the smoked meat you ate."

"That's a lie. I didn't eat any smoked meat."

The waiter was writing in the notebook. "I got a tab right here says you ate smoked meat, fries, and a pickle. I got a restaurant full of witnesses. What have you got?"

Cane Man swore a little, then went silent. The waiter stared him down. Cane Man finally looked to Ryan, who turned his head away. Then he turned to me. "The fuck *you* want?"

I didn't say anything.

Cane Man turned and shuffled away in the snow. The waiter went back in.

"You eat today?" I asked Ryan.

He thought about it. "Had a Mars bar at lunch."

"C'mon," I said, "you might as well pack it in and get some food while you can." We went into Schwartz's. My glasses fogged. For once there were plenty of seats. We sat way in the back. We ordered the usual, exactly what Cane Man hadn't paid for.

The lights were bright, there was still a fair bit of noise even though it wasn't crowded. Conversations were yelled from the patrons to the cooks, from the cooks to the waiters, from the waiters to the cashier high up on his stool in the front window beside the door. French, English, Portuguese, even a little Yiddish. Plates and cutlery, sizzling grill, the door opening and closing. Our sandwiches came.

I gobbled mine, but Ryan ate slowly and left half on his plate. "Something the matter?" I asked.

He shook his head. "I'm saving this for Billy. He's across the street." He meant in Max's studio.

"I thought that was supposed to be just you."

"Yeah, but I can't turn Billy out. Besides, Max don't mind."

"Does he know?"

Ryan shrugged. "I guess so. Hey, why don't you come on over, I got something I want to show you. Something I've been working on."

We had the waiter bag the leftovers. Outside, the snow was still falling. Light from the streetlamps bounced around painfully. It was still night, but the street shone without shadows. Big plows were grumbling up the center of the street, smaller ones on the sidewalks. Trucks were being loaded with snow—they'd be at it for days, according to the weatherman.

We had to go down to Pine Avenue and up the lane, which hadn't been plowed. At least the snow covered the garbage and mud, which was all I ever saw there in the summer. But it was a hard slog on the uneven ground for a quarter-mile back to the rear of Max's. We cleared a path with our knees. Halfway there I was soaked from the upper thighs on down to my boots.

Ryan reached over the wooden fence, clicked something, and the framed door jerked open. He pushed it back, crushing away the snow behind it. I bent my head and followed him through, trying to step in the footprints he had left behind. I pushed the door shut behind us.

He started up the iron fire escape, waving his foot back and forth to clear each step. On the landing he reached around the corner of the building and into a light well affixed to the adjoining building. He hauled himself around the corner.

"What the fuck?" I said.

Ryan popped his head back. "It's easy, there's a one-foot drop to the bottom."

I reached over and found the window frame easily. I swung myself around the corner and placed my foot exactly where I expected to find the sill. Ryan had the bottom half open already and was hopping in as I crouched and followed him. We were inside.

I waited in the dark while Ryan shuffled around bumping into things. The light came on with a loud click. He was standing beside a wall switch. I stamped the snow from my boots. Over on the couch, beyond the partially sculpted stone, was Billy, one foot on the floor, asleep or passed out.

Ryan called, "Hey, Billy, it's us," but he didn't move. We went over to take a look. He was perfectly still, I couldn't tell if he was breathing or see his eyes fluttering. His good eye was closed. The bad one was popping out of his face like a dick through foreskin, but it had still managed to turn up. At least I couldn't see a pupil. On the coffee table beside him, his things were set out: an open bottle of Griffin, some change, a bus ticket.

The matches, the bent spoon, the plastic bag, the syringe—they were all there too.

"Jesus Christ, Billy." Ryan jumped on him in a panic.

Billy woke fighting. "Cocksucker! What the fuck?"

Ryan leaped off him, gasping. "I thought you were fuckin' dead."

Billy was wide-eyed, crouched with his fists up, red-faced with tension and anger. "The fuck? You fucking idiot." He relaxed, but he was still angry.

There was one shabby chair. I sat in it; Ryan took a pillow and sat at the short end of the coffee table. "What did you want to show me?"

"Oh, yeah," said Ryan, who got up, shuffled through a pile of stuff tucked against the wall, and brought out some papers.

Despite Ryan's habitual tremors, the lines of his drawings were elegant and fluid. The pictures were simple, almost

outlines really, big loose suggestions of figures, objects, buildings. The people were all naked; their feet were never on the
ground, and their limbs seemed to float away. They were like
cartoons, the colors indicated by the thick strokes in different
pens. I couldn't see anything different about these, they were
just like any others of his I'd seen—beautiful.

"What am I looking at?"

"You're looking at the wrong side."

I turned them over and saw charcoal sketches of the studio
with Max's stone in it, newly delivered through the process of
sculpting, like a record of watching Max work. I glanced from
the statue to the sketches, and back. Ryan's drawings looked
less finished but more natural, yet the face emerging from the
stone was not a clean, young, hard face, it was a square grim
face, with broad flat cheeks and dead eyes. On some of the
sketches Ryan had scrawled odd birds or swirls in the air.

"Kind of grim," I said.

"I got the idea from the letters outside on the sign and
staring at that stupid statue. You ever see this old German
movie about the golem? Old Jewish legend from the ghetto?"

"I know it—I read Meyrink and saw the movie at Concordia." I peered at his drawings again and could now imagine
the little swirls as Hebrew letters. I looked at Max's stone, the
figure was still only roughed out but you could already see the
upturned face of an idealized man looking to the heavens, like
a worker in a Soviet poster, and even more prominent, the
rough mass of his up-thrusting phallus, like a prod, and I said,
"You know, Ryan, Max is an asshole. But you made art."

Billy opened his stamp and tapped the remaining few
grains out onto a clean spot on the coffee table. He picked
up the foil of Ryan's crack, found a few tiny rocks, put them
down with the dark powder, and crushed it all together with

the back of his spoon. It was a tiny pile. I took my dime bag out, dropped the last few crumbs of bud into it. Billy mashed it all up. I gave him my papers and he deftly slid the powder into the crease of the Zig-Zag. He rolled, licked, lit. We smoked. I went to the fridge. Max had a few bottles of beer in there. I grabbed three and twisted off the caps.

By the time I brought them back to the coffee table, I wanted to leave. Billy One-Eye was snoring; Ryan's head was down and he wasn't saying anything. I suddenly felt extraordinarily tired, like if I didn't move soon, it would be too late.

I woke with the feeling, but not the memory, that I'd heard a sound. I was high, and upon opening my eyes in the semi-darkness of the candlelight, I sensed the speed with which the universe revolved around me. Had I dreamed it? What have I been dreaming?

It was an effort to keep my own head still and focus. Ryan was still in the wooden chair, slumped over, and Billy was stiff as a corpse, like he had been when we entered.

But there—shuffling steps in the kitchen, where the light was still on, and a draft came from the open window.

Open. I had closed it. Ryan had asked.

Then I heard the window slowly closing.

I struggled to clear my head, unsure what to do. But it didn't matter. I was drugged, I felt as if I were in a cocoon or a womb. I could wriggle and kick and perhaps turn over, but I couldn't manage to lift myself up and I struggled simply to maintain consciousness.

A figure filled the kitchen door, a big man blocking the light. He entered the studio and loomed behind Max's statue. He was almost as big, but soon disappeared in the shadows behind. I heard him stomping around, and then approaching us. He was standing behind the couch I was on, but I couldn't turn my head to look at him. I was lying on my side, looking across at a passed-out Billy. Ryan was only visible in my peripheral vision.

As I lay there, trying to get up and keep my eyes open, I saw him lumber out from behind the half-formed statue, almost staggering, leaning on something; it looked like a staff. Or—wait. A cane. Cane Man. He must have followed us.

I couldn't sit up to ask Ryan or Billy. Both were snoring, as I had been. I could only watch behind my heavy lids, which opened and closed slowly, as Cane Man approached. He must have stubbed his trailing foot on the sculpture—he swore when it shifted weight and thumped the floor; the couch beneath me swayed like a canoe, and I twitched instinctively, my hand flopping and knocking an empty beer bottle off the coffee table.

I felt like the ground was gone and I was falling backward, then I got the darkness with the electric sparkles, and suddenly the world was black again.

Billy got up like a dead man. Ryan was dancing around, freaking out, like some animal caught in a trap, swearing spittle across the room in a ragged arc.

Billy was staggering over, not really conscious, just doing what Ryan was screaming at him, going over to fight with Cane Man.

He was just standing there, sizing things up. He glanced at me on the couch, then looked away quickly. He brought his attention toward Billy, who was slowly making his way toward him, hunched over and leaning on things as he walked—the arm of the couch, the coffee table, a chair beside it. Cane Man then turned to Ryan and brought his cane high above his head, swinging down on Ryan's skull with both hands.

Ryan collapsed and screamed like a girl. Billy roared and straightened up, like a bow unstrung. He rounded his fist and delivered an underhand punch into Cane Man's left kidney. The guy went down on top of a whimpering Ryan, who yelped upon impact. Billy lost his footing and also fell face-first onto the pile.

Beyond the statue, the light from the kitchen shone across the end of the room. Everything seemed to glow faintly, and light spilled like fog into the darkness. It seemed almost to pile up at the base of the statue, spilling around it in swirling eddies and shining from within rather than being illuminated from without.

Then my attention was caught by the Cane Man's movements, and when I blinked, my eyes were focused on him, down the long trail of the couch with my feet so tiny in the distance, and beside me the stained and crowded wooden coffee table, the empty bottles and cans, towering over the ashtrays, matchbooks, lighters, forks, packs of cigarettes, and other debris like skyscrapers over crowded streets, and I could faintly make out his outline in the darkness behind Ryan, passed out in his chair, head bowed and leaning back into the corner with his palms together under his cheek and his knees drawn up.

Cane Man seemed to stumble on something in the darkness, maybe even bump into the chair, because I heard a tiny rumbling like thunder down a long tunnel. Ryan squeaked and leaped up off the floor, grabbing hold of the couch to anchor himself.

Cane Man came into the light, his face a red scowl. Ryan was yelling. Billy roused too, but with lids lying low and bags under his eyes. He grabbed Cane Man's arm but fell forward at the same time.

Ryan dodged out of the way; Billy ran forward a few un-steady steps, though he recovered with his arms spread like he was about to rise from the earth. Cane Man fell forward onto the floor where Ryan had just been.

I saw Billy run out of my vision like an actor dashing into the darkness in the wings of a theater. I saw Cane Man's big frame scrape the wide wooden planks of the floor, and then from the right side of my peripheral vision, I saw Billy jump back on top of Cane Man, stomping his head and his face, hopping around on one foot.

A sound like a carbonated waterfall roared in my ears, and the statue, still radiant and diffuse against the darkness, sailed across my vision from the left and dropped upon Cane Man like a lover upon his betrothed, and there was an echoing boom as the great phallus found its mark, the torso smother-ing the now prone Cane Man, the shoulder popping his skull like a blueberry between your fingers just as Billy, without turning about or flinching a muscle, suddenly bounded back-ward away from the spread of brains, blood, and eyes trailing connective tissue and nerves like spermatozoa or comets.

Suddenly there was silence, which either lasted less than a second or an interminably long time, or both. Ryan ap-proached from the left and Billy approached from the right and all I could see beyond my distant and tiny feet was a gran-ite boulder rising to a point like a triangle and then the two of them slowly, and as if on purpose in synchronization, turned their faces toward mine.

They staggered and climbed over whatever was in their way and it took the two of them to lift me from the couch and drag me, one on either side, to the window. Billy took a handful of snow from the sill and smashed it all over my face, and then Ryan slapped me until I roused enough to help them get me over the sill, out the window, and onto the fire escape.

We slowly climbed our way down, acutely aware of how high we were, of what had just taken place, and of the need to get away as quickly as possible. We fell and tripped and scraped our way down the iron staircase, making too much noise. But this was Saint-Laurent, where strange noises were normal every night. We didn't arouse any suspicion.

Like drunken revelers we climbed up Saint-Urbain's hill toward Mount Royal, where Ryan and Billy pulled and pushed me up the stairs to my second-floor flat. When we got inside, my girlfriend woke and gave us a stony welcome. She took me from them, angry I'd brought them home—though in truth it was the other way around—and led me to bed. After I stripped out of my clothes and climbed under the sheets, I began to cry uncontrollably, like a child, great sobs blinding me. My girlfriend turned away from me, and left me to cry myself out.

When Max opened the studio door the next day, there was his glorious statue, his *ecce homo*, pinning the broken rummy to the floor, his phallus up the bum, so to speak. He called the cops, but they never made any arrests. The *Gazette* reported that a homeless man was tragically killed seeking shelter in the massive blizzard, and the city spent the next week clearing snow and ice from the streets.

My girlfriend never forgave me for letting Ryan and Billy crash with us that night. Things only got worse between us from there. She went off to Toronto and I stayed home. Ryan and Billy moved into a rooming house, which they could barely afford between their welfare checks, so they supplemented their income by panhandling. Ryan was back across the street outside Schwartz's, but he could never again stay the night at Max Ygoe's studio. He tried to sell his drawings; I even gave him ten bucks for one, though I can't tell what it's supposed to be. It hangs over the couch he slept on that night he saved me from being found unconscious and surrounded by drug paraphernalia at a murder scene.

Billy died later that year. He was found among some garbage bins behind the Belgian fries place in the heat of summer, near Duluth, a needle sticking out of his arm. Overdose was the verdict, yet Ryan swore to me that it couldn't have been an accident—Billy was too experienced and careful for that. According to him it must have been on purpose.

Later that year a guy started making a film about Ryan, a documentary about his fall from grace and his life on the street. And when it won an Academy Award two years later, Ryan and his buddies were watching the Oscars on the big screen at the Bar Saint-Laurent, so he saw his eventual triumph, and not long after he succumbed to the cancer he'd been ignoring for a couple of years.

WILD HORSES

BY ARJUN BASU

Mile End

Albertson wakes to the sound of horses galloping. He looks out his window, and yes, there are horses racing down his street. He watches them cross another street and run into the darkness, toward the condo construction site two blocks away. He pinches himself to make sure he's not dreaming. He can already see himself at work, saying, *You know what I saw this morning?* He will tell his story unless the media picks it up first, and they are sure to—someone's probably blogging about it right now. Either way, he'll still have a story. His story. And women love horses.

Albertson is the manager of a shoe store downtown, and all of his employees and customers are women. And these women are not the types to drag around their indifferent husbands, the kind of men who show distaste with aggressive boredom. No, Albertson's shoe store is for women, for girlfriends, the kind of women who will be impressed by horses running down the middle of a city street.

After a quick scan online and a survey of the local TV networks, Albertson finds no media reports about horses running wild though the city. There are no blogs, no status updates, no photos. The radio is silent on the matter of horses invading Mile End. In both languages.

Albertson's blood feels like it's changed color. *Why is no one acknowledging what I have just seen?*

He walks up his street, past the butcher with the grass-fed veal, the boulangerie owned by the tattooed guy, and the ceramics shop with the collection of fine art chopsticks. When he turns the corner, he sees orange-helmeted construction workers standing under the green loft project and condo developments that are surely going to change everything about this place. And then there, just beyond the construction site, is a hole in the ground, where fresh horse shit has been flattened by traffic. The unmistakable smell of horse shit steams from the hole, filling the air. It is obvious.

Albertson walks up to a hip young man wearing a tartan bowler hat and a skinny blazer, and asks, "Do you smell that?" The man stops and sniffs the air.

"What?"

"Do you smell something odd?"

The man in the bowler hat takes a good deep whiff. Deliberate. He's polite. "Like out of the ordinary?"

"You don't smell it?" Albertson is incredulous.

The man sniffs the air again and looks at Albertson before walking away, breaking into a trot after several paces.

Albertson wants to reach down and touch the horse droppings, but he has to get to work. He wants that horse shit to be horse shit, so he walks over to it, looks around, and puts his right shoe in the biggest pile. The give. It goes right through his brown Oxfords, right up to his brain. It registers as horse shit; he smiles triumphantly.

He returns to his apartment and changes into another pair of brown Oxfords, putting his single shit-encrusted shoe into a plastic bag and into the freezer. He goes to work.

At work he waits. He waits for one of his employees or a customer, anyone, to bring up the horses. Every time his phone rings, he expects a call about them. He checks the Internet constantly, his social media channels, the news. The city *must* know there are wild horses about. They are running up our streets at night, shitting near half-finished condos, and running some more. He has proof of these things. He smelled it. He saw the horses. He heard them and then he saw them and then he smelled them. That's three senses.

Albertson swims through the day and no one brings up the horses. The radio is silent on horses. He googles it, because at the end of day, if it isn't on Google, it isn't real. Nothing turns up.

He begins to entertain the possibility that perhaps there were no horses. He asks about horses on his Facebook page and receives no response. After he closes the store, he races home to inspect his Oxford shoes, and there it is. Horse shit. He has horse shit on his shoe. It wasn't a dream, it was real. He has a shit-covered shoe in the freezer. It's his link to an event he knows happened. To a specific reality.

Albertson goes to the park to investigate. He walks up to a dog owner who is waiting for the inevitable to drop out of her animal's backside. Albertson approaches the woman and her dog cautiously.

"Were you out last night?" he asks, which is the wrong way to approach a stranger, he knows, but he can't take it back.

"Excuse me?" she replies, looking at her dog as it squats, getting in position. She knows she's trapped. She can't get away. Not yet.

"Sorry," Albertson says. He stammers a bit and pushes his hair back. "Last night. Here. Did you see them?"

The woman is distracted by her dog. It's not doing what it needs to do. The thing is a small mongrel, definitely some type of terrier.

"The horses," Albertson clarifies in a soft whisper. He feels like a dissident in Communist Germany. "They galloped down this very street. A herd of them."

She smiles sympathetically. "Are you crazy or is this an elaborate pickup line?"

Her dog has shifted position, walked to another spot a foot away, and is trying again. Albertson can sense its exertion. "I wish," he says, still whispering.

"You wish what?" she asks. "You can do it, Bella. Go on."

"Early this morning. I saw them. I heard them. I even stepped in their poop."

She puts a finger to her lips to shush him. "Don't say that," she says, lowering her head. "We're not supposed to talk about it."

Meanwhile, Bella squeezes out a small turd, something small, even for a little dog. She seems satisfied, however, and comes over to sniff Albertson's pant leg.

"Good girl!" the woman chirps. Bella looks up and wags her tail.

"We're not supposed to talk about what?"

"There were no horses," she says, giving Bella's leash a yank and walking away without bagging her dog's poop.

At the other end of the park, Albertson spots another dog walker, an elderly man with a robust German shepherd. The dog takes note of him as he approaches, and sits, alert. Albertson slows his walk.

"She's friendly," the man says, but Albertson decides to stay where he is, twenty feet away.

"I was wondering if I could ask you a question," he says to the old man.

The man pets the dog as it walks in circles, sniffing, completing its picture of the world. "Shoot."

"Were you walking your dog this morning?"

The man's face freezes. It's subtle, but Albertson notices. "Do I know you?"

"I'm wondering if you saw anything odd this morning."

"What kind of odd?"

"Out of the ordinary," Albertson says. He is sinking into code speak.

The man's face hardens. "What are you going on about?"

"I'm sorry to bother you," Albertson says, turning to leave. He has to look at his shoes again, in the freezer. He needs to confirm the events. Because now he's not sure. Again.

"Sorry I couldn't help you," the man calls out.

Albertson turns back around. "Something odd is happening," he says.

The man takes a step toward Albertson and then stops. "Perhaps you need some sleep," he offers gently.

"Horses," Albertson whispers.

"Horses?"

"Wild horses. A herd of them. Galloping down the street. Early this morning." Albertson feels out of breath now.

"Something like that would have showed up on the news, no?" the old man says, and this triggers in Albertson a kind of low-level panic. He feels his ears get warm, tingling.

"Y-yes," he stammers. "You'd think." Albertson turns and walks away, slowly, back to his apartment. He knows what he saw, but he needs to look at his shoe again.

Back at home, Albertson opens the freezer. There is his brown Oxford encrusted with horse shit. He opens a beer, sits down on the couch, and turns on the TV. He searches for news of what he saw, for some form of evidence, but finds none. He opens his laptop, scours the Internet, but nothing shows up—his search takes him everywhere but to the place he wants to go. *Nothing.* Less than that. Disappointment. A feeling that he is not himself, that what he knows is wrong, that everything he thinks about himself, everything he dreams, is all wrong.

A dream would not have covered his shoe in horse shit. That stuff is real. Everything else isn't.

Across the street from the shoe store is a lingerie boutique owned by a middle-aged Indian woman. She comes in for shoes every few weeks, and Albertson attends to her personally. Mrs. Sen has large feet and stands a head above Albertson. She often makes a point of noting how rare it is for an Indian woman to be her height. Albertson always feigns surprise, and Mrs. Sen buys her giant shoes—she's been partial to Mary Janes lately—and returns to her boutique, but sometimes she doesn't. Sometimes they go out for lunch and talk, and she tells Albertson about her childhood in a village north of Calcutta, and the unfortunate skateboarding accident that killed her first husband, and how her new husband is a judge who has bad breath and always interrupts her, and how she doesn't know what to do with him, but won't leave him because they're invited to all the good parties, and she quite enjoys her new social life.

Today, Mrs. Sen enters the store and takes a seat on the divan. Albertson puts down his coffee and walks over to her.

"Mrs. Sen," he says, smiling.

"We're having a dinner party, you know."

"And what will you be wearing?"

"No, no, I'm not here for shoes," she says, laughing. "I'm here to invite you."

This is an odd thing, Albertson thinks. Beyond their lunches, Mrs. Sen has never invited him into her social orbit. "When?" he asks.

A pair of shoes has caught Mrs. Sen's attention, a pair of muted-blue open-toed pumps. "Oh my," she says.

"I'll have to check if we have your size."

Mrs. Sen turns sharply to him as if he has just said something amazingly rude. "I don't want them."

"I can check."

"Friday night." She stands and takes a look at the shoes again. "Can you order them?" she asks.

"For Friday?"

"I don't need them for Friday. It's nothing fancy. Some dentists. A doctor. The usual lawyers and judges. A city councillor. The lady who owns the nice café in the food court. She has a young boyfriend who's a musician."

"I can order the shoes," Albertson says.

"Thank you. Bring wine if you want."

As Mrs. Sen steps into the damp light of the mall, she calls Albertson over, and he rushes to her. She leans in, motioning him to come closer.

"Did you see the horses?" she asks in a whisper. Albertson's eyes radiate fear and awe, but also community. A communal warmth. Bathed in cold.

Albertson picks up a Beaujolais. He doesn't know a thing about wine, can't tell the difference between names or regions or grapes. The girl at the SAQ looks like she's just turned eighteen, but acts like she's been drinking wine forever. He decides not to ask her about the horses. He's convinced that everyone around him knows something about the horses, something he isn't allowed to know. That his understanding of this isn't permitted. By someone. By someone important.

Mrs. Sen and her husband live downtown on Sherbrooke Street, in an ancient high-rise, built when the city was prosperous. Back then, if you said you lived on Sherbrooke Street, it meant a lot more than a street name. It meant more than money, class, or anything like that. If you said you lived on Sherbrooke Street, it meant that, because of your address, you had inexhaustible power. That if you'd told someone the world revolved around you, they would have had to consider the possibility. All because of your address.

Albertson announces himself to the elderly doorman, who gets on the phone, nods, and welcomes him in. The doorman escorts him into a tiny elevator that smells like lemon-scented wood polish.

Albertson knocks on Mrs. Sen's door, and she answers with a look of momentary confusion—Albertson is not on her regular guest list, after all. He holds out the wine bottle awkwardly in his hands.

"The girl said it was a good year for Beaujolais."

"What girl?"

"At the SAQ. I know nothing about wine, unfortunately."

She accepts it and studies the label. She puts the bottle down on the side table where Albertson imagines it will sit, forgotten. "Come in."

He takes in the apartment's decayed grandeur, the vaguely yellowish lights and dimly lit corners populated by exotic statues, bookcases, and half-dead plants. The apartment smells like the elevator, mixed with some unidentifiable odor coming from the kitchen, a collection of spices he can't quite make out.

"Let me introduce you to my husband."

She takes his arm and leads him to a room with three dignified-looking men, all in gray suits, standing and talking, each holding a tumbler of Scotch.

"Am I early?" asks Albertson.

Mrs. Sen stops walking and looks at him oddly. "No. My guests are late. Annoyingly so. My husband just arrived himself. He's in his study."

She opens the door to the study and her husband, the judge, is standing in the middle of the room, also holding a tumbler of Scotch, watching television.

"Louis, this is the young man who sells me my shoes."

The judge turns to face him. He studies Albertson and Albertson studies him and neither man learns much. Louis is wearing a gray suit; it seems to be a uniform.

"My wife owns a lot of shoes. You are a very lucky man."

Mrs. Sen nudges Albertson toward her husband. Albertson allows himself to be nudged.

"Mrs. Sen has an eye for footwear," says Albertson, uncomfortably.

The judge takes a sip of his Scotch and turns off the TV. "Nothing about the horses," he sighs, smiling.

Albertson is confused, yet intrigued. "I have questions about the horses."

The judge walks to a corner and sits on a chair. "What kind of questions?"

Albertson turns to look for Mrs. Sen, but she is gone. The door is closed. Albertson is alone in the room with the judge. "I have a shoe in my freezer at home with horse shit on it."

Louis's eyebrows reach north.

"I heard them, but there's nothing on the news, the Internet, the radio. Nothing. Not even the people on my street saw anything." Albertson lowers his voice: "They act as if I shouldn't bring it up. And I've only brought it up with a few of them."

The judge stands and walks to an alcove in the wall and opens a door. "Would you like a Scotch?"

Albertson nods.

The judge pours the Scotch and hands it to him. "Have a seat," he says, pulling a chair from the corner and placing it in the center of the room.

Albertson sits.

"Wait here," says the judge, leaving the room.

Albertson sips his drink and closes his eyes. He sees the horses again, feels them rumble through his chest. When he opens his eyes, the judge is before him. This time, he's with one of the men in the gray suits. "This is my colleague, Bertrand."

Bertrand is older than Louis, with thinning white hair and brown marks splotching his temple. He holds out his hand to Albertson and shakes firmly. Bertrand leans into Albertson so close that he can smell the old man's stale breath. Albertson tries to pull his hand away, but he can't; the old man's grip is surprisingly fierce.

"Tell me about this shoe," Bertrand says.

Albertson feels as if he's about to be sick. Bertrand has Albertson's hand, but it feels like he has all of him. Albertson feels engulfed.

"Tell me about your shit-covered shoe."

Albertson remains silent, diverting his eyes from the old man's glare.

"Fine, tell me: do you ever eat sausage and then lie down, feeling like you're about to choke or at least suffer from incredible heartburn?"

Albertson has no idea what this means, and doesn't know why he's here, in this room, in this house. Who are these people?

"Do you sometimes dream in one language, but when you try to recall the dream, you realize that you've forgotten said language?"

Albertson senses a kind of poison running through his veins. He feels the world tilting on its axis. Maybe even changing direction.

"Does the television always come on before you enter the room?" Bertrand twists his face as he asks this. He doesn't seem like the type to watch TV.

Albertson searches out Louis, but only now does he realize that the judge has left again. "Are you going to kill me?" he whimpers.

Bertrand loosens his grip on Albertson's hand. His face softens. His eyes become grandfatherly. "I just want to hear more about your shoe."

Albertson sits up. He can feel the sweat covering his back in tiny dew-like droplets. "My shoe is covered in horse shit."

Bertrand shakes his head emphatically. "No, it is not."

"Just one shoe."

Bertrand raises his hand. "Stop."

"I put it in the freezer," Albertson says. "Why would I be lying?"

And then Bertrand's hand coils into a fist, and that fist connects with Albertson's mouth with the intensity of a meteor hitting earth.

Albertson awakes in a dark room. The floor is damp with humidity. He touches his mouth and confirms he's lost a tooth. He faintly hears someone, somewhere in the darkness. He stands quickly, and hits his head on the low ceiling.

"It's a low ceiling," a voice says.

Albertson doesn't know if he should speak or not. He wonders if any of this is happening at all.

"You saw the horses too, I'm guessing."

Albertson trusts no one. He's just decided this.

"I saw the horses," the voice says, "running through Mile End. Down Maguire. Then up de Gaspé. Crazy shit, huh?"

Albertson wants to speak and admit everything. He wants to trust someone.

"Though I guess the real Mile Enders don't consider that part Mile End anymore. More like Mile End Adjacent."

Albertson wants to say something.

"And then the old men, those crazy old men. Especially that Bert dude. He punched you too?"

Albertson wishes he had a match right now, so he could see this invisible person he doesn't trust, the only other person who might believe his story. "Why are you here?" he finally asks.

The voice laughs. "I don't trust anyone either," he says. In the silence, one can hear two men trying to figure out the world. "I went down to the cop station on Laurier. I asked them about the horses. They took it down. I filled out a fucking form. And that night, I met Bert."

"How did you meet him?"

"He knocked on my door," the voice says. "Of course he had my address: I'd given it to the cops."

"How long have you been here?" Albertson's going to ask his way to a place of trust.

"I don't know," the voice replies. "It's always dark. They bring food every two hours. Little bits: chocolate bars, bag of chips, croissants. Pretty good croissants, I have to admit. Not like grocery store stuff. They went to a real boulangerie and bought real croissants. But it's always dark. That way you lose track of time."

"How many snacks have you eaten?"

"That's a good question." Albertson hears the man rustle and imagines he's sitting up or stretching out his legs. There's no way to know, and Albertson now realizes he has no idea how large—or small—this low-ceilinged cell is.

"So you don't know?"

"I'm counting."

Albertson figures he's been in here less than two hours, unless he was passed out a long time, which is possible.

"More than twenty-four."

"Snacks?"

"More than twenty-four snacks," the voice says. "So that means two days, at least."

"And how long have I been here?"

"Maybe an hour. They threw you in with the last snack."

"You've been here two days?"

"At least."

"The horses were . . ."

"Two days ago."

"Three."

They both contemplate this. Could they be speaking of the same horses? If Louis is a judge, who is Bertrand? Who were the other men in gray? What does Mrs. Sen have to do with all of this?

"Do you know Mrs. Sen?" Albertson asks. He feels unsafe asking this.

"Never heard of her."

"She owns a lingerie store downtown."

"Sorry."

"Don't be sorry," Albertson says, feeling his defenses fall and his trust growing, like some creeping vine.

"My name's Phil," the voice says.

Albertson doesn't give his name.

"I don't blame you," Phil says. "This is all fucked up. It doesn't feel real."

Albertson wants to stretch out. He wants to believe that none of this is happening. "I have a shit-covered shoe in my freezer," he says.

Suddenly the lights go on. Phil is standing in a gray suit, grinning. Through a trapdoor come Bertrand and Louis.

"What the fuck?" Albertson shouts, because he has no other words. He has no frame of reference. He has nothing, he realizes. Because he saw some wild horses running down the street, he is at the mercy of these seemingly powerful men. Because in a city like Montreal, even the implausible is not surprising.

And then Bertrand punches Albertson hard in the mouth.

Albertson wakes up in a motel room. He knows it's a motel room, the aesthetic tells him so. He's seen this kind of room in movies. He reaches for the phone on the bedside table, picks up the receiver, and doesn't hear a dial tone. He stands and walks to the windows, pulling back the blinds, but the windows are covered with black tape. He goes to the washroom, and pisses a long fluorescent yellow. The window in the bathroom is covered in black tape too. He flushes the toilet. He notices that there is no shower curtain. He walks back to the bed and sits down. There is no TV. There is no radio.

He lies back on the bed and runs his tongue over his swollen lip. Bertrand has punched him in the mouth twice now, and he doesn't even know who Bertrand is. He's never disliked anyone as much as he dislikes Bertrand. Not even the ladies with smelly feet who insist on trying on shoes two sizes too small, who insist that Albertson pry such shoes on and off their grotesque feet. But even they are nothing compared to Bertrand. The man has physically assaulted him. Twice. He is responsible for the loss of a tooth. And much of his dignity. Albertson hates him.

He could use some food. He's craving a cheeseburger. And then he understands the craving because he can smell meat. He can smell the fried promise of a *casse-croûte* close by. He could be on Saint-Jacques. He could be in Brossard or Laval. He could be anywhere. But the smell of the *casse*-croûte tells him he's still in Quebec. There's some comfort in that. Some.

The front door opens and Bertrand walks in. Albertson reflexively sits up.

"I won't punch you again," Bertrand says. He grabs a chair and brings it over to the bed and sits before Albertson. "No more punching."

"Why are you doing this?" Albertson doesn't expect an answer, or at least one that makes sense.

"The problem is your shoe."

"What about it?"

Bertrand sighs. "Louis is a very important man. This is what you don't understand."

"What does this have to do with the horses?"

"You should shut up about the horses."

"So there *were* horses."

"Of course there were horses. You saw them."

"But no one else did."

"That's not true."

Albertson relaxes again, despite the man's proximity. "Do you work for him?"

Bertrand looks around the room. "Do you understand what is happening?"

Albertson considers the question. He considers it ridiculous.

"Mrs. Sen is worried about you, or *for* you. She knows what Louis can do. His capabilities. How high up this goes. How wide."

Albertson watches the dust float about the room. It's a

dusty room, as if it's been empty, devoid of any sort of life, for a very long time. "What's going to happen to me?" he asks.

"My friend . . ." Bertrand's voice fades away, perhaps to a place where he doesn't have to punch people, strangers, for having seen a herd of horses running down a residential street. Perhaps he doesn't know the answer. Perhaps he's not even a cog in this, merely the hired help. Perhaps his not-knowing is all that keeps him innocent. Because knowing would get him in trouble as well, on the receiving end of punches and waking in a dusty motel room on the edge of the city. "You are here for now," he says. "Safe. You are safe here."

Albertson wants to laugh. The humor of the thing finally hits him. "This is a weird version of hell," he says.

Bertrand shrugs. "It's nothing. It's Montreal. Are you hungry?"

"I want answers."

Bertrand stands and heads for the door. "I'm tired of punching people," he says, and then he is gone.

Albertson wakes up in the back of a car. He has a headache, and as he gropes his head in pain, he realizes he has been struck—he has a giant welt on the back of his head. He is alone in the car. The car is old and smells like the inside of a musty garage. And then he looks around, and sees he's in a musty garage. It's dark, and he can't tell if it's dark because it's night or because the lights are out.

He opens the door and stumbles out of the car, waiting for his eyes to adjust to the darkness. He makes out a wall and heads toward it, slowly, like a toddler learning to walk. He kicks something metallic-sounding, and hears it ricochet off a surface. He finds himself by a wall covered with cobwebs. Albertson thinks that every single awful thing that is ever going to happen to him has happened. He hates spiders.

He reaches along the wall, feeling his way through the cobwebs, over chipped paint and cracked Gyprock. He feels a light switch, and flips it on. A lightbulb casts a jaundiced yellow glow over the place, and yes, he's in a garage, except it looks like it hasn't been occupied in a long time. Along the opposite wall is an old worktable and some tools, but other than that, the only thing inside the room is the car. It's a cab, a rusted Ford Fiesta that looks like it was never a very good cab—surely a Ford Fiesta is too small to be a licensed cab, even in a city like Montreal with such awful taxis.

He sees a spider crawl along the floor. The garage door is weighed down with a concrete weight that's bolted to a chain. Whoever put him in here—and he's guessing it was Bertrand—doesn't want him to leave.

The light goes out. Albertson reaches for the switch, but it doesn't work now. *Where was that spider?* he thinks. He hears a sound, like someone turning on a loud stereo system. Suddenly the garage is bathed in a spectacular array of lights, a disco of color; they seem to light the universe. Albertson shields his eyes, but the room is too bright. And then he hears music. Dance music. Electronic, synthetic, pulsating. The lights dance in synchronicity to the beat, and now he is surrounded by both light and music. His body is inside this thing, this aura—he cannot escape what is around him because he has been made a part of it. He runs to the car and gets back in, but there is no relief from the wash of light and ocean of music. He closes his eyes and holds his head, knowing he must escape—it is the only way.

Albertson abandons the car and heads for the garage door, but it is weighted down, far too heavy for him to lift.

He's only one man, alone and under assault, and he's entered some crazy alternate reality. And for what? Because he saw some horses on the street? More than some, sure, a lot, that was a lot of horses, but what does it matter? Who cares about these horses and what he saw? Where is this garage? Why are these people doing this?

Why haven't they killed me? he wonders.

Albertson stumbles over to the worktable and peers underneath it. He sees a key. He takes the key and studies the garage door, the chain, the concrete weight. The chain and weight are held together with a lock. Not even a large one at that. He puts the key into the lock and the tension of the chain is released. It whips out, and the garage door flies open.

It is day. Albertson looks around and is running as soon as he is on the street, in a part of town he doesn't quite know. It's suburban; the street signs are different. He figures he's far from home. He runs. He runs past closed office buildings, warehouses, and derelict garages, much like the one he was just in. He turns onto a busy street with buildings inhabited by commerce. There's traffic on the street, and Albertson hails a cab. When he gets inside, he asks to go home.

He steps into the apartment and of course Mrs. Sen is sitting there, in the dark, on his love seat, waiting for him. At her feet is the bag with the shit-covered shoe.

"I should probably laugh," Albertson says. He goes to his fridge and grabs a beer, joining Mrs. Sen in the living room. "I should, shouldn't I?"

Mrs. Sen nudges the bag toward him with her foot. "Tell me about this," she says.

Albertson takes a pull of his beer. It feels like liquid gold going down his throat. He thinks he should probably eat, except he's not hungry. "Tell me what's going on," he says.

Mrs. Sen sighs. She lets out a lot of air and sits back on the love seat. "Mr. Albertson . . ." she says, like she's apologizing.

"You invite me to your place, and before that, you say something about the horses. So you got my attention. And then your husband, the judge—he's a judge!—has his goon attack me. So I wake up in a dark room. And then I wake up in a motel. His goon is there, and attacks me again. So I wake up in the back of a cab in a disco garage . . ." Albertson pauses to see if Mrs. Sen has anything to say, but she just stares at him with a kind of maternal blankness, as if she were expecting disappointment. "What the fuck, Mrs. Sen?"

"Louis is my second husband."

Albertson knows this. He finds it odd that she would make this point now, after all he's confronted her with. This is not a response. This is nothing. A non sequitur. *Why is Mrs. Sen in my apartment?* he asks himself, knowing an answer is impossible.

"My first husband was a cardiologist. Dr. Sen. A very accomplished man. But he died, as you know." She lets the information sink in. Again. She knows he knows all of this. "I've been married to a cardiologist, and now a judge."

Albertson thinks back to when he's sold Mrs. Sen shoes. He thinks of the ungodly amount of shoes she has bought from him. The Imelda Marcos amount of shoes. Her lingerie shop is always empty; she's married to a judge.

He thinks that a normal person would go to the cops, but he doesn't trust the cops. Not in this city. Not if a judge has old guys ready to punch him and stuff him in cabs and take him to disco garages. For the first time, Albertson is thinking of a conspiracy. Something vast. An ocean. The kind of conspiracy that doesn't seem like anything until the anvil of it falls in front of you. Those horses were real but he's not supposed to know about them. Bertrand told him that this went far and wide.

"Why is your husband's friend punching me in the mouth?" he asks Mrs. Sen.

"My husband wanted to stick to law. He was an excellent lawyer. He's told me that so many times."

"Mrs. Sen!"

"Once, I lost my nail clippers. I found them two weeks later in a bottle of Tums."

She's lost her mind. Albertson can see that now. What she's doing here is another matter. He's not even sure how she knows where he lives. The judge has placed her here. To scare him? What has he done to his wife? She's a shell, empty, discarded. A void.

He reaches over and takes the bag with the shit-covered shoe. It's been out awhile now, apparently, and it's starting to smell. The horse shit never dried; he put it in the freezer still fresh, and now it's thawing out. He stands and takes it to the fridge. Except his bag is still in there. He opens the bag in his hand and it's one of Mrs. Sen's shoes—a shoe he once sold to her—and it is also covered in horse shit.

"My husband hates those shoes," she says.

He turns and she is standing at the door to the kitchen.

"He says the color doesn't suit the shape, or something. He's a very intellectual man. But he doesn't really have good taste in shoes."

Is she crazy or speaking in code? Albertson's head feels like it's being struck by boulders.

"Are you even old enough to remember cassette tapes?" she asks him.

The light in the apartment changes. Night is coming. Albertson realizes he doesn't know what time it is. He doesn't even know if he should be tired or not.

"I cannot patronize your store any longer," she says. "I am forbidden."

Albertson imagines the moment before a jumper gives in to the physics of their reality. The feeling of utter loss, and freedom.

"Keep my shoe," she says. "You might need it. I'm almost sure you will."

She turns to leave. Albertson can't even bring himself to call out, to ask her to wait, to ask even a single question.

Albertson wants to call someone, but he doesn't trust his landline or his cell phone. He is likely being monitored, likely at this very moment. He paces. And then he thinks of his neighbors. What if they report him? All this pacing. It must be driving them mad. He lies on his bed. He tries to sleep. But he can only think of Bertrand and his gray suit. He keeps imagining Bertrand punching him, in slow motion, over and over. With this image, he finally falls asleep.

The phone rings. Albertson is startled and sleepily reaches for the phone.

"Don't speak," he hears. He thinks it's Mrs. Sen but he can't be sure. "Just listen. Hold on." Albertson pinches his arm to make sure he's awake. "*The granola is in the pantry behind the cornflakes!* Sorry," she says. "Louis can't find anything in this house. He's useless."

"Mrs. Sen?"

"Yes."

Albertson doesn't trust the phone.

"There's a horse festival happening, up in Little Italy. Have you heard of this?"

"What?"

"*I said behind the cornflakes! On the third shelf!* Sorry, what did you say?"

"I didn't say anything."

"Le Festival des Chevaliers, or something. My god, there's a festival for everything in this city."

"Why are you telling me this?"

"You know why," Mrs. Sen says.

"No, I don't know."

"It's new. It's a horse festival. It's in Little Italy. It has some government money from the city, and a lot of business money. Mostly construction companies."

Albertson wishes he'd never seen the horses. He wishes he'd never stepped in horse shit. "When?" he asks.

"It starts tonight."

"I haven't heard about it."

"Me neither," Mrs. Sen whispers. "Louis told me."

She hangs up. Albertson puts his phone down and closes his eyes. The sleep never comes. He knows what he must do.

Albertson heads up Saint-Laurent toward Little Italy. Mile End's not far, but Little Italy is on the other side of the tracks and the crumbling underpass. The city is always claiming to fix the underpass, but then pleads poverty, makes the next neighborhood over seem farther than it is—Little Italy, and Mile Ex, a made-up neighborhood next to Little Italy where you can find beer gardens and restaurants serving foraged food, where bands consist of Casio keyboards, laptops, and two people smoking e-cigs. A neighborhood not really made by hipsters, but one created for them—both of these places are psychologically far from Mile End, even though they are nothing more than a twenty-minute walk, at most.

Before Albertson can notice the new faux diners, kitchen design stores, and *dépanneurs* serving artisanal toast, he's in Little Italy, past the marble gates and into the neighborhood. There's a sign for the horse festival, and in the park he finds people milling about, looking handsome, sipping wine. In the grandstand, Albertson sees Louis, surrounded by important-looking people; some of them are wearing top hats and fedoras. They are the only ones in the grandstand, above everyone else, and they have access to a microphone. Everyone in the park is listening to Louis. He's the one speaking. The important-looking people are standing behind him, looking important. Albertson doesn't see any horses.

The crowd claps. Louis has finished speaking.

Banners snap in the breeze. There are hundreds of people in the park—families, well-dressed couples, small children wearing designer clothing. Italian music plays over loudspeakers. Albertson makes his way toward the grandstand. He shouldn't be here, he realizes. Louis might kill him. But he wants to see the horses, wants to confront Louis when the horses come out. Nothing can happen to him here. He's safe. There are cameras and microphones. The park is well lit. Albertson smells grilled meat, and at one end of the park he sees smoke. A balloon flies above his head, toward space, free from the pull of gravity.

Albertson walks in Louis's direction. *Why are judges such big shots?* he wonders.

Louis sees him and smiles. Albertson stops. He has to confront the man. The breeze shifts, the smoke from the grills swirling around him, and he finally realizes that this festival is serving horse meat.

The people are here to eat horses.

Albertson thinks: *So what?* You can find horse meat all over this city. You can find the stuff in the grocery store. On menus in not-particularly-ambitious restaurants. People eat horses here. People eat everything here because people like to eat. There are no foie gras protests in Montreal.

"It's quite something," Louis says, surveying the park with a father's pride.

"Those horses I saw . . ." Albertson says.

"You did not see horses."

"Let's not play that game anymore."

"You saw a run for freedom, perhaps." Louis is still smiling. He's won.

Albertson doesn't know what Louis thinks he's won, but the smile is the smile of a winner. Albertson feels hands on each of his arms, and he is slowly being led away. Two very large men in black T-shirts and dark sunglasses lead him behind the grandstand. "What is going on?" he asks.

Louis, who has followed them, stops smiling and sighs. "My wife visited you?"

Albertson sees Bertrand. He is walking toward them, a glass of red wine in hand. He puts the wine down and extends his hand. Albertson shakes it. "Your wife visited me, yes. But you knew that."

Frank Sinatra plays over the loudspeakers, "My Way." Albertson wants to laugh. At this touch. "No media," he says. "Nothing. How are all these people here with no publicity?"

"Look at all the television cameras," Louis says.

"Why didn't the television networks cover the horses, then?"

"The horses you didn't see?"

"I have proof I saw them."

"And how is it that no one else saw these horses? How is it that no one in your entire neighborhood saw these galloping horses that you claim to have seen, Mr. Albertson?"

Albertson doesn't know. He can't even pretend to know. "My question is why you've gone through all this trouble."

"Did you read the papers this morning?" Louis asks. He knows Albertson hasn't. He's asking rhetorical questions to prove he's in charge.

Bertrand takes a page from that morning's *La Presse* from his back pocket and unfolds it. Right there on the front, the headline reads: "The Police Cavalry Has Gone Missing."

"We had a problem with a supplier," Louis says. Bertrand refolds the page and puts it back in his pocket. "Not a *major* problem, but enough of one. And one of our sponsors said he could fix it. He had storage space too. One of his projects."

Albertson wants to go back to sleep. "Your wife has a shit-covered shoe as well."

"I never liked those shoes," Louis says.

Bertrand cracks his knuckles. Albertson does his best not to flinch.

"I have discussed your situation with many people, obviously." Louis's tone has changed. Now it's business. Now Albertson thinks that perhaps he will die. Right here. Surrounded by well-dressed families eating horse burgers, steaks, and sausages. "We have made some decisions."

Albertson knows he can't run.

"We have wondered how best to purchase your silence."

"Who would believe me?"

"This is true. But still. We are fair people. I am, after all, a judge of the Superior Court."

Albertson waits for laughter.

"You have been the manager of that store for . . . how long?"

"Almost ten years," Albertson says.

"You know shoes. Ladies' shoes. My wife is very fond of you, of your expertise."

Albertson wonders what has happened to Mrs. Sen, or if she has always been off. He can't recall now.

"We don't want trouble."

Albertson expects to die any second now.

"You will get your own store," Louis says. "A boutique. Whatever you want to call it."

"Montreal doesn't need another store selling ladies' shoes," Albertson says.

"We have picked out a spot. It's very well located. Near all the new construction in Griffintown. Or, if you would prefer, there is a spot on Laurier, on the Outremont side. But that's a tricky street, and it's not so good for your customers."

"I don't even have a store."

"No, but you already have clientele."

Albertson understands. It has all been fixed. Not only is he going to live, he's going to own a business. It's going to be patronized by some wealthy women. Louis has secured everyone's freedom. Except Albertson does not feel free.

"All the paperwork is done and awaiting the relevant signatures. All the legalities and financials. All the construction permits."

Albertson feels like he's about to shit his pants.

"You will combine your contacts, your skills, with certain contacts that my people bring to the table. It will be a massive success. The media will be tremendous. We will make sure of it."

Albertson just wants to faint. He wants to be tough and he wants to yell for help. To scream. "All that for horse sausages?" he asks.

Louis smiles again. Bertrand steps forward and punches Albertson in the face for the final time. Or maybe not. One never knows in the shoe business.

PART II

Bloodlines

DRIFTWOOD

BY IAN TRUMAN

Hochelaga

"He started saying shit like he knew Bloods or something."

I was in my brother's kitchen. It was a Hochelaga kitchen, which meant the counters hadn't been changed since they were built in the thirties; the old windows let cold air in throughout the winter, and the wood walls were about to crumble under the weight of chipped paint. I couldn't even imagine how many people were *dealt* with, how many deals were brokered, and how many problems were fixed in a kitchen just like this one.

That's why I was here: to fix things.

My brother and I were in trouble. Not that we were the ones who caused it, but growing up where we did, you often ended up with friends who dragged you down on their way to hell. There's that saying, *You don't choose your family.* Well, sometimes you didn't choose your friends, either. Sometimes an idiot sticks with you whether you want him around or not. Julien was that kind of friend: too useless to make it and too stupid to get rid of.

"How the fuck does Julien know any Bloods?" I asked my brother.

"He doesn't. At least not really. He said he knew a full-patch one, though."

"Bloods don't have patches."

"That's what I told him."

"Well, even if Julien does have connection with the Bloods, why is that bad for us?" I asked.

"Because he ran his mouth off to the wrong people. He was bragging about how he knew us, how he could sell drugs out of our bar, and how he could use his Blood friend to provide him with the dope."

"But why would the Hells forfeit their power in Hochelaga?"

"That's the thing: they didn't. I got a visit from the Hells today. They wanted to know what the fuck was going on and why they were hearing these rumors. They asked if I knew the guy yapping his mouth, and I had to say yes, because I do."

"So now we're fucked."

"Well, now they want a meeting."

"Fuck!" I paced the kitchen and picked at my nails. "And Julien's Blood—is he legitimate?"

"I'd be surprised if he was. He's probably just some fucking wigger from Laval."

"A wigger from Laval?"

"I mean, he may have access to some weed, but I'd be surprised about anything else," my brother said, staring through the cracked kitchen window. "Legitimate or not, the Hells now think we're willing to go behind their back to try and get a sideline going."

"So what, now you'd like *me* to fix this?"

"I just want to brew beer, man. I don't want anything to do with crime, you know."

"Yeah, I know," I said, sighing. "I'll look into it, all right? Don't worry."

We gave each other a hug.

I walked out the back and into the alley. I lit up a smoke as I headed toward Ontario Street. *Don't worry!* I thought. *Shit.*

The noises of the city surrounded me as I made my way north—two cats screeched beneath a porch; an ambulance cried in the distance. Two forty-year-old hookers were out looking for their next fix. A bunch of kids were having a late lunch at La Pataterie, the way they always did. The smell of grease and potatoes filled the street. You had to watch your step as pigeons were busy pecking at a poutine on the sidewalk.

Our bar was three blocks over, heading west. It was neither a dive bar nor a biker bar. It was a fancy place where the newly rich flocked to after they moved into the neighborhood.

Eight years ago the city renovated that fancy plaza over on Valois Street. Shortly after that the first condos started popping up around it. We just happened to be the lucky owners of a commercial lot within walking distance of those condos.

Our father had bought the place in '86 when no one would have even pissed on it. He ran a shoe store out of it, and when the nineties came, he turned it into a Prill discount store, which was the kind of place you went to as a kid when your parents were on welfare. And there were a lot of welfare kids back then.

Then the biker wars came and whoever had enough money to leave left. We stayed behind. The war wasn't as bad as people made it out to be, but everybody was damn glad when the Hells won and the city passed anti-bunker laws. Not that we cared if the Hells ran the place or not; we just wanted the war to be over so we could live without the stigma of *being from Hochelaga.*

A few years later, wealth came back to the city, for better or worse. Rents went up, vacant lands and factories got turned into condos, and the former factory workers were forced to leave the island or swim with the current. My brother and I were just driftwood. Nothing more. We were just driftwood that happened to float up with the tide as the rest of the trash drowned underneath it.

We felt lucky about that.

But running a discount store that no one but hipsters would walk into was not my brother's idea of a future.

When we opened our bar, we had a narrow window in the history of the neighborhood, where the dive-bar crowd was catered to by the bikers, and the newly rich were looking for a place to park their asses on a Saturday night. If they had built that plaza five blocks over, we would still be selling crap that was made in China. But we got lucky. College students, designers, accountants, artists, and lawyers who wouldn't dare admit that they couldn't afford Outremont anymore needed a place to drink just like the rest of us. My brother wanted to build that place.

So we did. After an eight-month class at ITHQ, my brother was a certified microbrewer; six months of technical business school, and I was deemed fit to run a restaurant. We turned our father's old discount store into a fancy *microbrasserie*, equipped with wooden tables, white stools, pretentious wall art, and even a stuffed beaver for the hipsters.

Soon after opening, the Hells came to see us. We told them that what we cared about was brewing good-tasting beer, and that we didn't think our bar was the right place for them to peddle drugs. The crowd we attracted wasn't exactly the target market for the drug trade, with the notable exception of the lawyers, who knew better than to buy dope out of a bar in Hochelaga. We promised the Hells that if they didn't sell drugs in our bar, no one would.

These arrangements worked for the Hells under two conditions: one, that we didn't sell the same beer that they did, which was no problem given our menu was elite brews only; and two, that none of our drink specials would come under $6.99. Those prices would separate the haves from the have-nots, and ensure that we didn't steal the Hells' clientele.

This deal worked perfectly for the both of us, until now. Now some guy from *way back when* was fucking up our thing, and got the bikers to doubt our word.

Fuck!

Julien was white trash the way you'd imagine white trash to be. He made a living stealing his mother's welfare money, while also cashing in his own check at the same time. He and his mom had somehow scored a four-and-a-half in an SHDM project building, with a nice view of Notre-Dame Boulevard's trucking lanes and the Lantic sugar mill. It was the kind of apartment you'd expect a guy like Julien to have. He worked the loopholes from generation to generation, and for a guy who could barely read, his maneuvering was rather impressive.

Most of the time, Julien was inoffensive, and when he was, we let him be. He just had too much time on his hands. He mostly wasted his days in Davidson Park, playing cringe-worthy songs on that shitty guitar of his, the one with a porn photo taped to the back of it. I remember when he first found that photo. He just walked into the corner store one day, didn't even pay for the magazine. He started flipping through the pages right there in the store. When he found a chick that had tits big enough for him, he looked at the teller and said, "Hey, I like this one. I'ma take it, all right?" He tore out the page, put the magazine back in the rack, and walked out like it was a thing to do.

As I said, Julien was too useless to make it, too stupid to get rid of. Until now.

* * *

I walked into my bar. The place was full for a Wednesday. Twenty people, maybe. The weather was cool, and we opened the bay windows up front. Customers were flipping through menus, discussing what kind of beer they were going to try next. There were couples in their thirties with money to spend, a few suits, a bunch of college students slumming it out in the safest way possible.

"Hey, Richard," the barmaid called to me. She was twenty-three and a part-time student who tried to run an independent art gallery with her tip money. I nodded in response and sat my ass on the last stool.

Hey, Richard, I thought. My name felt like a name for another time, but at thirty-seven it wasn't terribly uncommon. Nowadays kids had fucked-up names like Anne-Crystelle or Marie-Lianne. Take the barmaid's name, for example: Sophie-Andrée. I always thought it sounded horrible, but she had an ass like you wouldn't believe, and as a rule of thumb, a barmaid needed a fine ass more than a good-sounding name.

"Give me a blonde, will you, dear?" I asked her.

I watched her walk to the taps, checking out the curve of her thighs in her black dress, listening to the click of her boots as they smacked the tile. Her turtleneck ran soft and tight across her chest and down to her breasts. I liked the way she was leaning back on one leg; it popped out her calf, rounded up her ass.

Wasn't there that saying, *Don't fuck where you eat?* Well, I was about to do exactly that. I was in for a shit night anyway. I was in for a shit day tomorrow. I was in for a shit week if you asked me. At this point, what the Hells would do to my brother and me was anybody's game. We could lose our money. We could lose our bar, and therefore, I could lose what was left of my sex appeal. The forties were knocking on my door, but I was willing to go a few more rounds before I counted myself out.

I made my move at closing time. I washed half her tables, picked up the empties, and asked about her tips. She said she did okay.

"Anything good for a night out?" I asked.

"Not really," she replied. "Besides, I got bills to pay, just like everybody else." She reached inside her purse. "Mind if I light up in here?"

"It's closed. Sure. How are classes?"

"I don't know." She sighed and glanced up.

They never do. "How about a drink then?" I asked.

She said, "Sure," as she blew out some smoke.

I walked next to her behind the bar. I poured her something old-school, a Fedora, a drink nobody knew about anymore. "Here. Taste this," I said.

She was leaning back against the bar, her short dark hair in line with her sharp chin, the cup of her breast just a shadow in the dim light. I looked straight into her eyes. She looked back and frowned at me sideways. With the faintest pinch of the lips, she dared me to flirt. I smiled slightly. She took a sip and didn't seem to like it. That was the plan.

"Sugar and whiskey?" she said, wincing.

"Don't like it?"

"Not really," she admitted. I was one-for-one.

"Maybe I'm an old fool, but I like it."

"Come on now! When was this drink invented? The *twenties*? You're not old enough to drink this!" she joked. "You're what? Thirty-five?"

"Thirty-three," I lied.

"See?" she said, taking a drag of her cigarette. "You're not *that* old." I was two-for-two.

"Then show me what you *young* mixologists are into these days."

She tapped her ashes on the counter, bowed her head sideways, and accepted the dare. "All right, let's see what we can come up with." She grabbed Taylor's Velvet Falernum, added some green Chartreuse liqueur, pineapple juice, and lime. I already knew I was going to fucking hate it.

I took a sip. "Not bad. Not bad."

"Right?"

"What else have you got?"

"Let me look." She turned back to the bar and leaned beautifully on her back leg.

Eyes on the prize, I thought. *Eyes on the fucking prize.*

I started scrolling through the bar's iTunes account. I wasn't gonna fuck with her taste in Lady Gaga, and she wasn't gonna fuck with mine in Pantera, so I started flipping through the songs, hoping to find an in-between. I glanced at her. She was already moving despite the silence in the bar, her loose leg stomping softly to the steady beat of a song she had in her head.

It was my job now to figure out what that song was.

The Killers? No—the Killers would make me seem old. The National? Maybe, but they were as exciting as watching fucking paint dry. Metric? I was gonna have to go with Metric. Metric was good fuck music no matter what anyone my age would say about it. "Gold Guns Girls" was too fast, but "Gimme Sympathy" was just right. I put in on. The first few notes filled the vast empty room.

"I love this song," she said as she looked at me. She put some ice into a glass. "*Get hot,*" she started signing. "*Get closer to the flame . . .*"

I was three-for-three.

She flipped a few bottles and handed me a glass of her concoction. At this point, I didn't really care what was in it, so long as it had alcohol. She kept singing, then poured herself a glass. I'd had two beers earlier, and I knew she had done a few shots before last call with some guy who thought he'd get her home by getting her drunk. We were just tipsy enough; it was starting to be fun.

On our fourth drink, Lana Del Rey started playing. I couldn't have planned it any better. Lana Del Rey was the kind of music that kept you awake while dreaming about twenty-three-year-old girls named Sophie-Andrée, who'd fuck their bosses at the end of a shift.

I approached her from behind, pressing myself against her back, locking my hands around her hips. She didn't seem to mind so I dove in further. I smelled her hair, felt her smile as I started kissing the nook of her neck. She turned around, smiled, and started kissing back. I grabbed her thighs and lifted her dress. She pulled it higher to get comfortable.

She wore black-laced Brazilian panties. Goddamn did she look good. It looked like a freaking heart at the bottom of her flat belly. A freaking heart around her ass, up to her thighs, and down inside her legs.

I swear to God—it was the most beautiful sight in the entire fucking world.

I kissed her again, lifted her, and sat her on the edge of the bar. I pushed myself against her. She moved her hair out of her face. I ran my hands inside her dress and down her back. I pulled her toward me. Then she forced me toward her. She grabbed my arms, scratched me, and kissed me. Then she looked at me and said, "I got condoms in my bag."

The sex was good but I hadn't slept; I probably wouldn't have anyways. It was nine in the morning. I was having coffee and a cigarette on the way to my car.

The meeting with the Hells was scheduled for ten. I needed to pick up Julien before that and drive all the way up to Rivière-des-Prairies, because when you're in trouble with these kinds of guys, you walk the extra mile.

Julien, being the idiot that he was, had no idea what kind of trouble he had gotten himself into. Maybe the Bloods had used him and his dumb wigger friend to poke around foreign territory. Because if Julien didn't actually know any Bloods, why would the Hells take his word seriously?

I found Julien at Davidson Park, where I had expected him to be. He was playing his fucking guitar in the shadow of the project buildings. No one else was there except two old drunks who lived in the homeless shelter down the street.

"Hey, Richard!" he shouted, playing a god-awful riff that was so out of tune it could have been experimental rock. "I'ma play a song for you, Richard."

"It's okay, Julien. I don't need a song."

"Ahhh, come on!" he slurred. "Hey, did I ever show you my girl? Let me show you my girl." He flipped the guitar and flashed a duct-taped photo of a young Filipina lying on a beach in paradise.

"I don't need to see your girl, either."

"Ah, come on, man! I'ma play you a song, all right?"

"You know about drugs?"

He stopped and looked at me in a snap. "Yeah! YEAH!" he said excitedly. "Ah shit, man! Ah shit! I knew it was coming. I fucking knew it was coming. Shit, man!"

"You want to sell at the bar?" I asked.

"Yeah, man! I'm your guy, man! You know? Anything you want I'ma keep it tight, you know? Shit's gonna be tight."

"And that guy you know?"

"Yeah! He's a Blood, man! In Laval. A full-patch Blood, you know?"

A full-patch Blood, I thought. What an idiot. "He's serious about this? This Blood. He seriously wants to sell in Hochelaga?" I asked.

"Yeah, man, he's fucking taking over. He said he can get me anything I need. He can get me weed, he can get me fucking coke, some GHB for the ladies, some E if you need it, peanuts—anything, man. Sometimes he just gets me this bag of pills, man. I fucking pop them and I don't even know what's in them."

"How do you know this guy?"

"We was just talking and he said that he had all this dope. I mean so fucking much of it he couldn't even manage to sell it off, you know? So I told him to tell the other Bloods that I had my boy who had opened his bar not that long ago, you know? I got your back, man. I got your back, you know? That's all me, baby."

God! I thought. He was in deeper than I had hoped. That painted me into a corner. If I didn't take care of him, then I could appear to be compliant in his lunacy. And if the Bloods, and whoever was behind the Bloods, seemed hell-bent on taking a piece of Hochelaga, then they would come after me if they really wanted the territory. Julien or not, they would do it if they wanted to.

But that territory belonged to the Hells until proven otherwise, so my only option was to bring this imbecile to them so they could deal with him. They could beat him, run down his wigger friend, run down their supplier. They could do whatever they wanted to him; I didn't care. All I wanted was to brew good beer.

"Get in the car," I told him.

"What for?"

"You wanna sell? You got to talk to the boss."

"I thought *you* were the boss."

I looked at him. "We all work for somebody."

"Right. Let me just bring her back to my place," he said, talking about his guitar. "It'll only take a minute, man."

"Put her in the trunk," I replied as I walked back to my car. He didn't move. "In the trunk, Julien. And quit fucking around."

I didn't like Rivière-des-Prairies, and not only because the borough had a bad reputation—I was from Hochelaga after all. No. I didn't like RDP because I didn't *know* RDP. I didn't know whose house not to piss on when I walked home drunk at night. I didn't know whose wife not to fuck or whose daughter not to stare at. I didn't know whose car not to scratch or who to vote for in order to keep the ball rolling.

That's what made it dangerous for me.

As dangerous as Hochelaga was back in the day, I knew how to deal with the danger, and that counted for a lot. I didn't know anything about RDP except that some of Montreal's most powerful criminals had homes there, as well as some of the city's highest-ranking officials. This combination could explain a lot about the corruption in Montreal.

We took 25 north, headed toward an address on Perras Boulevard. I only knew the name because it was the last exit before the toll bridge into Laval.

Julien tried to play it cool, leaning his arm against the open window. He had old, dirty jeans on, and some *Sons of Anarchy*–type T-shirt. *Such a goddamned fool,* I thought. He looked so bad I felt like it might have been a mistake to bring him. Was I really bringing such a poor offering in order to appease the gods of crime? I didn't know, but I couldn't exactly back down now, could I?

I put my shades on and lit up another smoke because I didn't want to make conversation. I was about to sell out the biggest idiot in Hochelaga. What the fuck do you say to that?

We found the small bakery in a dilapidated shopping center. There was a dry cleaner, a day care, and, at the edge of the parking lot, an old Italian bakery.

We were welcomed by a bouncer dressed in all black: black boots, black pants, black jacket, black-framed sunglasses, and black-ink hand tattoos. He didn't pat us down. He didn't need to.

A middle-aged Italian man wearing a white shirt with an unbuttoned collar and tan pinstriped pants sat at table, having a brisket with his coffee. "Welcome," he said warmly.

Julien sat down at his table. He leaned forward, arms resting against his knees, head bobbling for no apparent reason.

"Would you like something to eat before we begin?" the Italian asked. "You won't find anything like this in Hochelaga."

"Maybe in Mile End?" I responded, which was risky.

"All right, maybe in Mile End." He smiled.

I returned the smile. "Thank you, but I'm not hungry."

"Can I offer you an espresso, perhaps?"

"Latte, if possible."

"Good." The man turned to an old woman at the counter; she nodded and walked toward the espresso machine. The sound of steam running out of a nozzle filled the small shop. I looked around the well-kept store: there were pastries, vanilla cakes, Lavazza coffee bags, and the obligatory Montreal bagel.

"Anything for your friend?"

I looked at Julien. Goddamn, did he look stupid. I turned back to the Italian. "He's all set."

"Sit down, sit down," he said to me.

As I settled into the wood-backed chair, the old lady handed me my coffee, smiling as she departed. It was the most honest smile I had ever seen. Something in the way she moved, the way she rested the cup slowly on the table, her old hands still soft from years of care and patience, moved me. If she was this Italian man's mother, then the apple fell far from the tree.

"I assume you are aware of the circumstances leading to our meeting today," he said. "Let's have it then."

I took a sip of the latte. I enjoyed it for a short moment, but then it was time to get down to business. I pulled an enve-lope out of my jacket. "You will find eight hundred dollars in here as a gesture of good faith, to cover expenses pertaining to your men's time, as well as yours, of course."

He nodded in approval. Eight hundred was a good num-ber. Less than that would have meant we were either broke and expendable or that we didn't know how things ran prop-erly in the city. Any more than that meant we couldn't hold our ground and, therefore, why would they even care about us? Right?

He waved toward his bouncer, who approached and ac-cepted the envelope.

"Now," I said, "as you know, it has come to our attention that certain, shall we say, rival organizations, have taken steps to trade illicit products within our neutral establishment."

"I am aware, yes."

"And I want to assure you that my brother and I have had no involvement whatsoever in these arrangements The per-son next to me, Julien, had, in fact, single-handedly decided to contact these criminal circles so that they could provide drugs to sell in our establishment."

The Italian man listened in silence. He looked pleased.

He glanced at Julien and said, "You have the necessary contacts to initiate such a trade?"

Julien beamed, as if he'd been handed the keys to the fucking city. "Yeah, man! I mean, my man here didn't even need to ask, yo! I'm holding him down, man. I'm holding him down, you know? I got shit covered. My main man's a Blood, I mean. And he said he could provide anything we needed. Weed, coke, E—just ask and I'll call him and shit's done."

"This friend of yours," the Italian said to Julien, "what's his name?"

"Turcotte. Pete Turcotte."

The Italian looked at his bouncer.

"Rings a bell, vaguely," the bouncer said. "I'm guessing he's from Saint-Vincent-de-Paul."

"That's it. That's him. Saint-Vincent-de-Paul in Laval."

The bouncer continued: "Probably pushing a little weed to his welfare friends, nothing more, but it rings a bell."

"I see. This complicates things," the Italian said, sipping his coffee. We peered at each other. "And you know this man?" He nodded toward Julien.

"I'm afraid we grew up on the same street. Our relationship is merely due to geographic proximity, and has nothing to do with the actual business or friendship."

"Hey!" Julien said. "What the fuck's up with you all of a sudden?"

The idea that he was the scapegoat for this whole thing might have just started to sprout in his dumb fucking head. I could have asked for the Italian's lenience. I could have mentioned how stupid he really was. Hell, I could have gotten the guitar out of my trunk as proof. But Julien had fucked with my livelihood, and that required retribution.

"For all I care, you can beat him, maim him, kill him. I don't care."

Julien jumped out of his seat. "What the fuck, man!"

My arm rose to the sky, finger pointing like the Old Testament God. "Trust me," I said as harshly as I could. "You want to sit yourself back on that chair and shut the hell up. *Right now!*"

He sat down, shoulders slumped forward like a scorned child.

I took a deep breath to calm myself. "My wish, *Monsieur*, is to remain independent. My brother and I happen to be beer enthusiasts, and that is the main reason why we even care about our brewery at all. We like brewing it, we like serving it, the people, the noise, the staff, the waitresses—that's really all there is to it. While this incident is unfortunate and undesired, you can see that we took swift and immediate steps in order to ensure our neutrality. If you wish for us to handle Julien for you, we would be happy to do so, but the bottom line is that it remains your call to make, not ours. We will be happy to live with any decision that you make at this point."

"Richard," Julien pleaded, "don't do this, man."

The Italian sighed and looked at me, then Julien. Maybe the Bloods did want to start a turf war, and he'd need to beat some information out of Julien. Maybe the Bloods didn't want a turf war, but two idiots they had allowed in their outer circles could provide an opportunity to reopen certain negotiations. Maybe I didn't want to think about the real reason why this meeting had been called for in the first place. The silence started to weigh heavily, and I just wanted it to be over.

"We'll handle it from here," said the Italian. "It was a nice gesture: the envelope, him, the way you presented your case. It was well put together and you seem honest enough. We'll handle the rest."

"Richard," Julien muttered.

I didn't look at him.

"The coffee was flawless," I said as I got up. I took my last sip and put on my shades.

"Thank you. It's appreciated."

As I walked toward the door, the bouncer nodded at me politely. I nodded back. I started to feel like I had gotten us out of it. It looked that way for a minute. Maybe the two pieces of driftwood from Hochelaga could rise with the tide and become rich, honest men on their own terms.

I was inches from the door when the Italian said, "But of course, you have to understand that this business . . ." I stopped and turned around. "This trouble of yours, *him*," he added, referring to Julien, "is going to take a certain amount of our time."

Fuck! I thought. *Goddamn fucking fuck!* It hit me like a wrecking ball. I wanted to scream. I wanted to smash a wall or Julien's face. I couldn't let it out, though. I couldn't let it show that I had been fucked. Not now, not ever. *Stay classy*, I kept thinking. *Stay fucking classy.*

I swallowed my pride and said, "Of course," as calmly as I could.

"Now exactly how much *time* this is all going to take will be entirely up to our friend's collaborative spirit. So do not bother yourself with worrying quite yet." He got up from his chair and put his jacket on. "We'll get in touch with you when we know for sure. Go now, enjoy the rest of your day. It's a beautiful day outside. Go and enjoy it."

There was nothing else to say. I had just signed up for a lifetime protection plan, and I couldn't get myself out of it.

We were fucked.

"I'm sorry," Julien tried saying to me. I didn't answer. That goddamned idiot had gotten me into so much trouble. So much *fucking* trouble. I didn't want to answer. It could get ugly and this wasn't the time and place for me to lose it.

The Italian walked up to me. The bouncer approached Julien.

"Thank you for your time," the Italian said as he opened the door. "Don't worry about a thing."

I could hear the first punch hit Julien as I walked out. I heard him whine, cry, plead, and shout. I didn't feel bad. Not for a minute.

I got in my car, lit up a smoke, and started the engine. After I made it to Maurice-Duplessis Boulevard—that's when I lost it, and I lost it bad. I started punching the steering wheel, punching the dashboard. I punched my own fucking head, shouting, "Fuck, fuck, fuck, fuck!"

It wasn't gonna do.

I still had Julien's guitar in the trunk. I still had his fucking guitar. I still had his shitty guitar that was out of tune with the broken stings and the cheap porn glued to the back of it. I still had his shitty fucking guitar.

I was going to nail that fucking thing to the wall in my bar. I was going to nail it right over the bar, right over the fucking bar as a reminder of things that are and things to come.

Shit! I said to myself. The light was green again. *There is no such thing as independence in this world.*

JOKE'S ON YOU
BY CATHERINE MCKENZIE
Saint-Henri

I.
A Murder Is Announced

The sky above my grandfather's funeral was low and cloud-covered. Hovering around the gravesite in a far wing of the Mount Royal Cemetery, I felt oddly claustrophobic, like we were tucked into the back room of my father's favorite bar. Only it was raining, our breath marking each of us.

There weren't many people in attendance, just our immediate family and a few of my grandfather's golfing buddies. The sad fact is that when you die at ninety-three, there aren't many people left to pay their respects.

No funeral, my grandfather had always said. But despite the bleak weather and the sadness that weighed me down like a wet cloak, I was glad we'd ignored him. He never wanted to be a bother, but he was a man worth making a bother for.

We held black umbrellas handed out by the funeral home. Rain dripped off my umbrella's edges, creating a wet circle around me in the freshly turned dirt. I shivered inside my grandfather's old trench coat, which I wore because he'd once told me, in that prairie-plains accent of his, that it belonged to me after he died.

"You use this after I die," he said, pinning a slip of paper with my name on it into the label. I would've preferred the paintings from Spain that brightened the hall, but a trench coat wasn't the sort of bequest you denied. The coat was too big for me, and it smelled of aftershave, mothballs, and cheap gin. He and my grandmother would drink gin and tonics nightly; none of the rest of us would drink them unless absolutely necessary.

I had trouble concentrating on what the nondenominational pastor was saying. I hadn't being sleeping well lately. My brain whirred awake at night and most of the time I lay in a racing panic before the sun was up. My sleep symptoms, combined with a constant, nagging catch in my throat, were telltale signs of depression, so WebMD told me.

Oh joy, I thought when that result turned up, but of course there wasn't any joy, only a long flat line representing the time I had to get through every day until I could retreat into my bed and hide under the covers.

After the pastor said his final words—*Ashes to ashes, dust to dust*—and my father lifted a spade, placing a dash of earth on the cheapest coffin he could get away with purchasing, we trudged down the hill to the waiting cars. My brother and I climbed into the first one, shutting the door firmly behind us. *No parents welcome here* was written as firmly in our actions as it was on one of the signs we'd affixed to our bedroom doors as teenagers.

Two days of togetherness had been two days too many.

As the car wound through the cemetery, my brother began complaining about something our mother had said that morning. I murmured a one-word response. That was another thing about me now, how I seemed to speak with the volume off, my words only loud in my own head. Everything that mattered seemed to take place between my ears, and even the reality of death was just a bump in the feedback loop.

We reached my grandparents' house. It was low-slung and pink, hugging the corner of Vendôme and de Maisonneuve. Anyone who's seen *Jacob Two-two Meets the Hooded Fang* would recognize it; it's where Jacob lived. Filmed in 1978, my grandfather still talked about the thousand dollars he'd made renting out the house for the shoot.

When we got inside, the house smelled like a gas fire and economy catering. Covered in plastic wrap on the dining room table were egg salad sandwiches, interspersed with a few smoked salmon rounds and some sad-looking crudités.

"Your grandfather wouldn't want us to spend any money on a reception," my father had said before my grandfather's body went cold, trying, but not succeeding, at hiding his naked desire to start perusing the bank statements.

It was a good thing there weren't very many people coming.

In the elastic band of time, it seemed only a minute before the doorbell rang. My brother's wife's parents entered along with the next-door neighbors. The living room was small, and soon the noise felt unbearable.

I needed to flee. So I did.

I stole up the stairs and crept along the dark hall to my grandfather's bedroom. It smelled like his coat, which had hung in the closet until earlier that day, when I'd stopped by to retrieve it.

He and my grandmother enjoyed sleeping in separate rooms, he had told me without embarrassment years before. Her room was down the hall—this was his private domain.

I sat on the edge of my grandfather's bed. His bedside table was littered with his last haul from the library: a new Robert B. Parker novel, an old Dorothy L. Sayers book, and Agatha Christie's *Curtain: Poirot's Last Case*. He was the one who introduced me to mysteries as a child, and was largely why I worked as a private investigator now.

The September rain spat at the window. I pulled an envelope from my pocket—it was a birthday card from my grandfather I hadn't opened yet. He'd written the address poorly, one of the 0s looking like a 6. My neighbor received the card, and handed it to me two weeks after my thirty-eighth birthday. I'd put off reading it, as if he wouldn't really be gone if I didn't consume his last words to me.

But the earth had already covered him over and that wasn't going to change.

I kicked off my high-heeled shoes, which I thought were a good idea to wear for the occasion. They went with the coat, you see, along with the black sheath dress I felt poured into. Bright red lips completed the look.

Fake it till you make it.

My feet felt like they'd been dipped in ice after an hour by the graveside. I wrapped them in my grandfather's afghan, which sat folded at the end of the bed. I peeled open the envelope and pulled out a card with a faded bouquet of flowers across the front—not a birthday card, just one of those generic ones you get on sale once the holidays are over. I smiled through the lump in my throat as I turned the cover to read what was inside.

I did not die of natural causes.

II.

Last Rites

I spent another compressed night turning those words over in my mind. Was my grandfather trying to tell me that he'd been murdered? If so, who murders someone in their nineties? How would he know it was coming? And if he knew it was coming, why wouldn't he tell me more directly, or go to the police, do something to stop it? What was I supposed to do with this information? Why had he sent me this card?

For a few dark minutes I thought about ending my own life unnaturally.

If you're thinking about suicide, you're supposed to go to the hospital immediately. That's what the Internet told me when I googled *thoughts of suicide*. Google didn't say how many other people had searched this, but I felt some small comfort in knowing that I wasn't the first.

My problem was this: how do you know if you're *really* thinking about killing yourself? Is it the first moment it enters your mind, even if only for a minute? Does it have to take root, live there for a while? Does the method have to be worked out in detail?

I didn't know the answers to these questions. I only knew that I thought about it for four minutes and thirty-seven seconds after I read the bit online about the hospital, then put that thought away.

In the clear light of day, I was certain I didn't want to go through with it. But my grandfather's card lingered in my mind, so going to see a doctor seemed like a good idea.

My grandfather didn't have an autopsy. There were no suspicious signs surrounding his passing, just an incredibly old man dying in his sleep. Our family doctor had confirmed the death when my grandmother called him to the house. The house call was unusual, but he'd been my grandfather's doctor for the last thirty years, and so he came.

Dr. Wheelbarrow's practice was in a suite of offices in Westmount Square. I showed up without an appointment, but I knew from experience that if you were willing to sit there long enough, he'd generally fit you in. After two hours of playing SimCity on my iPhone, I was called into his office.

The doctor greeted me and told me to disrobe.

"Oh, I'm not here for me," I said, clutching the edges of my sweater. "I wanted to know if there was anything suspicious about my grandfather's death."

"He died from natural causes."

"I know, but I thought maybe . . . Are you sure there wasn't anything unusual?"

He sat back in his chair, tapping his finger against his lip. "What are you getting at?"

"Can I confide something in you?"

"Of course."

"I have reason to believe my grandfather didn't die naturally."

"And what reason is that?"

I realized how silly it might sound, but forged ahead: "He told me."

"He told you?"

"Yes."

"How?"

"He wrote me a letter. A card. For my birthday." I described what the card said. How I'd gotten it after he'd died.

"So he knew he was going to be murdered before it happened?"

"Well, he was suspicious, obviously."

"My dear girl."

"Okay, I know. It sounds ridiculous. But why else would he have written that to me?"

"I can't answer that for you, my dear." He glanced at his watch. "I have patients to see."

"I'll go, but if something occurs to you, will you please let me know?"

"I'll think on it."

III.

A *Solution, Perhaps*

I spent a fruitless day at the office catching up on paperwork from my last case—a missing dog, a hundred-dollar fee; does anyone dream of this for a living? But really I was turning over my grandfather's puzzle. It's a joke; it's for real; he was losing it. All of these seemed equally plausible, and I felt dumb with the weight of it all.

That evening I sat through a stiff dinner with my father and grandmother, both of them drinking their meal while I pushed lasagna noodles around on my plate. I felt like a failure, like my grandfather had finally asked something of me after a lifetime of giving, and I'd come up short.

When we were done eating, I cleaned the dishes as my father escaped out the back door. Then my phone rang.

"Hello?"

"Hi, it's Dr. Wheelbarrow."

"Oh, hello. Can you give me a second?"

I ran up the stairs to my grandfather's bedroom and closed the door behind me. Even though my grandmother was nearly deaf, some instinct told me she shouldn't overhear whatever it was the good doctor had chosen to call me about.

"I'm back," I said.

"I really shouldn't be doing this."

"Doing what?"

"Telling you this. He's entitled to his privacy."

"But he wanted me to know."

"That's the conclusion I've come to as well."

"So, there *was* something?"

"Yes, though not what you think."

"What was it?"

"He had some tests a couple months back. He had a blood clot in his lung. It wasn't operable. It was only a matter of time before he died."

My stomach fell away. Is this what my grandfather meant? How could it be?

"I'm sure I'm not the first person to say this to you, my dear," the doctor continued, "but I think your grandfather was having a laugh, sending you that card. You see, he *did* know he was dying, and you know how he liked his little jokes."

"Yes, I see. Thank you."

I ended the call and threw the phone down next to me on the bed. I pulled the card out again. Looked at the misshapen 6 that kept it from being delivered to me on my birthday, two weeks before he died. What would I have thought if I'd received it on my actual birthday, as planned? I'd have laughed it off, called him, and told him that he only *wished* his life was so interesting.

I looked at the books again on my grandfather's bedside table. All that detective fiction, including one by his favorite, Agatha Christie, about Poirot's last case. If memory served, Poirot murdered someone and then killed himself because he knew he was dying, and couldn't think of another way of stopping the killer. I remembered how one of the first books my grandfather had given me as a teenager was another Christie classic, *A Murder Is Announced*, where an upcoming murder was advertised in the local paper.

My grandfather was dying. As the doctor had said, he liked his little jokes.

I picked up my phone and dialed a number.

"Hey, Jane?" I said to my neighbor when she answered. "That card you gave me the other day, the one whose address was misdirected—you sure someone didn't give that to you?"

She hesitated, then laughed. "He said you'd figure it out!"

"Who said?"

"Your grandfather. What a sweet old man. He came to me about a month ago and asked me to hold onto that until I'd heard he died. Then to give it to you, and pretend it had been sitting in my mail for a few weeks. Said how much he liked puzzling out mysteries with you and he wanted to leave you one last one. Did I do something wrong? He said you'd find it fun."

I closed my eyes. "No, it's fine. Fine. Don't worry about it."

"He left you something else too."

"He did?"

"Yeah, hold on." I heard the phone click down, followed by rustling. "Here it is. You want me to open it?"

"Sure, why not."

An envelope ripped. "It says: *Dearest girl, bravo. You'll forgive your old granddad, now, won't you? Love always, Grandpa.*"

I thanked her as the tears started to roll.

Maybe now, I thought. *Maybe now I can move on.*

IV.

Motive

"You actually thought someone killed Grandpa?" my brother said the next night huddled under one of the funeral umbrellas, sharing a cigarette. We were outside Grumman #78, an upscale taco place in a downscale location on Rue de Courcelle just below Westmount. My mouth tasted like margarita salt and stale tobacco. I passed my brother the butt.

"You don't think it could happen?"

"Not really. I mean, why?"

"Money, obviously," I said. "Grandpa's loaded."

My brother looked amused. He'd suggested we get dinner

in order to escape from the hotel room, which was bad code for escaping from his wife and kids. Perhaps this attitude explained why I remained childless myself.

"So who were you thinking had done it?" he asked. "Couldn't be Grandma. She inherits everything either way, and it's not like she didn't already have everything she wanted."

"What about Dad?" I asked. I hadn't let myself get this far in my thinking, not before I knew it was all a joke. I'd wanted to make sure he was actually murdered first. Because if he was, the list of suspects was nasty, brutish, and short.

"But he's going to inherit too, isn't he?" my brother said. "When Grandma dies?"

"Knowing her, that might take awhile. Besides, Dad has debts." I passed on my turn at the cigarette. "I think he might owe a lot of money, in fact."

"To who?"

"He's been gambling again, and maybe doing drugs."

"*Please.* Our dad?"

My brother always saw the bright side of things. He moved away when he was nineteen, before he'd ever taken the time to figure out where our dad disappeared to at night or why our school fees were never paid on time. My brother had also not walked into a seedy bar and seen our dad hunched over his stool, yet still in full command of every regular's name in the place. My brother hadn't had the embarrassing experience of his new partner already knowing his father, because he'd been cleaning up dad's puke for years in the after-hours place where he ended his evenings.

"You don't live here. You don't know," I told him. "And with Grandpa out of the way, he could control the money through Grandma. She doesn't have a head for that sort of stuff, always left it to Grandpa."

"This is all just theoretical, right?"

"Of course. Don't worry about it."

My brother threw the cigarette to the ground and stubbed it out with his toe. "Business has been slow recently, hasn't it? Grandpa wanted to give you one last project. That's all."

"He did."

"One last project," my brother repeated as he opened the door. "That sounds like him."

I followed him inside and my nostrils filled with the smell of fresh fish tacos. I could already taste my next margarita.

V.

A Deep Corner of a Dark Bar

After dinner, my brother walked me up de Courcelle. We stopped outside the Bar de Courcelle, our hands shoved in our pockets, warming them against the night. It was about five minutes from raining, and the air felt wet.

"You going in?" he asked.

"Probably."

"You think that's a good idea?"

"Probably not."

"All righty then. You need me to come with?"

"Better off alone."

He shrugged his shoulders. "Say hi to Sam for me."

I faked a laugh and pulled the door open.

The Bar de Courcelle was home to twenty-something hipsters and music I couldn't identify. But my ex, Sam, worked behind the bar, and tonight I couldn't resist my desire for company.

I squeezed between two burly guys with beards and knit beanies, and placed my hands on the smoothed-down bar top. I still felt the absence of my wedding ring; I'd taken it off nine months ago, but the skin underneath remained stubbornly puckered and pale. My heart felt that way too.

"And what can I serve you, young lady?" Sam asked in a two-beer voice, without looking me directly in the eye.

"You still working that line?" I said.

A smile flashed when he realized who was speaking. "Oh, it's you."

"Just what every girl wants to hear. Whiskey back."

He grabbed the bottle and poured the shot. "Sorry to hear about your grandfather."

"Thanks."

"I always liked him. I should've called."

"Probably."

I took the drink and tossed it down. Sam had the bottle ready to pour me another as I set the glass back down. I resisted the temptation to place my hand on his forearm, feel the warmth of his body travel through me.

He watched me for a moment, a look of concern crossing his face.

"What is it?" I asked.

"Did you know your father's been in here?"

My heart sank, barreling past the effects of the whiskey.

"He has? When?"

Sam was leaning on the bar now, focusing only on me, which was always dangerous. "The man just lost his father, jujube. Cut him some slack."

"The man didn't give a shit about his father. What is it? Cards? Numbers?"

Sam wiped the bar with the towel he usually kept across his shoulder. "I hooked him up with a card game a few nights back."

I set my mouth in a grim line. "Which game?"

VI.

Walk of Shame

In the early glow of morning, I found a left-behind pair of panties in the back of Sam's underwear drawer. He lay flat on his back, his arms flung over his eyes to keep out the light slanting through his bare windows.

In my younger days, I would've slammed the drawer loudly, made sure I did something to wake him up, provoke some kind of reaction. But I knew how that scene went. He'd be distant and wanting me out of there, or he'd be affectionate, tell me to move back in. Either way, it ended the same. Too much drink, too much bed; nothing that could survive outside these four walls in the full, bright glare of life.

And I was so tired of the dark.

I got dressed in the living room and twisted my index finger and thumb once around the puckered skin on my left hand and left soundlessly.

Outside, I stood on Sherbrooke, staring at the mountain. Some of the maples near the top were already starting to change color. I knew from experience that the trail of red, orange, and yellow would make its way down the hill until it was a beautiful riot of color.

My grandfather loved the fall. When I was small, he used to rake huge piles of leaves for my brother and me to jump in. I can still remember the smell of wet earth and slightly rotten grass. The way the leaves were wet and slippery. The snap of the enormous orange garbage bags as he opened them, threatening to scoop us up with the rake.

I swiped my tears away and turned north.

I wasn't sure what was driving me. Perhaps I felt like I owed my grandfather, who always took my father's behavior badly. If his death had caused my father to teeter off the wagon, I owed it to Grandpa to hoist him back up.

My first stop was the poker game Sam had set him up with. I was fairly sure my dad had left it only moments before he'd shown up at the graveside, and promptly beetled back there as soon as he could. These games were mobile, and went on for days. The janitor who swept the floors at the McAuslan Brewery—and played bouncer for the game that took place in the basement, among the brass vats and empty bottles—was open to the twenty I pressed into his hand.

And so I followed my father's trail across the city.

He wasn't in the flour-dust room above St-Viateur Bagel. As I chewed my still-hot poppy seed bagel, the man who ran the poker game there said it had been awhile since he'd seen my father, which could mean anything from several months to several hours. Time was money, piled up or torn down. Everything else paled in comparison.

My next stop was above the Portuguese chicken place on Rachel—Rotisserie Romados. As I walked up the stairs, feeling the airborne fat coat my skin, I wondered why so many of these bootleg poker places were linked with some of the better food Montreal had to offer. Must be the ready-cash business, the perfect front for ill-gotten gains.

A large man in a black T-shirt told me my father had been there overnight while I was wrestling with my past. He wouldn't tell me if Dad was winning or losing, but I knew my father's patterns well enough: if he was winning, nothing could get him out of his seat. So, he was losing, and wandering, hoping to find a lucky streak, imbued with that magical thinking that keeps gamblers coming back to the table.

One more hand, one more card, and I'm made.

I pulled my grandfather's coat tight against my body as I stepped back out into the ever-present rain.

VII.

A Love Story

It was coming on five p.m. by the time I made it back to Westmount. I found my grandmother in the living room, sipping a gin and tonic, a bowl of nuts and Chex mix on the chairside table. I noticed that her skin seemed papery under the lamp; she seemed so much older than the last time I'd looked properly.

She was flipping through the day's *Gazette*. I thought I heard her swear under her breath.

"What's that, Grandma?"

"Bullshit," she said, this time more clearly.

I wasn't sure I'd ever heard my grandmother swear before, and I wondered what the paper could possibly contain that would get her cursing. She hadn't said a word since my grandfather died, her muteness a testament to her grief.

"Is everything okay?" I asked.

"Nothing ever changes," she said. "It's all the same."

I sat down in the armchair next to her. "Ain't that the truth."

She squinted in the way she did when she wasn't sure she'd heard me. She'd been a beauty, my grandmother, in her youth. Even now, in her midnineties, traces of her beauty remained.

"Where've you been?" she asked.

"Wandering around, really."

She sniffed the air around me. "You smell like sin. Your father been gambling again?"

I looked at the floor. Someone had left their muddy print on the rug. I added it to the mental list I was keeping of all the things we'd have to take over now that Grandpa was gone.

"I'm not sure."

"Don't you lie to me, girl. You always were a terrible liar, even as a little thing."

"Did I lie often?"

"All the damn time."

I smiled. This new, swearing version of my grandmother was a hoot. "How awful of me."

"Your father was such a sweet little boy."

"I know."

I'd seen it in the photograph albums and the old reel-to-reel movies they'd made. A happy kid. Earnest. The kind who always put his hand up in class and stayed in at recess to help clean the erasers.

But something had broken somewhere along the way. When I was younger, I thought the cause of that break was me.

"I hate to ask this, Grandma, but has my dad been asking you to sign checks or do you keep a lot of money in the house?"

"What are you getting at? I know better than to write checks to your father. Learned that long before you were born." She picked up her glass and drained the remainder of its contents. The ice rattled in the bottom as she shook it.

"Would you like another?"

"Why not?" she said. "You'll make it like he did?"

Her eyes were brimming, nearly spilling over. Seventy years she and my grandfather had been together. Day in and day out. All the rubs of life, its joys too. I couldn't imagine that level of commitment, strength, sticking power.

I gave her a quick hug, almost knocking the glass out of her hand.

"I'll make it with love."

VIII.

Finis

"I hear you're looking for me," my father said, startling me as I made my grandmother's drink.

On TV, or in movies, there's any number of ways to tell that someone has been up all night doing something dissolute. Unshaven, wrinkled, hair askew. But what the screen can't convey is the sour mix of whiskey, sweat, and greasy food, the bitter taste of coffee that followed him like a cloud, the damp reek of sex he didn't have time to shower off.

Those scents told me he'd found his winning game, that it had lasted just long enough for him to pay a one-hour hooker before someone alerted him I was on his trail.

"You could at least make an effort," I said.

He ducked his head behind the fridge door. "An effort to do what?"

"Hide what you've been up to."

"Why should I have to hide?" He straightened up, a milk carton in his hand, as if that wholesome drink would dissipate the cloud of deceit that followed him.

I turned away from him in disgust, and reached up into the cabinet for another glass. I poured gin into it, straight. Right then, I didn't care what it would taste like. I only cared about the effects.

"That's not how she likes her drink," my father said, his voice slushy.

"It's for me."

"That's not a good idea."

"Why do you care?"

He slammed the carton down. A splash of milk flew up and onto the counter. "Goddamnit, how could you say something like that?"

I turned to face him. Despite all the years of estrange-ment, anger, and suspicion, the little girl inside of me wanted to dive past the cloud of scent and into his arms, capture that safe feeling I hoped was more than a false memory. But my father was a drunk gambler, which meant he was an excellent liar and manipulator. I should know.

"Forget it, okay? Just forget it." I picked up the glasses from the counter and tried to move around him. He was standing there like a stone. I wondered for a moment if he'd fallen asleep, but his eyes were still half open. "Dad?"

"Yeah."

"You going to move?"

"Oh, sure."

He stepped to the side, then swayed into me, knocking my glass to the floor. The gin spread across the dirty linoleum. "Oopsie," he said, grabbing a cloth off the front of the stove and leaning down. "I'll clean it up. You take that drink out to your grandmother."

"Let me make another first."

"Just leave it, I'll make you another one. A better one."

I nodded. As I stepped over him, some of my grandmother's drink sloshed against the side of the glass and landed on my hand. I raised it to my lips to siphon it off. God, it tasted awful, way worse than I remembered. Bitter, and not just from the tonic.

Oh my god. *Oh no, no, no.*

My mind flew past the present to the many conversations I'd had, years ago, with my father about difficult-to-trace poi-sons. He had an obsessive personality, and at one point in time, when I was a teenager, that's what his brain got stuck on. He'd made it into a bit of a game: what was the best way to hide a slow-acting poison so you could administer it without the victim knowing?

My hands were shaking as I walked into the hall and put the glass down on a table. I found my phone in my purse and started an Internet search.

My eyes raced past the symptoms: *Thinning skin . . . Blood clots . . . Stroke . . .*

Oh, Grandpa, I thought. *You were right.*

COYOTE

BY BRAD SMITH

Westmount

They gathered at the Sunflower Diner in the mornings, never before ten because they weren't the kind to get out of bed early, even to go kill something. The core group was generally the same, a dozen or so men most days, although the number could double, depending on who was working what shift where. They'd have breakfast before heading out, slopping up egg yolks with Wonder Bread toast, and calling for more coffee, those bottomless cups.

They were older, the majority of them, half-assed farmers who called themselves retired even though they had never worked full time, having years ago rented out the acreage they'd inherited from their fathers to the big US cash croppers. They still called themselves farmers, living on the fat of the land rather than off it, but most had worked other jobs sporadically over the years, and nearly all of them had wives who worked. The men drove big pickup trucks that served no practical purpose other than a participation in some vehicular pissing contest. Splattered with mud, like some badge of honor, the trucks had loud diesel engines and tires the size of Volkswagens.

From time to time, Joanna would see some of their working wives in town, driving their husband's trucks. They practically needed stepladders to climb in and out of the monstrosities.

Breakfast was leisurely and long, the conversation revolving around sports—the Maple Leafs, the Canadiens, and sometimes the NFL. The weather, if commented upon at all, was quickly determined to be *fucked up*. They didn't need to talk politics; they all voted the same way so there was nothing to discuss. Some days it would be close to noon before they left the diner, Ben Dubois deciding when it was time to go. Anybody walking into the diner wouldn't exactly pin Dubois as the leader, and the other guys wouldn't readily admit it, but he was certainly their captain.

He would sit in the same corner booth as always, not saying much, too busy concentrating on his eggs, pancakes, and sausages, cleaning up his own plate before helping himself to the scraps on someone else's. He would then sit back, toothpick in his mouth, a slight look of contempt on his face, some undisclosed disdain for his surrondings. He couldn't care less about hockey or football, and the weather was going to do whatever it wanted. But Dubois held himself in such a way that suggested he knew more about the matters at hand than the rest of them put together, and if someone came up with an inordinately stupid statement, all eyes would turn to his reaction, even if it was nothing more than a condescending smirk.

Leaving, they'd stand in the parking lot for a few minutes, light the cigarettes they weren't allowed to smoke in the diner, and watch the sky, deciding what concession to hit first, rifles in the racks, whiskey in flasks tucked into their hip pockets.

The hunting had started just a few years earlier, so Joanna had never known about it. She had come home in the spring, and didn't notice the bunch until late fall, when the crops were off the fields, the leaves off the trees. One afternoon, washing dishes in the kitchen sink, she spotted trucks parked alongside the road, north of the farm, exhaust pipes puffing smoke rings into the cold November air. Homer was just two days quit of the latest round of his chemo, and was in the front room by the fire, trying to stay warm and positive, his skin as gray as day.

"What's with the trucks on the side of the road, Dad?"

He didn't look away from the flames. "Dubois and that bunch."

"What are they doing?"

"Coyote hunting."

It was pure serendipity that Joanna was even there, in the house, her marriage having finally collapsed at roughly the same time that Homer's cancer came back. The disease thrived as the marriage had not. Her leaving had been anticlimactic, and Richard had said as much on their final night together. He compared their relationship to a baseball player batting .180 over the course of his final season, with everybody, including the player, knowing it was over.

Joanna hated sports metaphors, and that this was the best he could come up with after fourteen years made her resent him even more than she already did.

They'd spent some time in counseling, even changing therapists twice, as if the therapist might somehow be the problem. The last one was a sunny blond woman named Nathalie. She had a degree from McGill, and legs like a *Vogue* model. She brought things to a close when she called Joanna at work to tell her that Richard had sent her a text asking if she wanted to get a drink. It was the first time Joanna had ever heard of a marriage counselor advising a client to run for the hills.

Which is precisely what Joanna did, although the hills turned out to be the fields of her youth, less than an hour south of Montreal, in Howick. She took a leave of absence from her job at Dawson College. Her father's illness provided a convenient excuse, although most of her colleagues were aware of her domestic situation. Who knows—maybe a few of them received a text from Richard too. Maybe a few even responded.

She came home to her old bedroom, to the familiar smell of the house and the barn and the land. She cooked for her father, drove him to Montreal for his treatments, and in between, she frantically cleaned a house that hadn't seen much more than the occasional pass of a corn broom since her mother died seven years earlier. In what even she recognized as a cathartic state, she suggested painting, papering, and installing new flooring. Homer would have none of it. He wanted things to be as they'd always been—his walls and his floors and his health.

Joanna should have known better. She had tried a similar tactic when Richard began his wayward drift, spending less and less time at home, showing houses to prospective clients in the evening instead of the day, attending real estate conferences he'd eschewed in the past. Meanwhile, Joanna renovated and redecorated the house, knocking down the wall between the kitchen and dining room, making an en suite bath and walk-in closet in the bedroom for the kids they'd never have. The renovations had been expensive, even for Westmount, but money was never the problem.

By early December, Homer felt well enough to wander around outside for a couple hours every day, looking for jobs to do. One sunny morning, Joanna found him on an extension ladder, cleaning leaves from the eave above the front porch. She'd made him climb down, to his disgust. Since then, he'd reluctantly confined himself to whatever chores he could find at ground level.

* * *

One gray afternoon, Homer was changing the oil in his pickup truck when Ben Dubois rolled into the driveway. Joanna was in the kitchen making soup from the carcass of a chicken she and Homer had eaten over the weekend. When she heard the rumble of the exhaust, she saw Dubois sliding his girth out from behind the wheel. Ralph Acton emerged from the passenger side, shoulders slumped, head hanging down like a cartoon character. Homer straightened and wiped his hands on a rag he drew from his coveralls. Joanna could tell by his step that he was not happy with the interruption.

The three men were standing by the tailgate when Joanna came out of the house wearing Homer's old wool jacket, which he'd once worn when doing his evening chores. Ralph Acton nodded as she approached, but looked away quickly so he wouldn't know if Joanna nodded back.

Inside Dubois's truck bed were three dead coyotes, two of them small and brown, the third large and yellow. Their hides were thickly matted where they had bled out, their eyes glassy, tongues swollen. Dubois glanced at Joanna as if she were a child interrupting the grown-ups, and then didn't look at her again.

"The big one near got away," he said. "We ran him around the beehive bush and he went through a culvert on Mill Road. Billy Logan just pulled up to the intersection there, got out with his .222, and put a slug through his hindquarters." Dubois pointed to the shattered hip of the dead coyote. "Spun him around like a whirligig. Son of a bitch kept going, though, just his front legs working. Made the mistake of crossing my path, so I hit him in the ribs with my rifle. He was done like dinner. Lookit the size of him, Homer."

Homer nodded. It seemed to Joanna that he was trying to

muster some enthusiasm for the matter at hand, but couldn't quite do it. Changing the oil in his pickup was the job at hand. The cancer had made him more focused, she'd noticed, whether he was cutting the grass or clearing the vegetable garden—whatever the task of the day was, he did it relentlessly, distractions be damned.

"What do you do with them?" Joanna asked.

Dubois, looking at Homer, smiled, making a point of not acknowledging the question or the woman who'd asked it.

Ralph watched Dubois, needing direction, then reluctantly took it upon himself to reply: "We dump 'em at the landfill."

Joanna kept her eyes on Dubois. If he wouldn't look at her, she wouldn't stop looking at him. "You're not serious," she said.

"Girls," Ralph chided, "always against us boys and our hunting."

"Right," Joanna said. "Except I was shooting and skinning out rabbits and ducks when you were still shitting your pants, Ralph. We ate what we shot."

"I ain't going to eat no coyote," Ralph said.

"A little bit of the city come home to roost, I see, Homer," Dubois said.

"You don't sell the hides or anything?" Joanna persisted.

"Ain't worth nothing." Ralph again.

Now Joanna turned to him. "Then why shoot them?"

Ralph grinned. "Just what we do. Right, Dubois?"

Dubois stepped to the tailgate, lifted the front quarters of the large coyote, and stared straight into the dead glassy eyes. "That's right. It's what we do. And we do what we want." He dropped the carcass carelessly, the animal's head banging onto the metal of the tailgate, and turned to Homer. "We'll let you get back to your truck, Homer. Got a feeling you'll be getting an earful over supper tonight."

Joanna waited until the vehicle was out of the driveway before turning to her father. "They ask your permission to hunt here?"

"Yeah," Homer answered, slowly adding new oil to his engine.

"You approve of it?"

"I guess I don't disapprove of it."

Joanna stared hard at her dying father.

It wasn't until breakfast the next morning that the subject came up again. It seemed Homer had been thinking it over.

"A coyote will kill young calves and lambs," he said, having finished his single piece of toast, both hands on the coffee cup before him. "Helps out the farmers, keeping their numbers down."

"Except these days you can drive fifty kilometers in any direction and not see a single cow," Joanna countered. "And when was the last time anybody in this county raised sheep?"

When Homer took a sip of coffee, his watch slid halfway up his wrist. His forearms had once been like fence posts. "They're just a nuisance."

"So are telemarketers," Joanna said. "We don't shoot them and toss them in a landfill."

Homer smiled. "It's an idea though."

Joanna stood and cleared the table. "I'm not opposed to hunting. But these guys aren't doing it for meat. It's nothing more than blood sport. Sitting in their goddamn trucks along the road with the heaters going. Ralph Acton smelled like a distillery yesterday. Dubois too."

Homer got to his feet. "I guess it's become a bit of a hobby with them. I told them years ago they could hunt here." He grabbed his jacket from a hook on the door. "Hard to untell them now."

Five or six years into Joanna and Richard's marriage, Joanna had lunch one afternoon with a colleague from the college. They went to a newly opened café a few blocks away on Sherbrooke Street, near Atwater. Joanna's mother was in failing health at the time, and the woman told her that she'd lost both her parents in the past couple of years. The woman had inherited her parents' house, an old-style ranch on three acres at the city's edge. A young man and his wife had approached the woman immediately after her widowed mother died. They impressed her with a story of how they were about to get married, looking for the perfect place to start a family. The woman had sold the house to them without putting it on the market. The couple immediately sold the property to a city realtor, who promptly turned the three acres into a subdivision. The realtor was Richard. Joanna hadn't taken Richard's last name, so the woman did not know he was her husband.

Joanna kept the story to herself for a long time, not knowing how to bring it up, and not knowing if she wanted to. She deliberately avoided becoming better friends with the woman, fearful that the truth would eventually come out. Of course, when Joanna finally broached the matter with Richard, she did so during a late-night argument, the details of which she couldn't remember. When she had accused him of screwing over her friend, Richard mocked her. If the woman had done due diligence, he said, she would have known that subdividing was not only possible but quite likely. Besides, if Richard hadn't moved on the property, somebody else would have. He told her this in his usual forceful manner, silencing her with his tone.

* * *

The trucks continued to appear throughout the winter. Joanna occasionally heard gunshots in the distance. There were days when she saw the trucks but didn't hear shooting; those days were rare. Neither Ben Dubois nor any of the others pulled into their driveway again to show off their kills. That might have been because Homer was rarely outside anymore, the combination of sickness and cold weather keeping him housebound.

Joanna did have an encounter with Dubois in town one day, in the parking lot of the food market on Bridge Street. In a town of less than a thousand people, it was inevitable that they would see each other eventually. It was late in the afternoon when Joanna walked out of the store, carrying her heavy grocery bags, and spotted Dubois talking to another man in the lot. His truck was parked next to Joanna's Honda—not coincidentally, she guessed. He watched her as she approached, his face red with drink, his tiny eyes narrowing. The other man sulked off the moment Dubois diverted his attention, like he had been waiting for a chance to take his leave.

"There's the girl," Dubois said. "How's Homer?" It was more of a demand than a question.

"Getting by." Joanna opened the hatch and started to place the groceries inside. Dubois drew near; without turning, she smelled the whiskey on his breath.

"Some of us been thinking we'd like to come see him. Thing is, we don't feel all that welcome."

"Why not?"

"Makes you feel that way, being judged." Dubois paused but couldn't help himself. "Especially by the likes of you."

Now she turned on him. "I beg your pardon?"

"You heard me. You're from here, same as the rest of us.

Don't matter if you go off and live in the city awhile, until you figure out you can't hold onto a man and you come running back. You're still from here. But all of a sudden, you act like we're beneath you."

It surprised her how angry she became. There was something about him, some inborn visceral hatred, that she recognized, and it was the recognition that bothered her, more than Dubois himself. It was as if she wanted the concept of someone like him to be completely alien to her.

"Nothing is beneath me," she said. "I'm talking to *you*, aren't I?"

And then she was in the car, pulling away, not looking over to where he stood, legs spread, his mouth slack with liquor, an ever-present grin on his face.

Christmas came, and then New Year's, neither day delivering anything remotely festive. Joanna cooked, but Homer had no appetite, so she ended up eating too much and tossing things out.

In late January, the doctors decided that further treatment would be pointless. Homer passed his days in the front room by the fire, first in his leather recliner and lastly in a bed the hospital brought over. He read mostly nonfiction books, and watched movies Joanna got from the library in Ormstown. He said he wanted to make it until spring; he died the day after Easter Sunday.

The funeral was on that Wednesday. They filled a little church with friends and neighbors, mostly people Homer's age, some still upright and relatively strong, but most bent and worn, leaning on canes or walkers. Homer's last surviving sibling, Doug, didn't make the trip from Victoria.

Richard wasn't at the funeral either. For that Joanna was

mostly grateful. She didn't want to see him at a time when she was so emotionally fragile, but his absence clarified his incredible selfishness. He knew her father had died—she had left him a message on his cell, and had regretted the call immediately after she put the phone back in its cradle.

Richard did show up six weeks later, pulling into the driveway in a black BMW Roadster Joanna had not seen before. She was planting string beans in Homer's vegetable garden along the south wall of the barn. When she saw him, she moved the sticks and twine over a row, running the corner of the hoe to cut a valley in the fresh-tilled dirt. As he approached, he made no comment about what she was doing. If someone were to ask him about it later, Joanna would bet that he wouldn't remember what she was doing when he saw her. He said hello and got to it.

"I've been wondering how you were getting along," he began.

"Fine," she said. "Thanks for asking."

"I meant with the farm," he elaborated. "How close are you to putting it on the market?"

Joanna straightened. "You thought I might list it with you?"

"No," he said. "Find somebody local. I need to know when you're going to sell."

"Why do you need to know that?"

He gave her an incredulous look. "We're married, Joanna. The place is half mine. I could use the equity for a project I'm starting."

Joanna looked at the cutting edge of the hoe. "You think you own half of my father's farm?"

"The law thinks I do," he replied. "We were together fourteen years."

"And now we're not."

"Now doesn't matter," he said. He waited a moment. "You'd better talk to your lawyer."

She went back to work as he got into the BMW and drove off.

After a few minutes, she sat down on the grass in the shade of the barn. She felt like she'd imagined him there, that it hadn't really happened. In the garden, the beans were partially planted, the rest still in the envelope by the watering can. She realized she'd been planting the garden without even considering if she'd still be there when things were ready to harvest. She was planting the garden because it was time to do it.

She got up and started for the house. It was past noon, and she thought she would eat something. Movement caught the corner of her eye as she rounded the old machine shed. A skinny brown coyote was crossing the field to the west of the house, the field planted in red clover just six inches high. The animal was mangy, its tail nearly bereft of fur.

It seemed to Joanna that she sensed the shot an instant before she heard it. It rang out like a thunderclap during a sudden summer storm. The coyote lurched sideways as the bullet hit it, then took two steps forward and collapsed.

Joanna glanced toward the side road and spotted Ben Dubois's truck before she saw him. He came out of the trees, his gun in the crook of his arm, walking toward the dead coyote. He noticed Joanna in the yard as he approached. He gave her a quick look of dismissal. Even in the distance, she could see him smiling, knowing she'd been watching.

She had left the double doors to the storm cellar open when she'd retrieved the gardening tools earlier. She walked past the house to the edge of the property, waiting for Dubois to pick up the coyote before calling to him. He had the animal's rear legs in one hand, preparing to drag it away, when he heard her voice. He hesitated, then started over, leaving it behind. When he was near enough, she gestured toward the storm cellar.

"You like to kill things. How are you with rats?"

Dubois looked wary as he approached, but now he smiled into the darkness of the cellar. "Don't tell me you've changed your way of thinking."

"I just want it dead."

"Rat's no different than a coyote."

"Maybe you're right," Joanna said. "Give me the gun. I'll kill it myself."

Dubois did so, liking the idea. When she had the rifle in her hands, she swung the stock as hard as she could, crashing it across his temple.

Later in the day she heard him yelling, and then calling out, promising vengeance before seeking conciliation, and finally pleading with her. She kept the radio on to drown him out. He was still making noise when she went to bed, alternating back and forth between dark threats and offers to bargain, before finally stopping. Joanna went to sleep; she assumed Dubois did too.

When she went into town late that afternoon, she heard that Ben Dubois had been reported missing. The police had found his truck on English River Road, two kilometers from the farm. There were no leads, although the prominent theory was that Dubois had suffered a heart attack while hunting, and was lying in the woods somewhere. When Joanna got home, she buried Dubois's rifle in the heavy loam of the barnyard before going down into the basement to give him a bowl of water. He howled as he heard her come near, first calling her a fucking whore, then sobbing, begging for forgiveness. He told her he was starving and beseeched her to give him something—anything—to eat. She slid the water beneath the door and left.

A few hours later, she stewed some meat and gave it to him, along with a piece of bread. She could hear him eating from behind the door. The next morning, she went out to the smokehouse where she had hung the dead coyote. She hacked the back leg from the carcass and took it inside, where she cut the meat into pieces and made more stew. She figured there was enough there to last Ben Dubois a couple of weeks.

After that, she didn't know.

THE CRAP MAGNET
BY PETER KIRBY

L'île Sainte-Thérèse

My buddy Mike brought me over to L'île Sainte-Thérèse in his boat. It was two in the morning. Pitch black. The only light came from the stars. I needed a place to hide out for a while, and Sainte-Thérèse was the perfect spot. Only a ten-minute boat ride from Montreal, but it's another world, a tiny island that no one controls, except the squatters who have been living there since the fifties. The police and the authorities gave up on the place years ago. Mike said the cottage was empty and I could stay there as long as I wanted.

That bastard cop, Luc Vanier, was pissed at me. He had me marked for a double murder, but couldn't prove anything. So instead of letting it go and moving on, he put out word that I was cooperating, that I was going to make a deal with the prosecutor in exchange for a free pass and a spot in witness protection. In my line of work, that's a death sentence.

That's why I needed to drop out of sight. I needed to figure things out.

The first night, I took a quick look around outside but it was darker than a blacked-out basement. I locked the doors and put chairs against them. I slept in a sleeping bag under the dining room table but I didn't sleep well.

In the morning, I took a good look around. The cottage was surrounded by trees that had been cleared back, like a bunker in a green parking lot. In two hours, I counted about twenty different ways people could approach the cottage through the trees. If you're sneaking through the woods trying to find someone, you won't be hacking a new path, and I wasn't expecting Indiana Jones. If anyone was going to show up, it would be guys as freaked out by the forest as I was. I found a spot on the deck where I could see the approaches funnel into the clearing, a spot where it was still a short run into the woods if anyone showed up.

Mike's father must've been some kind of handyman; he had a nice collection of tools in the shed. There was a wrench the length of a baseball bat, with most of its weight at the business end. There were a couple hammers, a mallet that could crush a skull, and an axe. I dropped them onto the forest floor, covering them with leaves and making sure I remembered where I hid them. I also hid two old baseball bats in the undergrowth beside some trees. I found a serious chef's knife in the kitchen that I wrapped in a dishrag and stuffed into my pants. I had to cut a small hole in the pocket to get it to sit properly.

I kept the sleeping bag under the kitchen table. Every night after I finished eating in the last light, I would turn on the television in the living room and sit in the kitchen. Sitting in the dark isn't much fun, but it's safe, and when you're looking out into the night from a dark room, you see everything. Guys who creep into houses at night always go for light, like moths. Most of the time they're right; the target will be sitting in his La-Z-Boy, nursing a beer, watching Jay Leno, not a clue what's going on until it's too late.

It took me awhile to settle into the cottage. In the city, you develop a filter. You ignore all the normal stuff, noticing only what's odd—like the guy trying too hard to appear drunk, or the fool who looks you in the eye but turns away a second too late. On the island, all the activity made me twitchy at first. Nothing stayed still. Shit was happening all over the place. Fat brown birds rooted around trees, making more noise than rats in a dumpster. Squirrels with stripes up their backs sprinted through the grass like they were trying to escape something awful.

Eventually I figured out the patterns, relaxed, and focused on the stuff that stood out.

Like the golden-brown flash that sliced through the trees. By the time the dog came bounding into the clearing, I was thirty feet into the woods. A red ball on a short rope went flying over his head, and he chased after it. It was a Labrador, I think. The dog grabbed the rope as the ball hit the ground, turned in a big circle, and headed back to the brunette behind him. Her hair was loose and curly, and she wore jeans and a white T-shirt. She had a farmer's tan. She grabbed the rope and threw the ball in a slow arc toward the house. The dog took off after it. I scanned the woods behind her. She was alone.

I was ten feet behind her before she noticed me. She wheeled around to face me, terrified. I tried for a disarming smile and said, "Hi."

"You made me jump," she said, backing away. "I didn't know there was anyone here. It's been empty for weeks."

"I'm staying here for a few days, maybe longer." Before I could reach out for a handshake, the dog was sniffing my crotch. "I'm John Webster."

The fear in her eyes was obvious, but the dog was friendly enough. I grabbed his head and looked him in the eyes. His tail waved back and forth. I peered up at her, keeping my eyes on her face, avoiding the body scan. She was attractive, but worn-looking.

"I'm sorry for disturbing you," she said, turning to the dog, "Come on, Hoagy."

"Carmichael?" I asked.

"What?"

"Hoagy. Hoagy Carmichael, the singer. That's the dog's name?"

"How did you guess?" She almost cracked a smile. "My dad used to sing 'Stardust' all the time. That's why I picked the name. Reminded me of my dad, I guess."

Hoagy was bouncing around, and she was warming up to me.

"Want a drink?" I offered. "All I've got is iced tea and coffee, but iced tea is good in this heat."

She looked past me into the woods. "Sure, iced tea sounds good. I'm Maude," she said, reaching out to shake my hand. As she did, I noticed fingertip bruising on the inside of her arm.

We sat on the deck. She wasn't relaxed, constantly twisting a cheap ring on her finger that looked like a purple flower. She had other bruises, fading but still obvious. She kept glancing back over her shoulder at the woods. I could have told her I would see anyone before they arrived, but I didn't.

"So you live on Sainte-Thérèse?" I asked.

"Yeah, about half a mile through the woods." She pointed in the direction she'd come from.

I'd seen the house. It was a crap magnet, a worn-out looking shack surrounded by junk, like an old all-terrain vehicle on cinder blocks, rusting parts on the ground like it had spilled its guts, a refrigerator lying on its side, empty beer cases, rusted appliances. It was the kind of place that brought down the neighborhood. But there wasn't any neighborhood, so who cared?

"So we're neighbors, Maude," I said.

We made small talk. Then I saw movement. Hoagy was on his feet running toward it. I dropped off the deck, moved to the woods at a right angle to the dog's path, and made a wide circle through the trees. I came up behind a stocky guy in green pants and a camouflage T-shirt, carrying a shotgun in his right hand. Hoagy made crotch contact with him, and turned to run back to Maude.

Camo-boy stepped into the clearing and yelled, "Maude?" It wasn't a *Hey, darling, where you been?* More of a *What the fuck are you doing here?*

I moved quietly toward him. Here's a rule: never surprise a guy who's carrying a gun, unless you're close enough to jump him. He probably felt my breath on his neck before he heard me.

"Afternoon," I said. I was getting good at this friendly neighbor speak.

He spun around and backed away from me. Another rule: if it's a choice between invading someone's personal space and giving him room to lift and aim, go for invasion. I had maybe forty pounds on him. I reached out and grabbed the gun. He wasn't happy.

"These things make me nervous," I said, grinning. "So I have a rule: no guns on the property."

He didn't argue when I cracked the gun open and lobbed the two cartridges in his general direction.

"John's the name. Want to join us for iced tea?"

It took him a few seconds to process everything. Eventually he said, "Sure."

We walked back to the cottage.

"My name's Ace. Me and Maude live back over there," he said, pointing over his shoulder.

Ace was trying to be nice.

I left him with Maude on the deck and went for another glass. When I got back, they were silent. Hoagy was sleeping in the shade.

Right away, Ace started to explain himself. He carried the gun because you never knew who you might run into. Maude had been gone awhile, and he had gotten worried. Then he started into the questions, too many questions. He was trying to figure out where to slot me in his limited universe. I was thinking how to pull his wires to leave him safe. Maude was watching both of us with a who-gives-a-shit expression.

At some point Ace felt comfortable enough to stake his claim: "Me and Maude, we've been together for a long time. We love this place. That right, Maude?"

"Sure, I suppose. It can be nice here sometimes," she replied.

Ace waited for Maude to say more, but she looked away. He rolled his eyes. "Women. They're never satisfied, know what I mean?"

"I've known some pretty satisfied women in my time." I looked him in the eye, let him understand. Then I let him off the hook: "But I've never been able to satisfy one myself."

When they were leaving, Ace acted like he had made a new friend, full of the we-should-do bullshit of fishing and drinking beer.

Doing nothing on Sainte-Thérèse wasn't easy. I was thinking too much. I couldn't help it, but I started going over every hit I had done in the last fifteen years. In my business, forgetting is what keeps you going; you just do the job and move on. Yet with nothing to do but sit around, I started reliving the old jobs, and there had been a lot. I even did a priest once, for paying too much attention to an altar boy. I gave him a knife through the ribs, right after he gave me absolution.

Don't get me wrong—I wasn't feeling guilty. They all deserved it. It was more like, *How did I end up doing this?* The only reason I could come up with was that some moron had paid me. It wasn't personal. I hadn't felt anything personal in years.

Maude came back three days later, early in the morning. I was having a coffee on the deck and saw Hoagy coming through the trees. I disappeared into the woods. She didn't notice the coffee cup as she crossed the deck and went into the cottage like she owned the place. I was back in my chair when she came out.

"A regular Houdini," she said, her eyes hidden behind big movie-star sunglasses. She had washed up. Her hair was clean, and it looked like she had ironed her T-shirt. When I brought her a coffee, I smelled flowers in her hair. She cradled the mug in her hands, tucking her feet under her chair. She hardly protested when I lifted the sunglasses off her face. Her right eye was ringed with dark bruises.

"You got him mad by taking his gun off him."

"That's bullshit."

"It's the way it is."

"You could leave. Walk away."

"Walk away?" She stared at me like I was an idiot. "He'd come after me. He'd kill me. I've learned to put up with things, to be satisfied with whatever little escapes I can get."

She looked me in the eye. I was today's little escape.

I grabbed her hand and led her into the cottage, straight into the back bedroom. She let go of my hand, peeled off her T-shirt, and unclasped the front hooks on her bra. I stood and watched. She stripped off her boots, socks, jeans, and panties.

Then she came up and kissed me. She braced herself against me, wrapping both legs around my waist. I held her ass to support her. She took her time, testing me. Then she put her feet back on the ground and started undressing me. There were no questions, no hesitations, and I'm not the kind of guy who argues with women.

The sex was quick and rough. I let her scratch, claw, and grab handfuls of me, squeeze like she was causing pain. She was hitting me, solid punches, one after the other into my ribs while she played with my tongue in her mouth. She was slick with sweat, and my hands glided into her body's slippery crevasses as she pushed herself into me. We stared at each other in the final moments.

We lay naked on the bed, covered in sweat. I could feel her heart beating against my chest. Finally she stirred.

"Shit," she said.

"That bad?"

She aimed another blow at my ribs, softer this time.

Not even five minutes later, she stirred again. "I gotta get going, before Ace wakes up."

"You know, you don't have to take his shit, Maude. It's a free country. You can walk away anytime you feel like it."

"Simple as that, Mr. Webster? And what planet do you come from? I want to get away from this shithole more than anything else, but I also want to stay alive. I'm stuck here with a maniac who owns nothing but me. He won't ever let me go." She was pulling on her jeans.

"If you want, I can get you off the island. Get you to Montreal."

"I left once, two years ago." She put on her bra and stood up. "I got a job waiting tables. Not much, but it was all I needed. God knows how he found me, but he showed up when I finished my shift. He pulled me into his pickup. Literally picked me up and put me in the truck. We drove back here, and he beat me hard for three weeks. Who came to my rescue? Nobody. Not my fucking family, not the social services, not the police. I gave up. It's easier to be nice than to be beaten."

She let her words hang in the air, pulled her hair back from her face, and leaned over and kissed me, her tongue snaking deep into my mouth. Then she pulled back and kissed me on my forehead. "I have to get going before that fucker wakes up. Maybe we can do this again sometime."

She pulled on her T-shirt and left.

I lay there, anger beating in my chest. I thought I had lost that anger long ago.

Once, when I was a teenager, I met my dad on his drunken walk home. Every night he drank at the Bar Saint-Vincent on Ontario Street before staggering home through the alley. He was always angry, drunk or sober, but he was violent when he was drunk. He had stopped hitting me when I grew big enough to fight back, but he never stopped beating Mum.

I remember waiting for him in an alleyway called Sansregret. I always thought that was funny. He didn't see the baseball bat swing out from behind the dumpster and into his face; he didn't feel the dozen or so home runs I smashed into his disintegrating skull. Mum didn't cry when she heard he'd been killed.

Four months after Dad blocked the swings with his face, Mum had another shithead living in our apartment. When her bruises became regular, I realized there was nothing I could do. I gave up on the emotional stuff.

When I whack someone, it's business. I'm good at it, and you can't be emotional. If you want to make a career out of it, you have to treat it as a business.

* * *

Maude didn't come back. After a couple of days, I decided to pay a visit to the crap magnet. I knocked on the door. Eleven in the morning, and Ace was already hitting the booze.

"Just passing by," I said.

He wasn't so friendly this time. He told me that Maude had left him. She took the dog. He loaded his sob story with details—about his brother coming to help look for her, about the bus schedule he found in the house. Liars love details. They think the more details, the better the story. Honest people tell the facts, and don't dress their stories up like whores.

Walking back to the cottage, I thought about Maude. Ace didn't deserve her. She deserved some Henry Constant to take care of her, someone who wouldn't punch her in the stomach or slap her face with flat fists. She didn't deserve to leave without a goodbye.

It took me awhile, but I found the fresh earth covered with leaves and branches. I didn't have a shovel, but just kicking the dirt a few inches down was enough to expose Hoagy's back. Ace hadn't even dug a grave deep enough for respect. Kicking up some more dirt, I uncovered her hand, the one with the purple flower ring. I moved her pathetic burial back into place, spread some more leaves and branches on top of it, and went back to the cottage.

It was none of my business. It wasn't the first time I'd seen people turn up dead for no good reason. No point taking sides. There's no mileage in supporting the dead.

I should have walked away. But maybe I had too much time on my hands.

I went back to visit Ace first thing the next morning. He came to the door looking like shit, in boxers and a mangy vest, his greasy hair sticking up in odd places. I told him I wanted to go to Montreal for booze and food, and asked to borrow his boat.

"Sure, no problem, man. Long as we share some of the booze." He went back into his pigsty and returned with the keys.

Five hours later, I brought the boat keys back. I had a bag full of booze and a case of beer. His eyes lit up.

I let him outpace me—he didn't notice. After two hours he was feeling it. He rigged up a radio outside using an orange extension cord that ran through the kitchen window. He tuned the radio to a country music station that broadcasted from Kahnawake. After three hours he started talking about Maude, the heartbreak and lonesome country songs fueling his imagination.

"I loved her, man, I really did. Sure, we used to fight, but she was the best thing I ever had. And taking my dog too? What kind of woman does that?"

"Hoagy was *your* dog?"

"Strictly speaking, she came with the dog. But I loved that dog, man."

"I understand, buddy."

I walked off into the trees to take a leak. When I came back, I leaned over Ace and said, "Isn't it always the case? The ones you love are the ones who break your heart." I had just heard something like that in a song on the radio—it seemed appropriate. Ace looked up at me like I'd said something profound, his mouth open in awe. That's when I put all my weight into a punch I sent into his slack jaw. His head folded down onto his chest and he dropped the glass. He didn't even look surprised.

* * *

When he woke up he was sitting in the kitchen, strips of duct tape holding him to the chair. I knew he was awake when his breathing changed, but he kept his eyes closed. I waited on the couch while he tried to figure things out. The place stank of stale beer, cigarettes, and dog piss. I had a shovel across my lap, its shiny silver blade still sporting its new label. When Ace finally decided to open his eyes, he looked at me but said nothing.

"I'll be back in a bit, Ace." I smiled at him and left.

I came back with Hoagy in my arms, and dropped him at Ace's feet. Dirt and dried blood made the dog look like he was wearing a bad wig. Ace remained quiet, so I left again. I was back in thirty minutes carrying Maude over my shoulder. I sat her down in an armchair opposite him.

"Look who I found, Ace. Maude came back to see you."

"Listen, I can explain."

"Go ahead."

"It was an accident. I didn't kill her. She tripped and fell. I didn't know what to do. Wasn't any point calling an ambulance, she was dead. I knew they'd blame me."

"How'd it happen?"

"We'd been drinking. Maude liked to drink. It was one of those freak accidents, you know, like on *America's Funniest Home Videos*. But it wasn't funny. She was walking past Hoagy and he jumped up like she'd stepped on his tail. She tripped and went flying."

He was talking as though every word was a step toward escape; all he had to do was fill the room with words and he'd be okay.

"She hit her head on the corner of the stove. When she got up, she seemed fine. We went to bed, and she fell asleep right away. She'd had a lot to drink. Later, maybe three in the morning, she woke up and started vomiting. She was vomiting like crazy for about an hour, then she came back to bed and fell asleep. But in the morning she didn't wake up."

"Good story," I said.

"Yeah, a horrible accident."

I would have done the same thing in his situation: deny everything.

"I don't believe you, Ace. I saw the bruises on Maude. She was scared of you. You used to beat her pretty good, didn't you? What was it, recreational?"

"No way, man."

"So it got out of hand, and now she's dead. That's an accident. You didn't mean to kill her, did you? Just rough her up a little, right?"

"It was a fucking accident. It happened the way I said it. That's the truth."

"And what about Hoagy? I thought you loved that animal." I nodded toward the dog. The top of his skull was caved in, the hair around it matted with mud and congealed blood. "You must have done that with a hammer."

"Yeah. It hurt me to do it. But I didn't have a choice. Every time I let him off the leash, he scratched at the place Maude was, like he was trying to dig her up. He wanted to be with her, so I gave him his wish." He looked up at me with pleading eyes. "Listen, I know I've done wrong, but this ain't the way to deal with it. Why don't we just call the police? I'll tell them everything."

"I can't do that. It wouldn't really make things right for Maude, would it? You'd just repeat your sad little story, and get a few months for interfering with a dead body. But Maude's gone forever. So is Hoagy."

"But I didn't *mean* to kill her. You know how it is. We had a fight—pushing and shoving. But then she fell. It was an accident, I swear."

Fear makes people run off at the mouth. When talk's the only thing left, they'll say anything to unlock the leg-hole trap they're in.

"So why don't we ask Maude?" I said. "Look at her."

He did; she didn't look good. A worm was climbing out of her T-shirt. Under the dirt, insect bites covered her skin, which was washed out and ready to start peeling. Ace was sobering up.

I opened a bottle of vodka and poured half of it down his throat. He chugged it like he was proving something at a frat party. Then I went over to the counter, took a large pot from under the sink, and filled it with canola oil. I set it on the stove top, but didn't put the heat on. I started peeling some potatoes I had brought over. Ace had his back to me, but I could hear him straining to see what I was doing.

"Don't look at me, Ace, look at Maude," I said as I peeled. "Why don't you guys chat a bit while I prepare dinner?"

"Please don't do this. I admit it. It was my fault. I killed her. Please, for the love of God."

"Talk to Maude, Ace. I'm busy with dinner. You like french fries, don't you?"

He was quiet for a while, then I heard him say, "Maude, you wouldn't want this, would you? Not like this. Maude, tell him."

Maude didn't say a word. After an hour in the small cabin, she was beginning to smell pretty bad.

"I'm sorry, Maude. We had some good times together, didn't we?"

I chopped the potatoes into thick wedges and left them on the counter. "Another drink, Ace?" I asked.

He didn't say anything. I picked up the vodka bottle and slowly poured the rest of it into his mouth. I held his chin to make sure it all went down the right way. I poured myself a Scotch and sat on the couch.

Ace was crying now, sobbing like a child.

"What's the matter, pal?"

He didn't answer.

Some people would say I was toying with him, and maybe I was. It takes time for alcohol to get into your bloodstream. I had to fill the time. What's wrong with being polite? What's wrong with trying to make someone's last experience civilized? I was doing what felt right.

Ace hadn't given up hope, and I didn't need to take that away from him. There's a point when people finally understand the inevitable, when they realize there's no way out. Most people never get there—they refuse to cross the line. They keep pleading, hoping and praying for a miracle to happen. And it never does. Like most people, Ace believed what he hoped for.

"Why are you crying?"

"Because I'm sorry. I'm sorry for what I've done. I didn't mean to kill her, honestly. It was an accident. It ain't right to do this."

"Oh. I thought that you were crying for Maude."

"I'm crying for her too. If I could do things over, I would."

"Another drink would help you, Ace." I opened the second bottle of vodka and began pouring it down his throat. He struggled against it. It took a long time for the second bottle to go down.

He was stronger than I thought, but eventually his head lolled around and his eyes lost focus. Then he passed out. He was lucky he wouldn't have to deal with the hangover in the morning.

I went to the stove and put the heat under the oil. I left the potatoes on the counter. The cottage was a scene of domesticity ruined by tragedy, both Ace and Maude asleep while waiting for the oil to heat up. I took the duct tape off Ace and carried him to the couch. I left the cabin and waited at the edge of the woods.

Through the window, I could see the pot sitting on the stove. After a few minutes there were small whiffs of smoke, and there was no detector to wake them up. I had the battery in my pocket. The smoke darkened, and then an explosion of flames erupted out of the pot. In seconds, the flames took hold of the wall behind the stove and moved through the kitchen like something alive. A little while later I saw little puffs of smoke escape from under the roof. I watched the couch burst into flames, and with it, Ace disappeared into the smoke and fire. His face was the last thing I saw, the skin blistered and peeling. He didn't suffer. The fumes would have gotten him before the flames.

I stood watching at the edge of the trees, feeling better than I had in a long time. I realized then that I had a future. Maude was dead because I held back, didn't get involved. Well, that was going to change. I've got skills. I just need to use them properly.

POPPA

BY ROBERT POBI

Little Burgundy

I t was a shouldn't-be-there kind of noise that took Jimmy from a dead sleep to the edge of his mattress, a pistol in his fist as soon as he opened his eyes. He froze in the dark and cocked his head to one side, bringing his attention to the world beyond the bedroom. After a few breaths he heard it again—a chair sliding on the floor in the kitchen. Followed by a cupboard door closing. A drawer sliding open. The tap coming on.

Jimmy checked the clock—a little past three a.m. It wasn't a hit; hit men didn't drag chairs around and wash their hands in the middle of the night. Which narrowed the possibilities to a home invasion or Iggy. And since Iggy meant bad news at this time of night, Jimmy found himself hoping for a home invasion; he hadn't shot anyone in a while.

Christie woke up as the lights went on in the apartment. "Jesus, Jimmy. Don't you ever get any privacy?"

He put his hand on her ass, gave it a squeeze, and smiled into the dark. "Easter's usually pretty quiet." He got up, put on a robe, and left the bedroom with the pistol still in his hand. *Just in case,* like Poppa would say.

Iggy was at the other side of the apartment, at the kitchen counter. He was going through the preflight operation of adjusting knobs and wiping down stainless steel on the espresso machine. Iggy was a clumsy-looking motherfucker, but he was a surgeon when it came to making coffee. And hurting people.

The chrome-colored coffee maker burped and coughed and farted.

Jimmy flipped on the rest of the light switches, bathing the 2,000-square-foot living room in incandescent white.

Iggy stopped fiddling with the machine and dried his hands on a towel. "Sorry for showing up like this, Jim."

Jimmy waved it away. "I can sleep because I pay you not to." He stepped up out of the living room and put the pistol down on the granite countertop. He cinched the belt on his silk robe a little tighter and dropped onto one of the barstools flanking the island. "What's going on?"

Iggy picked up two tiny demitasses and put them under the portafilter. There was something tentative, almost nervous about the gesture, two characteristics foreign to Iggy. He turned a knob on the machine then looked up. "Tiny Rockatansky crossed the Champlain border an hour ago."

Jimmy reached for the phone: the boys needed to know that Satan was coming to town.

Jimmy faced the big window, hands in pockets, head tilted to one side. On a good day he could see Upstate New York from here, maybe even Vermont. Now the world stopped somewhere in the flickering image of Westmount below, an intermittent signal pulsing in the blizzard. The snow crippling the city looked like a Christmas movie effect, thick fist-sized clumps dropping from the sky that stuck to everything. CNN was on the tube in flat-panel silence, the chyron stating that the whole East Coast was shut down. Wolf Blitzer was shaking his head as if driving over speed bumps, soundlessly professing doom and gloom and loss of life. Jimmy often wondered when the pussification of society had started. People were afraid of a little fucking snow. It's wasn't like this was Aruba. It was February in Montreal. What did the sports fans expect?

It was all shut down, from New York up through Quebec. Chimneys burped pollution into the sky and a few cars did their best to thread their way through drifts and accidents. The handful of people who were out looked like astronauts, bundled up in coats that could be stuffed with pink fiberglass insulation. But for the most part, it looked as if a sniper warning had been issued across the city.

The snow-painted cityscape held very little of Jimmy's available attention; like a ticking clock, the blizzard was relegated to background noise. Jimmy was too immersed in doing what he did best: outthinking the other motherfuckers in the room. He had an almost preternatural problem-solving ability—it was this core competency, not nepotism, that had earned him his place in the ecosystem of his father's business.

Jimmy turned away from the window, back to the men scattered around the living room. Iggy stood back in the kitchen, brewing coffee, where he could see everyone. Jimmy brought his focus to Harold, who sat in a chair by the fireplace. Harold saw the world through the single prism of legality. He was not good at creative thinking unless it involved fancy legal footwork and a huge fucking invoice. He had been on retainer for Poppa for the better part of a half-century, and was very much one of the pillars of the old regime. Harold sat perfectly poised in his suit—no doubt a tailored Brioni—balancing the delicate demitasse and saucer on the arm of his chair.

"Through a friend in the DHS south of the border, we know that ten million just went into a Caribbean account owned by Rockatansky," said Harold.

Jimmy nodded. Rockatansky's contractual requirements were well known: half on signing, half on completion, boilerplate, and non-negotiable. Which left him crossing the border to do a hit for twenty million dollars. A big pile of money. *Poppa* kind of money.

Marcus—one of Jimmy's old-school captains—unfolded from the sofa and walked over to the window. "I got guys on every hotel in the city, from the Ritz-Carlton down to Motel Colibri. I have people checking out every apartment, loft, and room rented on the Internet in the past six weeks. Unless this guy's sleeping on a bench, he has to turn up."

"Except nobody knows what he looks like," Jimmy said, taking his hands out of his pockets. "He drives through a border checkpoint and we don't have a photograph. How is that even possible? This isn't Keyser fucking Söze." Jimmy looked around the room. There were a half-dozen men in here and he didn't trust a single one, not even Harold.

Harold finished his espresso in one poised tilt of his head, wiped his mustache on a linen napkin, and pointed at Jimmy in a we-need-to-talk gesture. "No one has ever seen Rockatansky."

When Jimmy was on his meds, his temper was pretty much under control. But when he wasn't, his reaction-proportion meter could be off; last fall he had put one of his Ferraris through the window of the dealership. He had taken it in three times to replace a piece of trim that kept falling off. On the third visit they had tried to charge him 969 bucks, saying that it wasn't covered by the bumper-to-bumper that came with the car. Jimmy smiled over the counter at the service manager, then pointed at the phone. "Call the police," he said.

The service manager just stared at him.

"Nine one one. Tell them that a customer just put a million-dollar car through your window."

The manager's expression was still stuck on skeptical when Jimmy launched the Enzo through the wall of plate glass, scattering the salesmen and destroying two floor models.

Jimmy stepped out of his car onto a floor frosted with broken glass. What was left of the carbon-fiber nose section was embedded two feet into the Cheetrock at the back of the showroom. "Better get out your *Reduced Price* stickers, assholes!" he shouted.

By the time the police arrived, the dealership had already decided not to press charges. They replaced his Ferrari, free of charge.

Jimmy reacted that way over a *car*. What they were dealing with now was a hit man hired to take out his father. The response had to be stepped up by orders of magnitude.

Jimmy spotted the Range Rover idling by the wall in the courtyard below, the wipers thumping away in a perfectly timed beat. The city was hidden in the blizzard and Tiny Rockatansky was hidden in the city, planning bad things.

It was impossible to think of Rockatansky without getting melodramatic. People liked to say shit like, *This guy is the deadliest assassin alive,* or, *That guy is the most notorious hit man who ever lived,* but either allocation would be hyperbole.

Rockatansky was a monster because he loved what he did. With him it was never business, it was always personal, and that made him infinitely more frightening. His résumé was a who's-who of top-tier alpha-male targets—from dictators in lost little banana republics to captains of industry to barons of crime. One of the tamer stories involved a former Dutch acquaintance—Mr. Van Dorman, the president of a shipping line—who stupidly refused to pay the second half on a job he had contracted. Rockatansky blew up the school where Van Dorman's grandchildren went; a dozen five-year-olds lost their lives. The device was packed with leaflets stating that Mr. Van Dorman should pay his bills to prevent bad things from happening. Six months later, his daughter and son were shot in their sleep. Four months after that, his wife was found dismembered in a parking lot, her driver and bodyguard burned alive in the trunk of the car. Two months on, Van Dorman was killed in his shower with an axe.

And that was just one story; there were plenty more.

Jimmy shook his head, thinking that if this wasn't so fucking serious, it would be sad; a pair of hundred-year-old guys playing cat-and-mouse. Only the cat wasn't playing, which was sad on a whole other level.

"I'm thinking I want to pull this guy's teeth out, one at a time, then piss in his mouth."

"What's first?" Harold asked.

Jimmy didn't have to think about it. There was only one piece of information they were missing. "I want to know where that money came from."

Harold was already shaking his head. "It's not important who hired him, only that he's here. What I suggest—"

"Fuck that!" Jimmy shouted, then paused and dropped his volume. "Look, just find this guy. Put one in his stomach and bring him to me in a hockey bag."

Harold smiled up at the roomful of stereotypes. "You heard the man, go find Rockatansky."

Harold and Jimmy shared the backseat while Iggy worked the big English sports ute through the drifts. The snowfall had ramped up along with the wind and the streets looked like the stage for an intergalactic conspiracy film—all that was missing was O. J. Simpson in a silver spacesuit.

Jimmy stared at the lawyer. "I have Tiny Rockatansky out there trying to find a chink in Poppa's armor where he can put a spear."

Harold kept his face turned to the window, more of that perfect posture again. "I understand that you want to unleash the dogs of war, but wait to see what your father thinks."

"I know exactly what he thinks."

Harold kept his face turned to the snowy terrain slipping by the tinted window. "I'm not so sure about that."

Harold was heading straight into the old man's room, but Jimmy hung back, nodding at his cell phone. Once Harold was inside, Jimmy called an associate in Ottawa—someone who owed him a lot of money. Without a greeting he asked the person at the other end to find out where the money in Rockatansky's account had come from. After a brief pause, the associate said, "Of course." Jimmy hung up, turned off the phone, removed the battery, and dropped it into his pocket. He straightened his jacket and walked into Poppa's room.

The old man looked like a patchwork cyborg Boris Karloff, but his knocks hadn't come from the effects-and-makeup department; he had earned every scratch, dent, and stich. Poppa had been visited by four car accidents, three shootings, two bombings, one poisoning, an attempted garroting, numerous cases of the clap, type 2 diabetes, a heart attack, shingles, a fall in the shower, a bout of colon cancer, and, finally, a stroke. By this point one thing had become painfully clear to all concerned: you couldn't kill Poppa, at least not with anything they'd tried so far. His refusal to display an expiration date had earned him the moniker of Old Man Bullseye in the Quebec press. But not even the old man could survive Rockatansky.

Poppa was in his chair—the only seat he would occupy for however many more breaths the intel-controlled machinery could coax out of his taxed mortal coil. But calling the contraption a *chair* was akin to calling an aircraft carrier a *boat*.

The mobile life-support system had helped him jump levels from a latter-day de facto crime boss to hard-core computerized Franken-Don. The doctors said that with the assistance of his new self-contained health station, he'd outlive the cockroaches in Keith Richards's drug chest.

An easy decade.

Maybe two.

Instead of the traditional wheelchair, the engineers had gone with an upright model based on Chuck Close's famous device, supporting the old man in a manner that made his grandchildren think he resembled Han Solo on a bad carbonite trip. Most of the general components wouldn't be available to anyone, corporate or government, for years. Some of the more specialized technology would likely never be available for mass consumption—it was simply too expensive. Being a billionaire helped knock down trade barriers and corporate secrets. And even where money couldn't do its evil little dance, Jimmy knew people who could rob almost anyone; anything was attainable.

There was more onboard computing power than NASA's latest communications satellite. Pulse and respiratory functions were priority one—his heart was wired to a dime-sized computer that regulated its beat, and his lungs were fed a better dose of air than most city dwellers got to smell in a lifetime. The setup monitored all major nervous functions, sending real-time readings to the specialized server at the Jewish General Hospital, where they were used to remotely optimize his OS.

The crown jewel in Poppa's mechanized cocoon was the communications hardware. The stroke had pretty much wiped his organic motor-skill software clean, only leaving him the use of his eye muscles and two toes and fingers on his left side. This diminished capacity was nonetheless a veritable treasure trove of digits for the tailored apparatus. The Bowers & Wilkens speakers delivered Poppa's end of a conversation in a slightly baritone Stephen Hawking voice that the software tinted with a digitized version of his original speaking voice. This unsettling by-product had been achieved by sampling his speech from more than ninety-one hours of heavily redacted recordings from surveillance files in the CSIS vault; Harold had subpoenaed the tapes under a medical emergency umbrella, citing their access as the only viable way to replicate some of the sick man's identity. The judge agreed; it was obvious Poppa was pretty much out of the food chain.

It was not the first time someone had written the old bastard off.

Poppa operated his speech program via eye movement and the good digits on his hand and foot-controlled cell phone and Internet, respectively. He could carry on silent phone conversations with his fingertips, send an e-mail with his toes, and blink out speech, a practice he had quickly mastered. His cell phone was piped into his head via Grado headphones and the Internet was displayed on a pair of glasses that functioned in much the same way as a heads-up display for a combat pilot. Transcripts of any part of his conversations—including e-mail and cell phone—were printed up and spit into a tray. The combined capabilities of Internet, e-mail, text, cell phone, and voice enabled the old man to exercise a twenty-first-century level of control over the financial empire he had inherited more than half a century ago—a classic example of the stone age meeting the space age.

It was *Allo Police* that had recently dubbed him Franken-Don. The *Montreal Gazette* had been less kind; Jimmy couldn't repeat what they had said about Poppa. But the *Gazette* was right: the old head of the family was gone and what was left in his place was a little troubling.

Jimmy stood between Poppa and the big window and even in this near-taxidermic state, his father still had a massive presence, like a regal oil portrait. The old man's hunting collection—glazed eyeballs and frozen expressions of carnage grinning off the exotic mounts—peppered the walls. In many ways, the rictus grins were not dissimilar to the old man's.

Before the stroke, Poppa swore he never wanted to live like this—*like a fucking space vegetable.* Yet here he was, the only time he had stepped out of character in his life. Jimmy wasn't sure if he saw his father's surrender to fate as some indomitable will to survive or a failure to accept the inevitable. A newfound strength or a newfound weakness? Whatever the logic, Jimmy had trouble reconciling his old man's life before the stroke with what he now saw in front of him.

Poppa's digitized voice cut through the perfunctory greeting Harold was still trying to hand out. *"Why are you . . . here?"*

Jimmy stepped in front of the lawyer. "Tiny Rockatansky crossed the Champlain border a little more than—" he glanced at his shimmering Rolex, "—four and a half hours ago."

For a few seconds, Jimmy thought the old man was blinking out a long response behind his glasses and he shifted on his feet to see past the yellow glare of the lenses. But Poppa was staring at him with avian concentration, unblinking. His fingers were still; he wasn't carrying on a phone conversation.

Harold stepped forward. "Tiny Rockatansky is—"

Jimmy put a hand on Harold's chest, his fingers splayed out over the silk tie. "He fucking remembers who the guy is." Jimmy was used to people thinking that Poppa was in some kind of vegetative state, even those who knew him, and it pissed him off. More underestimation at work.

Harold stepped back and looked down at his tie, as if Jimmy carried cholera. "Of course."

After a few long moments, Poppa's voice came back on in the controlled cadence of the computer. Jimmy knew that this probably should have come out as a yell but the software was not good at conveying emotion and, like e-mail, if you didn't know Poppa well, it was easy to misinterpret the cadence. *"What else . . . do you know?"*

This time Jimmy let the lawyer step up to the plate. "Ten million went into Rockatansky's account eleven days ago."

Poppa's eyes fluttered in a rapid staccato that the eye monitor translated into speech, delivering the old man's favorite word with passionless precision: *"Fuck."*

Harold moved away from the window and stood in the shadow beneath a Cape buffalo shoulder mount. His expression, like both the buffalo as well as the toxin-injected faces of the local Westmount hausfraus, never gave much away other than irritation.

Jimmy nodded. "Yeah. Fuck. We need to know where that money came from. There's only one person still alive who hates Poppa enough to pay twenty mil to put him down."

"Nikolai," Poppa's simulated voice said.

Poppa and Nikolai's feud went back to the 1978 Stanley Cup Playoffs and a ticket scam that should have been shared, but wasn't. At least the Habs won. There had been no bloodshed between them for a decade and change, and breaking the peace made no sense, at least not from any practical angle. Maybe Poppa would finally get that revenge he had been talking about for all these years.

If Poppa could have shaken his head, he would have. *"We know . . . who's responsible. There's only one . . . course of ac-*

tion." He paused and the only sound in the room was the gentle hum of his electronic life-support system. "*Harold, could . . . you wait outside.*" Even the software-imposed monotone could not present the statement as anything other than what it was—an order.

Harold opened his mouth as if to protest, then closed it. "Sure, Poppa, whatever you say." He left the room, stepping between a pair of men who took up several yards of well-tailored menace, and into the hallway.

Jimmy locked the dead bolt and went back to the window, to the blizzard-caked city. "What do I do?"

"*If Rockatanksy isn't . . . guaranteed the second half . . . of payment he . . . won't complete the . . . job.*" After a few metronomic pumps of the old man's artificial lungs, he said, "*You and I . . . spend a few minutes discussing . . . things. Then you walk out . . . of here and go to . . . war.*"

Another splendid view spilled out below him, rooftops and trees, all the way to Westmount Square and Saint-Henri, beyond the river in the distance.

Poppa had spent his life running this business—it had been his central obsession since inheriting the kingdom when his own father was shot down in front of the Ogilvy Christmas window all those years ago.

"*You will inherit . . . everything. What I need—*"

"Stop with—"

"*Don't interrupt . . . me,*" the old man's artificial voice interrupted.

Jimmy put his hands in his pockets and listened.

"*With that comes . . . a great responsibility . . . I know you have . . . respect in this . . . town. With that comes . . . enemies. Enemies who will . . . want what you . . . have. Now that I'm in this . . .*" He paused as his gaze shifted toward Jimmy, tears welling up in his eyes. *"Now that I'm in this computerized prison, they . . . think they can get . . . to me. Maybe they . . . can. But I don't want you . . . inheriting . . . a flaming ball of shit."*

"I'll burn this fucking town to the ground if anything happens to you."

Poppa blinked out his response. *"No . . . you won't."*

Jimmy was getting frustrated; he was a warlord but his old man's word was biblical. "What do you want me to do?"

"You kill Nikolai Bushinsky . . . and his sons . . . immediately."

From the time Rockatansky had been spotted at the border, Jimmy knew the situation would be boiled down to two options: fight or flight. And the second had never really been on the table.

"Rockatansky won't . . . fulfill his contract if . . . his employer is . . . dead," the old man's robotic drone continued. *"But . . . even if . . . he does, you'll have no . . . competition when I'm gone . . . Take out Nikolai and those . . . two retards he calls his sons . . . and then the town is yours."*

"Do we want to be subtle?"

Poppa paused; the only sound between them were his lungs inflating and deflating with computerized precision. Jimmy thought he saw a smile creep onto his father's face, a near-invisible flash of the man he had once been.

"Fuck . . . subtle. Do something . . . massive."

The blizzard had let up but the streets were piled with snow. East of Atwater, Rue Notre-Dame was relatively plowed, but most of the locals had yet to dig their rigs out and there weren't many parking places. Antennae stuck out of snow banks like snorkels.

The ersatz foodie crowd was smaller than usual; apparently the snow was too much of an obstacle in their search for the perfect Instagram photo. Still, the Burgundy Lion was crammed with hipsters who made too much noise under the assumption that talking loudly made them more interesting. Outside the restaurant, bearded guys in rolled-up skinny jeans and Cowichan sweaters smoked imported cigarettes and drunkenly pontificated about the latest Mac product. Across the street, the heavy-hitting Joe Beef and Liverpool House had started to empty out; many of the diners headed home for the tail end of the Habs game.

In front of Joe Beef stood a big guy smoking a cigarette, wearing nothing but a plaid shirt, jeans, ball cap, and three days' worth of stubble. His sleeves were rolled up, exposing thick forearms covered in koi tattoos. Nikolai Bushinsky came out behind him and thanked him for a splendid meal. Bushinksy had the look of an old-school mobster who had reluctantly stopped killing people; he wore an oversized three-piece suit and smoked a fat cigar. He was flanked by his sons, Josef and Vlad. Josef was a fat, heavy-lidded wannabe gangster, while Vlad was a small and lithe jazz pianist who played at several bars around town. Even to the casual observer it was obvious that they had spent the evening celebrating. They were all a little drunk, having put away seven bottles of good Burgundy wine. The three men scaled a snow bank and stepped into their town car, swearing and nearly losing one of their Gucci Horsebit loafers. Nikolai and Vlad got in back, Josef in the front with their driver, cursing his wet sock.

At the corner of Charlevoix, the Lincoln stopped behind a rental cube van. The light was red and the three Bushinskys were trying to decide if there would be any chicks at Chez Parée worth braving the elements for. Nikolai was of the opinion that it was smarter to go home and watch the end of the

218 // M<small>ONTREAL</small> N<small>OIR</small>

Canadiens game in the screening room. When they had all agreed to go home and watch the Habs, the roll-up door on the truck ahead flew up, exposing the biggest motherfucking antiaircraft gun any of them had seen outside of a *Star Wars* film. To be fair, the driver's reflexes were great, maybe perfect, but even a big eight with the gas punched to the floor can't back up faster than a double-snouted .75 cal can spit out death.

The car rocketed in reverse for about twenty yards before the massive gun opened up. As the first volley of fire mulched the engine block and front window, Josef detonated like meat-filled popcorn. The car fishtailed, swerving left and mowing down one of the groovy young people in front of the Lion before hitting the brick wall of the Corona Theatre. The big gun kept punching it, the rattle of brass in the bed of the truck tinkling like laughter just below the heavy barrage of the slugs.

The car shuddered in place as it came apart, hundreds of rounds smacking into the metal skin at supersonic speeds; red tracers lighting up the street like insects from a Timothy Leary nightmare. Somehow, Vlad rolled out of backseat and ran for the corner of Viger Square. One of his hands was gone and he stumbled along, drooling blood out of his sleeve and bellowing a single high-pitched shriek.

The gunner moved off the car, the red tracers stitching a line along the storefronts, shattering windows and whipper-snippering two hipsters down like plaid-clad dandelions. When the line of fire caught up to Vlad he danced in place for a few seconds, rounds vapor-trailing through him in a heavy black mist peppered with chunks of flesh and bone. Glass and stone and brick behind him exploded as copper-jacketed lead drilled through his body. Car alarms went off. A lamppost toppled. Vlad disintegrated before he could fall over and the line of fire swung back onto the town car.

But the Lincoln had already exploded. Nikolai Bushin-sky's arm stuck out the shattered back window, wrapped in flames, the index finger pointing at nothing in particular.

Jimmy stood looking out at the city in the exact same spot where, less than twenty-four hours ago, he had learned about Rockatansky. Only now Nikolai Bushinsky and his sprogs had been gunned down like 1950s goombas. Of course there were the nine dead bystanders if the police reports could be trusted. But there is a hidden cost to everything, survival in particular.

Harold was in the apartment, just in case the police came around. They wouldn't have anything concrete, not in any real sense of the word. Besides, no one really cared about the Bushinsky boys—just more criminal detritus subtracted from the gene pool of the city. Iggy and Marcus left the truck on the street, along with the antiaircraft gun; the weapon had been in storage since the seventies and the only one who knew about it was Iggy. And the truck had been stolen earlier in the evening. Nothing but a handful of dead ends.

The nine bystanders were the problem. Which meant at least one visit from the police. A few midlevel soldiers might get picked up. Maybe even smacked around. But Jimmy and Poppa would sit right here in the apartment, comfy and safe behind a thin veil of respectability. And a pile of money.

Jimmy watched the television for a few moments. *Pulse News* was on the scene, interviewing Dave McMillan, one of the owners of Joe Beef. Dave was a big guy in a ball cap and ap-parently didn't need anything more than a plaid shirt to keep warm. He threw a cockeyed and somehow weirdly cherubic smile at the camera. "I saw the whole thing. Four guys left the truck. Small, wiry dudes dressed in black, wearing masks—like ninjas. They got into two waiting cars—red Camaros. I think they were speaking Russian. Maybe Czechoslovakian."

Behind McMillan, a man sporting a CN cap and identified as one of the other owners of the restaurant jumped up and down, a meat cleaver in one hand, a Labatt Blue in the other. "Ninjas, tabarnac!" he kept repeating.

Jimmy smiled and nodded at the screen. "I like these guys. Iggy, send them ten cases of Scotch—the good Japanese stuff."

Iggy lifted his head, scanned the screen, and reached for the phone.

Jimmy watched the rest of the report then turned off the set. There wasn't anyone from the Bushinsky family left to come after him. No grandkids, nephews—no one of note. He had already reached out to mutual friends and they had happily jumped the fence.

Which left Tiny Rockatansky as the last pebble in his shoe.

Jimmy turned back to his apartment. The old man was in front of the fish tank, off to the side of the fireplace. Every now and then Poppa's fingers moved. At first Jimmy thought the old man was multitasking, but who would Poppa be speaking to at this hour?

Harold was in one of the chairs flanking the coffee table, a tumbler of Scotch in his hand and a concerned look on his face—from his perspective there was always a downside. After all these years, Jimmy still hadn't figured out if skepticism was Harold's natural setting or if he had adopted the stance because that's what Poppa paid him for.

"Thoughts?" Jimmy said to the lawyer.

Harold took a sip and shrugged. For a man who should have looked happy, he was missing a smile. "I think that Joe

Beef stunt opened a wormhole. You two have set things back fifty years."

A cell phone on the counter buzzed, and Iggy, who was doing his duty at the espresso machine, held it up. "It's yours, Jim."

Jimmy smiled at his old man, upright in front of the aquarium.

His father blinked. *"You did good . . . son. You get a clean . . . slate . . . to work with."*

Jimmy took his phone from Iggy's hand. He checked the display, then thumbed the screen.

After a terse greeting, his associate in Ottawa relayed information on the banking transaction—ten million US dollars that originated in a Grand Cayman account had gone through Luxembourg en route to Nassau. Not an unusual route or sum, but it was the only transaction that fit the description. It had been sent by a law firm in Toronto. She gave Jimmy a name and hung up.

Jimmy put the phone down on the counter and nodded at the bulge under Iggy's sweater. Iggy raised an eyebrow but handed it over.

Harold was pouring another Scotch when Jimmy came back in with the chrome .357 in his hand. The lawyer topped up the tumbler and returned to his seat by the fire. He kept his eyes on the pistol while he took a sip.

"I found out where the money came from, Harold."

"Oh?"

Jimmy raised the pistol. "Toronto firm. Dooley, Hall, Kerr and Reid. Heard of them?"

Harold's eyes scrolled up and to the right. He nodded. "Big firm."

"Remember the Place Ville Marie parking lot purchase? They notarized the papers for the seller."

Harold took another sip of single malt then said, "Good memory." He looked over at Poppa. "Aren't you going to—"

Jimmy pulled the trigger and Harold shuddered in place. His chest blossomed in a massive welt of red and he vomited up a rope of black blood that slopped into his tumbler and spilled onto his lap.

Jimmy walked over to the kitchen and placed the pistol in the sink. Iggy turned on the hot water.

Back in the living room, Harold made a horrible wheezing sound, then slumped over.

"*It was . . . me.*" The old man's voice chimed to life. "*I hired . . . Rockatansky.*"

Jimmy stared at the old man.

"*You have . . . a clean slate . . . a kingdom. Nikolai . . . just would have . . . been in the way. Harold and you were . . . a terrible . . . match.*"

"So you had me kill him for nothing?" Jimmy jabbed a finger at Harold's dead body.

"*You needed to . . . make a statement . . . I am . . . tired of . . . this prison.*" His fingers tapped away as he blinked out his thoughts. "*I am past the . . . point where even . . . the shitty parts . . . of long ago seem . . . better than . . . the present.*" His fingers stopped and his printer spat out a single sheet of paper. "*Visit me in your dreams . . . son.*"

Jimmy lifted the paper from the tray. It was a bank transfer order. Another ten million US dollars.

He had time to read it once before the window exploded. The heavy slug drilled through Poppa, through his magical chair, and into the aquarium, sending the candy-colored fish to the floor in a massive surge of water. Poppa teetered in place for a second before the second shot came whistling in and he died.

PART III

On the Edge

JOURNAL OF AN OBSESSION
BY JOHANNE SEYMOUR
Plateau Mont-Royal

Translated from French by Katie Shireen Assef

I've always been afraid of the void: a black hole, an empty glass, a vacant heart, a blank page . . . I have no confidence in the metaphysical platitude that the universe is allergic to vacuums and needs to fill the holes. I fear emptiness more than death itself. In my case, that's saying something.

Every inch of my apartment is taken up. Wherever my gaze falls, there's something interesting to look at—paintings, books, side tables, lamps, empty wine bottles. I hoard so that I am never without.

I live on the ground floor of a building in the Plateau Mont-Royal. In the summer, my backyard abounds with all sorts of plants and wildflowers. In the winter, I keep the curtains closed.

I have mistresses, one for each day of the week, and a few I cultivate for special occasions. I have many friends who fill the quiet moments—men, women, even children. I'm only alone when I write, and even then I'm not so alone; I have my characters to keep me company.

I've managed to control my obsession.

Until now.

I write in a popular café in the neighborhood, not because it's trendy, but because it's always crammed with people. I go early in the morning, sit at my usual table in the back, and stay until late in the afternoon. The owners tolerate me because I'm fairly well-known—they think I attract customers.

On one such day, I ordered a large latte and settled down at my table. I scanned the room as I plugged my laptop charger into the wall outlet. As usual, the assorted species of bobos and hipsters lined up along the counter to order their morning fix, while lumbersexuals wolfed down huge breakfast sandwiches as if they were actually going to spend the day chopping wood. That's the Plateau, for you—you're an artist, even when you're not. After I'd scanned the crowded café, I was ready to concentrate on my work. But then I saw him, the man who would lead me to my demise.

He was roughly fifteen years my junior, a handsome man, slender yet muscular, though I doubted he worked out much; he seemed naturally fit. He smiled at whoever would look at him, confident as he strode through the shop. I noticed he was carrying a laptop.

He sat down at a small table in front of the café. I wondered how he managed to find an available seat at this hour—the shop was swarming with customers. The barista, who normally stayed behind the counter at all costs, went over to the man and took his order, removing a small *Reserved* card from his table. I nearly choked on my coffee.

He took out his laptop and plugged it into the wall. Like me, he scanned the room before beginning his work. *Who is he?* I wondered. A lawyer? An architect? Is he answering e-mails? Playing around on Facebook or Twitter? One thing was for sure—he had a lot to write. The sound of his fingers clacking keys exasperated me. You'd have thought he was a keyboard virtuoso, the Mozart of word processing.

"Is everything all right, sir? Would you like a glass of water?"

I was sweating in streams, which is probably why the waitress stood before me, a concerned look on her face.

"No, no. I'm fine."

"Can I get you anything?" she asked impatiently.

"Another latte?"

She turned and walked back behind the counter, but not before I glimpsed the disappointment on her face. Would she prefer I free up the table? My table? The one I had occupied every day since the café opened?

Panic stung my chest.

I tried to tell myself that my imagination was taking me for another ride, but I couldn't help but think the worst. Would I have to find another café to write in? While in every other part of my life I'd set up escape routes, detours, emergency exits, here I felt totally unprepared.

"You okay?"

Mozart stood beside my table, staring at me. With a superhuman effort to not make eye contact, I said, "Yes, thank you. It's nothing."

I thought he'd go back to his spot at the front of the café, but he didn't budge. I finally looked up at him.

"You don't remember me?"

"No. I'm sorry." I wasn't sorry for anything. Why did I say that?

"Well, it's true that there were a number of us taking your seminar."

A *writer!*

"What can I do for you?" I asked. "I should warn you, I don't read other people's manuscripts."

Mozart smiled. "Don't worry. I just wanted to say hello."

Then he went back to his table and started clacking away

on his keyboard, as if his fingers had a life independent of his brain, or a direct connection to it.

The waitress set my second latte on the table.

"You sure you're okay?" she asked. "Something to eat, perhaps?"

Determined not to abandon my post, I said, "I'll have your lumberjack special."

She turned and walked away, and again I felt that she'd prefer I gulp down my coffee and get out of there.

I couldn't understand how I'd become persona non grata overnight. I'd never caused a scene at the café (well, once, but a long time ago), and my reputation maintained a pleasant status quo amongst my peers. So why did I suddenly feel like a leper?

I knew I was getting carried away. I attributed my state of mind to my usual paranoia, and tried to concentrate on my writing.

When I was starting out as a writer, I made a habit of rereading, each morning, whatever I'd written several days before. I thought of this as a kind of warm-up. And so I read over the twenty pages I had written in the last five days. A smile of satisfaction spread over my face. It was good. Very good. *Excellent*, even. Probably the best thing I'd ever written. My swan song.

The thought paralyzed me.

Was it a sign? Was I going to die? Was that what had colored this day from the very beginning? A presentiment of my imminent death? I shook myself out of it. I wouldn't give into paranoia. Why couldn't I write something exceptional without thinking I'd die because of it? I took a deep breath and read the pages once more. I was so moved that I could hardly believe I'd written these lines. Finally, I was writing the novel that would catapult me to fame, that would be my ticket to the hall of literary heroes, alongside Harper Lee, J.D. Salinger, Kerouac . . .

I placed my fingertips on the keys, ready to hear myself make the inspired clacking sound. I waited for the word that would prompt the avalanche, the inspired thought that would break the dam. Seconds passed, then minutes. Nothing. Not a single idea. No matter how many times I reread those lines, my thoughts stopped with the final period. Then, emptiness. An infinite void. Brain death. The café had fallen silent. All that could be heard was the sound of Mozart's fingers tapping away on his keyboard as if he were performing the "Minute Waltz."

It was intolerable.

My fingers were frozen in a grotesque position above my laptop while his were flying over the keys, light, bouncing, inspired. But who was this Mozart? He'd stolen my barista, my status as shop master, and now he was keeping all the muses for himself! He chose this moment to close his computer, walk up to the cashier, pay, and leave the café.

I should have taken a deep breath and let him go. But what can I say? I was panicked. I was about to crank out the novel of my career until this nobody, this poor man's Mozart, came and ran off with my inspiration. I packed up my things in a hurry, threw a few coins on the table, and left.

I didn't know what I had in mind, going out after him. I'd acted without thinking, gripped by panic, a sudden impulse. What was I supposed to do now that I was out on the street? The wind had risen, and a fine, icy rain swept over the sidewalk of Rue Mont-Royal. The autumn, crueler than usual, was making us pay for the splendid summer we'd had.

Mozart had turned right after leaving the café. I decided

to follow him. After all, he was headed in the direction of my apartment.

I was not dressed warmly enough, and shivered as the rain soaked through my clothes. The café was nearly ten blocks west from where I lived on Rue Marquette. It would be fifteen minutes or so before I was back in my warm apartment, which would be more than enough time to observe Mozart, if I didn't die of pneumonia first.

I quickly noticed the similarities between us. We walked with the same long strides, collar raised, hugging our computers to our chests. And we shared that dumb superstition about avoiding sidewalk cracks, which gave a jolting quality to our gait. Long strides punctuated by quick, jerky steps.

I felt myself come back to my senses, my anxiety dissipating. I began breathing freely again. My fear of dying or being unable to finish my novel vanished from my mind. I even felt like laughing as I realized how convinced I'd been that Mozart had stolen my inspiration. What idiocy! I lectured myself silently: *I know what's going on with you. You're getting old and you're afraid. Afraid to die without writing a great novel. Afraid that your readers will abandon you for a younger, more audacious, more talented writer . . .*

Mozart kept walking along, innocent, not suspecting he was the object of my scrutiny. I congratulated myself on my honest self-examination. I was pushing fifty and I clearly felt threatened by this young author; it was the way these things went. I simply had to learn to control myself. Remind myself that I was of an age to write a masterpiece, while he was of an age to commit novice mistakes. The thought made me smile, and I now felt for this Mozart. He would be flayed alive by critics, as we all are at one point or another, and his pride would make him pay dearly for it. I knew a thing or two about that.

Even as the weather worsened, my mood improved. To-morrow, everything would return to normal. I would go back to the café, sit at my usual table, and continue writing my masterpiece. I even wondered if I should run up and say a few words to Mozart before he disappeared down Rue Mont-Royal. I had been rude to him, after all. I was about to sprint ahead when I saw him turn right onto my street.

I had never seen him on my block before. He'd never set foot there, I was sure of it. Why was he heading in that direc-tion, today of all days? My heart pounded as I watched him from afar. I nearly fainted when I saw him stop in front of my apartment building. My hands were clammy and I felt short of breath. He hesitated, then stepped forward and rang my neighbor's doorbell. I stood paralyzed, right in the middle of the sidewalk. At any moment, he could have turned his head and seen me. But the door seemed to open itself then, and he disappeared inside. In that moment I found my legs again, and ran until I reached my door. After a few attempts, I managed to insert my trembling key into the lock and turn it. As soon as I stepped inside, I closed and double-locked the door.

I was overwhelmed by contradictory feelings. Mozart ter-rified, enraged, and thrilled me. I hadn't felt so alive in a long time. Or so crazy, either. I was obsessing over a stranger. Some of my own characters had been locked up for less erratic behavior.

I took a cold shower and holed up in my room. Like every-where in my apartment, the space was cluttered with objects. In the bedroom's case, books. The four walls were covered with books, and there was even a book motif painted on the wooden pillars of my bed. A writer in his nest. I turned off all the lights, except for a small lamp I always left on, a comfort-ing presence in the dark. I'd had the good idea of taking a tranquilizer before my shower, and so when I rested my head on my pillow, I fell right to sleep.

At first I felt a slow rocking sensation, nearly imperceptible, then an intense wave of vertigo that would have thrown me to the ground if I hadn't gripped the edge of the bed until my knuckles turned white. What was this? What was happening to me? I wanted to scream; my mouth opened in horror, but no sound escaped. I was at the center of a universe that was splitting into innumerable fragments. Millions of particles spiraled around me. I felt hell's funnel swallow me whole, but then I understood that it was me, with my mouth agape, inhaling the world. I was a black hole. An unfathomable void.

Aaaaah! Aaaaah! Aaaaah!

I screamed and screamed. Sitting straight up in my bed, covered in sweat from head to toe, I couldn't get a grip. The world around me had returned to its original form, but the nightmare kept playing out in my mind. I felt as if I were imploding. My physical self was dissolving, being sucked up by my inner void. Soon there would be nothing left of me but a gelatinous puddle of ectoplasm on my bedsheets.

I heard a loud, booming laugh through the wall separating my bedroom from my neighbor's apartment. Panting, I listened carefully. My neighbor had never laughed like that, never made a sound that reached my apartment. I lived next door to a tiny woman, discreet as a shadow. And yet this laugh . . . Mozart's face surfaced from the depths of my memory. I remembered now. He was at my neighbor's. Was he the one with this grotesque laugh? What did he find so amusing? The idea that Mozart was laughing at my expense slowly took shape in my mind.

Enough with this Mozart! I shook myself.

But the poisonous thoughts had already begun to do their

work. My anxiety gave way to a rising tide of bile that formed in my throat. A wave of rage came over me, so intense and powerful that even Mozart would have found it difficult to recognize me. I was in a state of complete self-defense. I would not let this man destroy my life.

I got up and went to the kitchen, where I started digging through the cupboards in search of a flashlight. Once I'd found one, I crept close to the back door, intending to spy on my neighbor. The night was pitch black, and no light filtered through her kitchen window. I approached the French doors of the dining room that opened into the garden. Everything was black. No human activity was visible. My bare feet were freezing on my neighbor's courtyard floor. I wore nothing but a T-shirt and a pair of boxer shorts. I was starting to have serious doubts about the legitimacy of my expedition, when I saw a shadow looming at the back of the dining room. I heard Mozart's delirious laugh once again. That was all it took. I charged at the door and knocked furiously until someone opened.

A harsh light erupted from the dining room, and for a few seconds I couldn't see anything at all. Then Mozart appeared in the doorway, pulling his bathrobe tight around himself, a terrified look on his face.

"What's wrong?" he asked, like a scared little mouse.

He stumbled to the ground as I forced my way inside.

I dashed toward the front of the apartment, where the living room and the bedroom were. Where was my neighbor? She had invited the devil in, she would have to get rid of him.

"What are you looking for?" Mozart asked, standing up with difficulty.

I wasn't going to reward him with a response. Who did he think he was? He had invaded my life. I was now an occupied territory, and had the right to defend myself. I hadn't spent all these years struggling to achieve modest literary status just to let some cocky young kid oust me without putting up a fight.

"You're not acting like yourself," he said wearily, following me into the living room. "You're worrying me."

We were strangers! How dare he judge my state of mind! And his head? Cocked on the side like a dog, questioning my presence in the house? Questioning my very existence!

I leaped at him, my flashlight brandished in the air. I remember hearing my neighbor in that instance, but her screams only echoed those of Mozart's as I hit him with the flashlight. He didn't budge. His stillness enraged me even more, so I hit him again. And again.

My neighbor kept screaming. "What are you doing? Stop!"

The room began to spin. I didn't understand why Mozart wasn't falling under my blows. Then, suddenly, he exploded into a million pieces, just like in my nightmare. And I saw my neighbor gripping my arm. She wouldn't let me go. I was afraid she would pull me away with her into the spiral.

Then there was nothing.

No sound. No image. Darkness. The great void.

When the authorities arrived, they found my neighbor unconscious on the floor, and me lying motionless at her side, half-dressed, my bloody flashlight in hand. There was no trace of Mozart. Despite my pleas of innocence I was later declared unfit to stand trial and placed in an institution. Mozart had disappeared in the night; the authorities did not believe he even existed.

But he did. And these words are my written testimony . . .

From far away, he heard the sound of someone clapping their hands. Who would dare to bother him while he was writing?

"Are you still there?"

He groaned.

"You were telling me that it started . . ."

He raised his eyes.

". . . when you began writing your magnum opus."

He screamed.

Two large male nurses grabbed him by the shoulders, and one stuck a needle in his arm. Before he lost consciousness, he heard the doctor say: "His hallucinations are almost constant now. I'm afraid his condition is irreversible. He will never leave this institution."

The older of the two nurses gripped the handles of the wheelchair and started pushing him out of the office.

"What is he doing with his fingers?" asked the younger nurse who had just started working at the hospital.

"He's typing on an imaginary keyboard. He spends his days writing stories that will never see the light of day."

The nurse looked stunned. "Why?"

"The man is a well-known novelist who has always struggled maintaining his sanity," intervened the doctor. "He was my patient long before his collapse. I thought I could control his illness with medication, but . . ." he paused almost theatrically, "one night, in a moment of delirium, he broke into his neighbor's home and attacked her. Luckily she survived; she said that he mistook her for someone else."

"What do you think pushed him over the edge?"

"I think the lack of inspiration drove him crazy."

"I guess we can't all be Shakespeares like you, doc!" The nurse pointed to the doctor's crowded bookshelves.

"Indeed, I'm fortunate to be able to pursue two careers successfully."

The young nurse approached the wall of books. "May I?"

The man nodded.

The nurse grabbed a book and read the blurb printed on the cover flap: "*Claude Chopin took the literary landscape by storm, eliminating his predecessors along his path.* Wow! Is that so, doc?"

Dr. Chopin smiled. The critics had never been so right.

THE SIN EATERS

BY MELISSA YI

Côte-des-Neiges

I didn't trust guys who were too good-looking.

Strange, since I was sitting to the right of a rather fantastic-looking patient at that moment. He had carefully combed dirty-blond hair, high cheekbones, and very white skin. Beautiful, but he gave me the creeps. He was perched on the edge of the bed with his legs and hands crossed, gazing steadily at the plastic surgeon.

Dr. Mendelson didn't seem to notice anything. "This is Hope Sze," he told the patient, waving at me. "She's a resident doctor, but she won't bother you." He flipped through the patient's chart, glancing at the *before* pictures, a big element in plastic surgery. "You're healing well. Lift your chin up."

I was a first-year resident finishing my palliative care rotation, but I was spending a day on plastics at Montreal's Samuel G. Wasserman Jewish Hospital, just for the heck of it. I didn't get to see aesthetic patients very often, because they pay privately, and don't want students descending upon them, but Dr. Mendelson said I could shadow him if I promised not to touch anyone, speak, or practically breathe. Dr. Mendelson was a gnome of a guy, with a deeply furrowed brow and a rumpled white lab coat. He was not exactly the kind of person you'd pick out of a lineup to perform plastic surgery.

This patient's *before* picture didn't seem all that different than what he looked like now. He'd paid for cheek implants and Botox, even though he was twenty-two years old, only five years younger than I was. The implants did give a foxlike sharpness to his features. As I assessed his new cheeks, his green eyes fixated on me in an uncomfortable way.

Dr. Mendelson took another picture and said, "Could you stand by the window? The light is better."

The patient posed with such alacrity that I figured he was either a model or a wannabe model. Dr. Mendelson snapped some frontal and side pictures, and the patient leaned forward to check his own image on the back of the SLR camera. "That's the best one," he said, pointing a thin, pale-skinned finger. He was glaring at the camera, which fit in with the *fuck you* image that most advertisements project nowadays. "Can I get a copy? You can e-mail it to me, or put it on Tumblr." His voice was high and thin, not as striking as his appearance.

I wondered what he did for money to afford plastic surgery at such a young age. Maybe it was just the bank of Mom and Dad. I wanted to ask him about his work, but since I was forbidden to speak, I glanced at his chart. His name was Raymond Pascal Gusarov. He was a Scorpio like me—not that it mattered—and we'd both recently had our birthdays. In fact—I took a quick look—he'd had surgery *on* his birthday, November 14, which seemed strange to me. *Yay, I turned twenty-two. Better have someone cut my face open.*

I've never been a big fan of plastic surgery. I just hope my Asian genes will protect me from the ravages of time.

"I don't put patient photos online because of confidentiality," said Dr. Mendelson, scribbling in the chart without looking up.

"I want it," said Raymond Pascal Gusarov, in a way that made me think he wasn't used to being denied.

Dr. Mendelson grunted. "I'll have copies made and leave them with my secretary."

"At least 300 dpi, so I can use them," said Raymond.

"Only the best for you," Dr. Mendelson replied indifferently. He held the door open. "You can pay the secretary for them when you pick them up."

Raymond cut ahead of me and offered the doctor his hand. "Thank you, Dr. Mendelson. I appreciate it."

Dr. Mendelson squinted at him. The light blinked off his glasses as he shook the patient's hand. "My pleasure." The doctor waved me through ahead of Raymond. I stepped up, because if the doctor's asking you to do something, you can't let a patient beat you to it. Twice.

The thought of Raymond Pascal Gusarov nagged at me for the rest of the day. I didn't know why. Most of the aesthetic patients are trim, fit, and obviously very conscious of their appearance. When Dr. Mendelson asked a young mother if she weighed a hundred pounds, she sniffed and said, "Please! Ninety-five!"

Raymond Pascal Gusarov's fox face seemed to follow me home as I hurried down Côte-des-Neiges, past Saint Joseph's Hospital. Even though I was surrounded by people spilling off the blue-and-white STCUM buses, groceries hooked on their arms, walking into businesses hung with tinsel and Christmas lights, I found myself checking over my shoulder, deliberately ignoring the Notre-Dame-des-Neiges Cemetery as I turned right and huffed myself halfway up the hill to my apartment. My grandmother hates that my new address overlooks a graveyard, despite my fancy digs and twenty-four-hour security guard.

I felt slightly better after I locked the door behind me.

As soon as I kicked off my boots and dropped my backpack onto the hardwood floor, I googled *Raymond Pascal Gusarov*. He came up right away.

The same green eyes stared out at me from a dozen different shots. Some of them were black-and-white, most of them color, nearly all of them professionally photographed. He looked younger in some of them, with a rounder face. Less fox, more chicken. But he never looked innocent.

He was on Twitter, Facebook, Tumblr, and Instagram. He had a fan page on Facebook with only seventy-seven likes. Even from our brief encounter, I figured it would really bother Raymond Pascal Gusarov that he wasn't more popular.

I scrolled through his fan page. He frequently posted pictures and videos of himself, little messages that I didn't want to think too much about, like: *I'M DOWNTOWN, BITCHESS!!!! Cum & C me.*

My phone buzzed with a message from Ryan Wu: *What's up?*

I had to smile. Ryan had just given me the world's most beautiful iPhone for my birthday. I couldn't look at it or touch it without thinking of him, which was probably what he had in mind.

I texted back: *I'm looking something up.*

Work?

Sort of. I didn't want to text anything else, because I'd just caught my third murderer, and Ryan thought that I should hightail it out of Montreal and join him in dull but safe Ottawa.

Ryan was calling now. I rolled my eyes before I tapped the green key to answer the phone. He knew me too well. "Hey, babe."

"Are you on another case?"

"Not officially."

His voice tightened. "I thought you were going to avoid those."

I didn't answer for a second.

"Right?" said Ryan.

"I'm just looking something up on the computer. I'm not getting strangled or anything like that."

"For once," he muttered, which I chose to ignore. "What are you looking up?"

I couldn't tell him without breaking patient confidentiality, but Ryan is a computer whiz—he could be so useful on this. "Let's say that I have someone that I want to look up online. How would I find more information?"

"What have you got right now?"

"Some Google images, his Facebook and Twitter accounts, plus a pretty website with some contact information."

"What are you looking for?"

"I don't know," I admitted. "It just feels fishy to me."

"You want me to do it?"

"I can't tell you his name."

"Okay. So what do you want to know?"

"I want to know more about this guy. I want to know where he lives, and if he's doing anything questionable."

I could practically feel him thinking through the phone. Ryan has a fairly massive brain, not to mention a long, lean runner's build, and—don't get me started. "You might try looking at the Exif," he said.

"What's that?"

"The Exchangable Image File Format. I'll send you some information about it. It not only stores the file format, it tells you the time, date, and GPS coordinates of where the picture was posted."

You mean you could Snapchat a naughty picture of yourself, and freaks could figure out where you lived? I ignored the niggling voice at the back of my head saying, *Isn't this an invasion of privacy? Are you violating the Hippocratic Oath? Huh, freak?*

Instead, I scanned and clicked the various articles Ryan sent me. "This isn't illegal, though, right?"

He laughed. "How is information illegal?"

Oh, Ryan. He was so innocent sometimes. I told him I couldn't wait to see him on Sunday, and hung up the phone.

Long-distance relationships officially suck.

I've never been a huge computer person. I like them, I use them, but I can't make them sit up and purr the way Ryan does. So I was pretty excited when I started tracking down Raymond's locations—mostly downtown and East Montreal, a few in the Plateau. Never Côte-des-Neiges where I lived. *Phew.* Because of its three hospitals and one university, my neighborhood's got a lot of students and immigrants, as Mireille, another resident, put it.

I turned back to Raymond Pascal Gusarov's social media accounts. I clicked on a few links he'd recommended, links that recommended other links, that recommended still more links, most of which were posts by users named TearsOfA-Clown and Heart's Blood.

TearsOfAClown had posted pictures of gerbils, hamsters, and other fuzzy animals. Strange. I would've guessed that Raymond Pascal Gusarov didn't love other living things as much as himself. Maybe I was totally wrong about him. Except TearsOfAClown started posting more photos. One hamster was clearly dead, its little body lying stiffly on its side.

In the next new photo, another hamster posed with a tiny chainsaw over the dead hamster.

My heart thudded. What the heck? Was this Photoshop? I couldn't tell. I've got no skills like that.

In the third photo, the dead hamster was decapitated. Its small golden head was sitting on the ground, severed side down, eyes closed, while the chainsaw hamster stood above it, wearing a miniature face mask.

More photos. More decapitated hamsters. The murdering hamster seemed to wink as it held its little chainsaw aloft.

Some of those hamsters, I'm pretty sure, had been alive up until the moment their necks had been cut.

Oh. Em. Gee.

What could I do about this? I thought this guy was as nutballs as you could get, but could we arrest him for cruelty to animals?

So far, I'd only put away people who'd killed other people. I could call the Humane Society, of course, but what if he said the animals were already dead? What if he claimed it was art? I felt sick.

Before attending medical school, my undergraduate literature class had read "The Sin Eater" by Margaret Atwood. Atwood correlated modern doctors with eighteenth-century sin eaters, who used to consume food and drink placed on a deceased body, theoretically absorbing the dead's sins so that he or she could ascend to heaven while the sin eater got a square meal. For a few days, I wandered around thinking, *Atwood's right; why am I applying to med school, anyway?*

Finally, I decided, *So what. Sins are interesting.* I made my peace with it. But sometimes I wondered, especially when I ended up confronting this level of insanity, if I had made the wrong choice. Not only was I absorbing the sins of the sick, but I was actively seeking out deranged murderers.

I took a deep breath. My phone buzzed again. This time it was Dr. John Tucker: *Yo yo yo,* he wrote.

Hi, I wrote back. If I ever needed Tucker's silliness, it

was now. Even though talking to him on this phone vaguely seemed like cheating. Again, maybe that was Ryan's point, since there was little love lost between him and Tucker.

What's wrong?

Again, Tucker seemed to know me too well. How could he tell, through a text? *I'm looking at something disturbing.*

Ryan? JK.

I rolled my eyes, as if he could see me in my white-walled apartment.

Are you on another case?

Slowly, I tapped out my response: *Maybe.*

I'm coming over.

You are not. I need to think. Bye

I turned my phone to airplane mode, so that neither of my guys could distract me. I started googling *animal cruelty in Montreal.* Then I called the local Humane Society. They took my name and number, but when I said I was calling about photos online, I could feel the guy's interest dimming. "Hamsters? In a picture? Okay."

"I know it doesn't sound like much, but I really think we should look into this."

He sighed. "I would love to look into everything, Ms. Sze." He pronounced it *See,* which was close enough. "But we just got a report of a guy beating his dog to death. We have to close down a puppy mill in another part of the city. And did you hear about le Berger de l'Étoile?"

I hadn't.

He sighed again. He sounded pretty wrecked, so I just thanked him and hung up. Poor guy. It seemed like the animal welfare system was as underfunded as the Montreal medical system. Or worse.

I looked up le Berger de l'Étoile, which turned out to be a

for-profit shelter that killed eighty to two hundred animals a day. Instead of hiring a veterinarian or an animal health care technician, a maintenance worker used the outmoded technique of intracardiac injections, ineptly. So the worker would have to inject up to twelve times, and even then, they'd basically throw the animals in the garbage, still alive.

I covered my eyes. I was heading down a rabbit hole here. I had to concentrate on Raymond Pascal Gusarov.

I Skyped Ryan, who picked up right away. I smiled at his blurry, pixelated webcam photo before I got down to business.

"Ry, I've got pictures, and I'm sending you the link. I need you to help me figure out if the pictures are real, who did them, and if we can sic the SPCA on him." I figured I could bring Ryan into my private investigation because the pictures were public, and I didn't know how to prove that they were from Raymond Pascal Gusarov.

"On it . . . Ugh," he said, clicking away, and then choked on his coffee.

"Sorry, babe." I hated to rope him into this too, making him into a sin eater when he could just work with nice, neat computers all day.

He waved my words away. "Let me see. Okay. I need an IP address . . . Okay, that's interesting."

"What?"

"His IP is 1.2.3.4. Obviously a fake. There's nothing there."

"He covered up his IP address?"

"Pretty much. Let me see what I can do."

While he worked his techno-magic, I busied myself combing through what I assumed was Gusarov's other alias, Heart's Blood, where he wrote stories about screwing other guys, slitting their throats, and eating their hearts. Dear Lord. I rubbed my eyes.

Ryan said, "Holy crap. He's using proxies here, bouncing from China to Sweden. Do you have a video?"

My heart was still pounding from Heart's Blood. "Um, I'll see if I can find one."

"Never mind, I'm on it. Videos are nice because they take up more bandwidth. YouTube won't give out an IP without a police warrant."

I wondered how he knew that.

"I pinged some of my friends. One of them commented on the background for the flying hamster. See how there's a streetlamp outside? It's got an unusual shape."

I squinted. It was especially blurry through Skype, but yes, one shot was of a hamster in a cape, in front of a window, with toothpicks through the eyes. I needed a drink of water. "How long's it going to take you to find out more about this creep?"

"It takes as long as it takes, Hope. It's not like TV."

"Too bad," I muttered.

Ryan's face stilled. "He's in Montreal. My friend found a match on Mapzest."

"I know."

"Is it that patient you were talking about?"

I didn't answer, which was probably enough of an answer.

"Be careful, Hope."

I heard a knock at my apartment door, and jumped. No one should be able to knock on my door since I moved into an apartment with a security guard.

I stifled a scream.

"Don't answer it," Ryan said.

"I won't." I was truly freaked out. Was it possible that while we searched for Raymond Pascal Gusarov, he was tracking us?

Was that how he got money for plastic surgery, at the age of twenty-two? Was he some sort of hamster-killing, heart-eating computer genius?

His *before* and *after* pictures weren't too impressive, but what if he'd started out as someone who looked very different?

"I'm going to stay on," said Ryan. "If anyone breaks in, I'll call the Montreal police."

Virtual backup. Good. Better than no backup.

I'd put the chain on my door, but I called down to the security desk first. "Hi, this is Hope Sze, apartment 8828. Did you let someone in the building who came up to the eighth floor? I didn't buzz anyone in."

"A man got buzzed into the twenty-third floor."

Shit. Of course, there was no stopping him from making his way to my apartment from another floor. Some idiot could have buzzed him in, and then Raymond Pascal Gusarov could decide, *Nope, I'm heading over to kill the detective doctor instead.* I'd gotten complacent, living in a prettier place. A killer is a killer is a killer.

"What did the man look like?"

"Caucasian, about five-nine, blond hair, slim build, jeans, navy jacket. Is there a problem? Do you need me to come upstairs?"

Someone knocked on the door again, harder this time. I squeaked.

The guard said, "I'll need someone to man the front door. Let me call someone."

While he did that, Raymond Pascal Gusarov could smash his way in.

"You want me to call the cops?" said Ryan.

A man spoke through the door: "Hope, I know you're in there. Let me in."

My heart seemed to pause for a moment. I recognized this voice, deep in my marrow. I unlocked my lips. "Tucker?"

"Are you okay? You weren't answering your phone, so I got Mireille to let me in. What's going on?"

I let my breath out slowly. He was talking loudly enough so that Ryan heard. "Is that Tucker?"

I nodded. "You don't need to call the police. But you may need to beat some manners into him."

"Will do," said Ryan, his lips pressed into a grim line, visible through the webcam. He didn't offer to hang up, and I didn't ask him to. Tucker and I shouldn't be doing anything that couldn't be witnessed in public.

I looked through the keyhole, and sure enough, Tucker stared back at me. Even through the fishbowl of the keyhole lens, distorting the sharp planes of his face, I couldn't help admiring his intelligent brown eyes and, yep, that stupid blond hair that he likes to spike with hair gel. "Are you alone?" I said through the door.

"No. I'm with you. There's just this door between us."

I undid the chain and swung the door open. "You scared the hell out of me."

"You didn't answer your phone or e-mail."

"I was busy."

He glanced behind me at my computer, and noticed Ryan. "I can see that. Hey, man."

They nodded at each other.

I felt like stamping my feet. This was not the time for civility. I wanted to kick his ass, no matter how attractive he looked in his dark-wash jeans. He pulled off his jacket and threw it onto my futon, making himself at home. At least he didn't try to kiss me hello on both cheeks in front of Ryan.

"When I say don't come, Tucker—"

"You know that's like waving a red flag in front of me. Strong like bull."

"That's a myth, about bulls and red flags," I said. "They're colorblind. They just don't like the movement, especially when the matador is spearing them."

"I know that," Tucker responded, and added something in another language, which was another one of his quirks that I wasn't going to respond to right now. "Talking about bulls is not the same thing as being in the bullring. What's this case you got?"

I realized that I might be able to share some details about Gusarov with Tucker that I couldn't give Ryan, since Ryan was a civilian. But Tucker couldn't do any of the computer wizardry. I needed both of them.

Shoot.

I ran my hands through my hair in irritation. It lay shoulder length; I hadn't had time to get a haircut. It was starting to get that blobby look. I caught Tucker watching me, a speculative cast to his face, his eyes arrested by the movement of my hands in my hair.

I lowered my arms and immediately glanced at Ryan, whose narrowed eyes shifted between Tucker and me.

I cleared my throat and explained, as best I could, that I'd met a creepy patient who was probably posting pictures of decapitated hamsters online, but the animal welfare groups in Montreal were overwhelmed and wouldn't do anything about it.

"Dr. Hope to the rescue, champion of animals and small children," said Tucker.

I wasn't in the mood for sarcasm. "You have a problem with that? Leave."

He seemed surprised. "No, I like animals. My family has a

dog. And you know what they say is the hallmark of an antiso-cial personality: fire-setting, cruelty to animals, and bed-wetting. We'd better catch this guy before he hurts anyone else."

"Hang on a second," said Ryan. "Bed-wetting?"

I nodded. "I know it sounds weird, but when they re-searched sociopaths, they found that they had these three things in common. That's just what the research shows. That and a lack of remorse. The average person does something wrong and feels bad. A sociopath might apologize because it's politically expedient, but really, they don't care."

Ryan cracked his knuckles. It startled me, even though I couldn't hear the noise as well through Skype. He hadn't done that in years. I guess the stress of detective work was getting to him too. "Okay. Let's get this nut."

Music to my ears.

Ryan doubled down on the computer side. Tucker asked me a few more questions about the patient, and I remembered that he'd considered doing psychiatry before he decided on family medicine. That could come in handy.

"It sounds like he could have body dysmorphic disorder. It's unusual for a man to get plastic surgery on his face at any age, let alone twenty-two," Tucker said, his brow pleated in thought. I tried not to register how yummy he looked when he was thinking. What can I say? Intelligence is a turn-on, even though he was stating something fairly obvious. "Maybe he doesn't like the way he looks. Maybe he's trying to change himself."

That was speculative, but I didn't want to interrupt his chain of thought.

"Maybe he's trying to hide himself."

Now he was getting into *woo-woo* territory, so I was re-lieved when Ryan said, "Got him. He's online right now, just posted another picture. He didn't manage to cover his IP in time. He's close to Saint Marc's Hospital, on Cote-des-Neiges."

I stiffened. Saint Joseph's Hospital, the Jewish Hospital, and Saint Marc's, the francophone children's hospital, are all within a twenty-minute walk of each other. My old apartment, Mimosa Manor, was basically next door to Saint Marc's, as well as the Université de Québec à Montréal. Fortunately, Saint Marc's was now a forty-minute walk from my new apartment. I licked my lips. "Can you give me his address?"

"I can give you his router address."

"Done." I wrote down the numbers and letters on a sheet of paper, then held them up for him to read and double-check.

Ryan nodded. "Now what are you going to do?"

"For once, I'm calling the police."

He sighed in relief. Even Tucker nodded. "I wouldn't go near this guy if I could help it. Are you doing plastics again tomorrow?"

"No. It was a one-time thing." I glanced at the IP address again. "Thanks, Ryan. I—" *Yikes.* I almost told him I loved him, right in front of Tucker, whose dark eyes silently bore into me. "I mean, thanks."

"You're welcome." Ryan grinned at my slip-up—he knew exactly what I was about to say. "You're calling the police right now, right?"

"Yup. Officer Visser. She's cool."

"You'll call me back after you're done?"

"Yeah. She'll probably need to talk to you anyway, since you're the brains behind the operation."

Miracle of miracles, Officer Visser was on that night, but she wasn't in the office. I tried to explain my investigation to one of her colleagues, who obviously wasn't interested. He said he'd give Visser the message.

I was dejected. I wanted to move on this guy—*now.* I

Skyped Ryan to update him, while pacing back and forth in front of the screen.

"You did all you could, right?" said Ryan.

"Sure." I was thinking about that IP address. Could I use it to look up the guy? I know I said I'd never climb back into danger, but . . .

Ryan's mouth clamped together. "Don't go there."

I nodded.

"I mean it, Hope. I'll never help you again if you keep endangering yourself. This is enough. Right?" His tone changed, and I realized that he was looking at Tucker now.

Tucker nodded. "I'll keep her on lockdown."

"You will not," I said, hands on my hips.

They both looked at me.

"You got a death wish?" said Ryan. "How many times do you have to run after killers, bare-handed?"

"I'm not. But I can't just sit here and do nothing."

"Sure you can," said Tucker, grabbing my hand a little too firmly.

Ryan watched us, eyebrows raised.

"Don't worry," I told Ryan. "I'm not going to screw Tucker while he's holding me prisoner."

"Pity," said Tucker in a fake British accent that made me laugh.

"Maybe I'll just hang out with you guys for a while," said Ryan. "Tucker? You following hockey?"

Tucker grinned. "The Habs just killed Phoenix."

Ryan scoffed. "I wouldn't call 3–2 killing them. They had to go to overtime."

"That's part of their charm!"

I glanced between the two and said, in French, "*T'es pas serieux.*"

"Crazy like a Coyote!" said Tucker, which I didn't understand at all, but it must have been a hockey reference, because Ryan responded, "Let's see how they do with the Predators."

While they talked about men with sticks, I tried to figure out what to do. The SPCA couldn't help me. The police didn't take me seriously. I only knew one other officer, Rivera, and he hated my guts. Now what?

I sat down at my computer to do more research. Surely I couldn't be the only person disturbed by an animal abuser? What did other animal-saviors do?

Traditionally, they went to the media and tried to get the newspaper, radio, and TV outlets interested. But nowadays, it looked like they went online. I followed their lead and started a Facebook group. I needed a catchy title.

"What are you doing?" asked Tucker.

"Can't talk. Working," I said.

He read over my shoulder. "*Help the Hamsters?* What?"

"Have you got a better title?" I snapped.

"Sure. *Headless Hamsters. Help Hammy.*"

Of course, Ryan wanted to get in on the action and was not impressed. "Do you know what you're doing?"

"I'm trying to do some detective work online. That way, I'm not risking my neck. I thought you guys would be thrilled."

Ryan stared at me through the camera and repeated, "Do you know what you're doing?"

"I can set up a Facebook group."

"But then the killer can find *you* through *your* IP address. Haven't you learned anything?"

A chill crept down my back. I stared back at him.

He shook his head and said, "I'll do it."

Throughout the next week, my dummy Facebook page received a lot of traffic. I was on my phone all the time, and not just researching articles. People wanted to join the Facebook group—IT folks, teenagers, whatever. I accepted them all, one at a time, before eventually making it an open group.

Then I got a private Facebook message. The subject was titled *yr group,* and the sender was Vladamir Kzurstan. The message read: *catch me if you can.*

I asked for Ryan's advice. He called me and said, "This guy's profile was made two hours ago. It looks like a setup."

My Internet research was driving me crazy. I had to do something.

On my second-to-last day of my palliative care residency, I asked Dr. Huot if I could visit the plastic surgery unit one more time.

The doctor's eyes twinkled. "Oh, my dear, are you thinking of changing specialities?"

"I'm just going for a visit."

Dr. Huot touched my arm. "Of course, dear Hope."

I rushed down Cote-des-Neiges to the Jewish Hospital. I had sins to eat.

I hurried to Dr. Mendelson's office. I had no idea if I'd be able to find him, but luckily, I spotted his rumpled lab coat walking into his office.

I stopped at his secretary and told her I needed a few minutes with Dr. Mendelson.

"You're not on the schedule today," she said, staring at me over the wire rims of her glasses.

"I know. You're right. But I need to talk to him about one of his patients."

She sniffed. "I'll check if he'll see you. He's a very busy man."

Two crucial minutes later, I was sitting in his office. His degrees hung on the walls, and his desk was covered with old-fashioned books and journals, leaving barely enough room for his flat-screen computer monitor, keyboard, and tinfoil-wrapped sandwich. I thought I smelled liverwurst, which always struck me as something one wouldn't eat willingly.

"What can I do for you?" he asked.

Ask not what you can do for me. Ask what you can do for the hamsters, spun through my brain, but I wasn't crazy enough to say it aloud.

"I think one of your patients is torturing animals, and maybe humans," I blurted out.

He choked and coughed, spraying a few crumbs.

I explained my accusations to him, using my phone to show him the proof. His eyes shot up, and he only read a few sentences of Heart's Blood's posts before he looked at me. "This is a sick man, but what does this have to do with me?"

"It's Raymond Pascal Gusarov, the guy with the cheekbones," I said.

"That one," he replied, sagging into his chair.

"What is it?"

"His credit card bounced. He never paid me for the surgery. I even had those photos made for him."

"Is he coming for the photos?" I asked.

"I left him a message that he couldn't have them until he paid for the surgery. He'll probably never show up again. He has thirty days to pay."

"If he doesn't pay, could you mention it to the police instead of a collection agency?"

Dr. Mendelson stared at me like I was speaking Kurdish.

"You know Al Capone?" I asked.

He blinked in surprise.

"He was a gangster who's probably most famous for ordering the Valentine's Day Massacre. But they never caught him for that, anything else either, like bootlegging or prostitution. What they got him for, eventually, was tax evasion. I wonder if we could catch Raymond Pascal Gusarov the same way."

Dr. Mendelson looked as if he'd rather stick leeches all over my face.

I licked my lips, but kept going: "You could report him to a collection agency too, of course, so that you could get your money back. But look, he just posted another photo now, see?" I held up my iPhone, but the doctor hardly glanced at the picture, which showed a hamster with an ice pick through its heart, pinned to the table, its little paws hanging in the air.

Dr. Mendelson looked at me coldly. "I'm not doing this for you."

My heart dropped in my stomach.

"I'm doing it for someone else." He picked up his phone and started making calls.

A month later, the police dropped by Raymond Pascal Gusarov's apartment.

Through the door Gusarov yelled, "Fuck you, pigs."

This did not endear him to the cops, especially when he started shouting, "You can't come in here without a warrant. Go away!" Then the officers heard someone in the apartment scream.

The police obtained a warrant, lickety-split. Dr. Mendelson told me that the person in the apartment was a minor held against his will.

"It's bad blood," Dr. Mendelson muttered. He crossed his arms and stared out the window overlooking Cote-des-Neiges.

We watched the cars stopped at the light and the people zig-zagging on the sidewalk, carrying their briefcases and gift bags.

I thanked Dr. Mendelson and tiptoed out of his office, barely catching something he said in Yiddish. His secretary had come to usher me out, and just before I left their shining office, I asked her, "What did he say?"

She pressed her lips together, but after a moment she told me: "*A shlekhter sholem iz beser vi a guter krig.*"

"What does it mean?"

She glanced at the patient coming in behind me and said, "*A bad peace is better than a good war.* Good day, Dr. Sze."

I turned to face the patient, a man whose gray hair and spotted hands belonged to someone in his sixties, but whose tight face seemed eerily younger. He smiled at me with gleaming white teeth.

MILK TEETH

BY HOWARD SHRIER

Rue Rachel

Max understood animals. His mother had always kept at least one cat in their East End flat, to keep the mice and rats to a minimum. He knew the cats could be cruel at times, batting around a trapped mouse or spider with one paw while pinning a tail or leg with the other. But they'd also rub against the back of his leg when he fed them. One gray tabby, Faigie—named for a maiden aunt with a sad bristle of whiskers—would curl in his armpit when he was falling asleep and rest her head against his chest, listening to his heartbeat.

Before he was old enough to find a real paying job but was strong enough to bale hay, Max spent three summers at his uncle Willie's farm near Shawbridge. Willie always had dogs roaming the property. One of them, Stella, took an immediate liking to Max. She was a blond Labrador mix, with huge swollen nipples up and down her chest. Max thought her eyes looked sad even when her tail wagged. Sometimes she would bare her fangs at the other dogs, snapping at their muzzles, asserting her place in the pack. Sometimes she'd let Max lay his head against her side in the tall grass behind the barn where he went to smoke cigarettes he filched from Willie's pack.

After he joined the police, he befriended a cop in the mounted unit, Marcel Aubin. They sometimes met at the stables on Mount Royal before heading off to drink. Max would watch Marcel groom his horse, Cassius, and marvel at the muscles rippling under its gleaming chestnut coat. The horse's eyes were darker than Stella's, coal black. They gave nothing away, though Max thought he knew something about the horse, watching it snort and shake its head back and forth as Marcel worked the curry brush over his sides.

Cats, dogs, horses. These he understood. It was people that baffled him.

No animal could ever have done what was done to Irene Czerniak in the summer of 1951. However cruel a cat might be, whatever strength a horse possessed, however vicious a dog might become, none would have hurt Irene that way. A cat might have clawed her. A horse could have kicked her. A dog—gripped in a foaming rabid craze—might have ripped out her throat. But only a human could have beaten her so savagely. Once Irene's body was finally found, after four agonizing days of searching, the pathologist, old Vaillancourt, had to append a second sheet to his report to list all the injuries inflicted upon her.

"It would have been easier to write what hadn't been broken," he told Max.

Hardly a bone had been left intact, he said. Her head had been pulped until it lacked structural integrity. Nearly every tooth had been cracked or knocked out.

Most of them were still her milk teeth.

Irene had just turned nine years old when she went missing from Avenue de l'Hôtel-de-Ville; she was a petite, dark-haired girl with two younger siblings. Her parents didn't really start to worry until nightfall. Being the oldest, Irene was independent and often went to visit friends on surrounding streets, allowed to go as far east as La Fontaine Park, where she'd watch the swans and boaters in the man-made lake. She knew when she ought to be home and always returned on time. Until August 3.

On the morning of August 4, a missing persons report was filed at the Boulevard Saint-Laurent police station. Two detectives took statements from Irene's parents while a dozen constables began canvassing the three-story buildings in her neighborhood: Laval, Rivard, and Drolet to the east; Rue de Bullion, Coloniale, and Saint-Dominique to the west. Under detective supervision, neighbors searched the laneways behind the houses. A police dog was given Irene's scent from a pair of her pink socks, and moved through the lanes, sniffing the ground, straining against her leash.

Nothing. No one had seen the girl since five o'clock on Tuesday night, when she left the flat of her best friend, Sybil Grauman, a block east on Laval, saying she was going home to help her mother prepare supper.

It was eventually the smell that led them to her. After nearly four humid days with temperatures in the high eighties, Irene's small body was found wedged into the crawl space under a shed at the rear of a three-story row house on Mentana, well outside the grid of streets they had been searching. The ground-floor tenant had not checked the rear, though a foul smell had been in the air the past two days. There were plenty of reasons why it might smell under a shed in a Montreal laneway—trash cans from three flats sat against the shed wall, and raccoons, squirrels, and skunks sometimes crawled under there to die. Once the tenant realized what he was looking at, a patrolman was on the scene in minutes. After the officer finished retching, he used the tenant's telephone to call downtown.

A few minutes later, the commander of the homicide bureau, Honoré Bellechasse, called Max Handler into his office on the second floor of the municipal courthouse.

"They found her," said Bellechasse.

Max had hoped someone else would get this call. Someone who hadn't lost his own kid, his only son, along with his wife, in a fire. "You know Rene is still out," he said. His partner, Rene Jamieson, was on medical leave, his left shin fractured by a bullet three weeks earlier. Wasn't that reason enough to give the case to one of the other old couples on the squad?

"Take Marois."

Max sighed. "No. I'll work it myself."

"Take Marois," repeated Bellechasse. "The newsmen are going to be all over this and I don't want anyone thinking I gave it the short stick."

Max sighed again. Bellechasse peered down at some papers on his scarred wooden desk and didn't look up again.

Marois was small, even by French Canadian standards, maybe five-six and 135 pounds. He had dark hair slicked back with Brylcreem and a pencil-thin mustache, his mouth a little sunken around his dentures.

"Boss says the parents are Hungarian," Marois said.

"Yes."

"You speak any of that? Boss says you speak a little of everything."

"Maybe ten words," Max said. "*Hello. How are you. Goodbye.* Like that."

"Is that a Jew thing?"

"What?"

"To speak so many languages."

"It's a Saint Lawrence thing. I walked the beat there for six years."

"It's okay I ask you that? I don't know any other Jews is why. You're the only one on the force, right?"

"I'm the only detective, not the only cop."

They rode in silence until Marois asked, "Do you know how to say *I'm sorry?* It'd be good to tell them that."

"The detectives at Station 4 speak English and French," Max said. *Sajnálom,* he thought to himself. *Sajnálom.*

They beat old Vaillancourt to the scene by a good quarter-hour. They were driving a 1946 Chevrolet sedan, while the pathologist had to lumber all the way north from Old Montreal in a '42 Cadillac hearse that served as his mobile forensic lab, the back half weighed down with chemicals, tools, and portable lights.

Max showed his badge to the pale constable guarding Irene's body, instructing him to bring out the tenant who had found her. "Get his story," he said to Marois. "See if you catch anything wrong."

While he waited for Vaillancourt, Max stood just inside the entry into the yard, as far from the body as he could. He smoked and scanned the yard slowly, from the property line to the shed. He looked side to side, up and down. Looked at the wrought-iron latch on the wooden gate, the semicircular line in the stone where the gate had been dragging of late.

He walked up and down the lane, looking at nothing, taking in everything. Once Vaillancourt arrived, Max would have to share the crime scene with him, his technicians, a photographer. He needed to be in it by himself as long as he could, just forming impressions, breathing in details. He was aware that people were watching him from their yards and balconies. They were going to have to canvass this area too, find out if anyone in these flats had a record of offenses against children. Somebody had to have seen something wrong. All it took was one. Maybe they wouldn't have the whole story, but a detail, a snatch of it. Someone might remember who walked through the dark. The make of a car, the smell of tobacco, an unwashed body, the breath of an ogre.

After half an hour on the scene, old Vaillancourt gave Max a grim preliminary report. He made it clear how much violence had rained down on Irene.

Max couldn't say offhand the number of dead bodies he had seen. Most of them stayed in his memory, which was considerable by both nature and training. He certainly remembered the first—a fifteen-year-old girl who drowned in the Lachine Canal back when he was a rookie patrolman. She got tangled in long weeds and only bobbed up when her body was bloated with gas.

Max had seen exactly nine dead children in his life, and could recall every detail about their crime scenes, autopsies, and investigations. Once he had caught the person responsible—and he had caught them all, six men and three women—he could tell you what they looked and smelled like; what they wore when they were caught and what they wore to court; the look in their eyes when they contradicted their own lie.

Irene Czerny had been in the hot, damp dirt long enough for significant decomposition, but not quite long enough to mask her youthful beauty. As Max gently felt Irene's head and bones, noting to himself the fractures, Vaillancourt smoked a steady line of Player's Plain, careful to flick his butts into the dirt and away from the body. Everybody was smoking to keep the smell out of their noses and give themselves something to look at besides the girl.

"I'm glad you're leading this case," Vaillancourt said, once the small body had been bagged and loaded into a morgue wagon. "You had to work harder than most to make homicide."

"I guess," Max said.

"When you find who did this, give him some of the pain he gave her."

"Whatever I can."

"Tell me about the guy who found her."

Marois pulled a notebook from his breast pocket and thumbed it open to a page in the middle. "Roméo Leblanc, thirty-six, married, four kids ages two to eight. Works as a baker on Rue Saint-Hubert. Leaves his house at five in the morning. Works twelve-hour shifts."

"So he'd get off at five o'clock at night, around the time she went missing. And he might have passed her street, depending on his route home."

"I think he's clean," Marois said.

"Based on what?"

"He looked me in the eye. He shook my hand. He spoke in a steady voice. Besides, he has kids of his own."

How did this man make homicide? Max wondered. Marois read crime scene details out of a notebook—Max had never carried a notebook in his entire career. If you couldn't commit a scene to memory, couldn't recall the details of an interrogation, what good were you?

Dead children. They could make a man fucking crazy.

Max left Marois at the scene to oversee the canvass and drove to Station 4, where Irene's disappearance had first been reported. He talked to a detective named Dagenais, and went through the statements he and his team had taken from the parents and neighbors.

"The mother says she was a good kid, good head on her shoulders," Dagenais said. "Swears she wouldn't have run away."

"And the father?" Max asked.

Dagenais shrugged. "Doesn't speak a word of English or French. Been here since the end of the war and can't be bothered, the dumb hunky."

"He strike you as off?"

"A *perv*, you mean? Christ, I don't know. He seemed broken up enough."

"They always do," Max said. "Even after they confess."

"Talk to him yourself."

"I'll do that. What about the neighbors?"

"Not much help. One of them told us the guy upstairs from her had a thing for young girls but he had the best alibi money can buy."

"He was in the can?"

"Yup. Drunk tank. Turns out the lady just doesn't like the guy. He plays his radio loud at night."

"Nothing else?"

"We got a call from a woman who said she saw a girl matching Irene's description walking on Rue Rachel with a boy around the time she disappeared. Five fifteen or five thirty."

"Rachel where?"

"Around Saint-Christophe."

"That's only two blocks from Mentana. Any description of the boy?"

"About Irene's age, maybe a little younger. Shorter, anyway. Wore a brown-and-white checked cap. Curly brown hair poking out."

"That's it?"

"It's all she could see."

"You ask the mother about boys?"

"Of course. She said Irene didn't play with the boys on the street. They mostly play hockey and stickball in the lane. She couldn't think of anyone who matched that description."

"I don't think a kid her age could have hurt her like that. You got anything else?"

"Another neighbor said she saw a guy out on the street the morning Irene disappeared. Thin, pale, thirties. Gave her the creeps."

"Why?"

"She wasn't sure. Said he stood across the street doing nothing."

"Nothing."

"That's what bothered her, she said. He was doing nothing."

"But this was in the morning and she didn't go missing until the afternoon."

"Right."

"Probably no connection."

"That's what we thought."

"She'd never seen him before?"

"No."

"You have her name?"

Dagenais thumbed through a spiral notebook and gave Max the woman's name and address.

"All right. Ask your constables if they know anyone matching that description in the quarter."

"Already did. Nothing."

Sonja Czerny sat at her kitchen table, covering her eyes as if a bright light were searching her out—only her hands could keep her from being blinded. Her husband sat next to her, elbows on the table, head in his hands. Every few seconds,

Sonja would take in a sharp breath and make a barking sound. Max wondered why the husband didn't get up and comfort his wife. Put his hands on her shoulders, rub them when they shook.

He started with a few questions about Irene's routine on summer days, the friends she hung around with, the places she went. All things he already knew from reading statements at Station 4.

Sonja answered all the questions. Her brown eyes reminded Max of Stella's. They had the same sad, searching look. A few times she hesitated and looked at her husband, Tibor. He wore a white undershirt and green pants that were the bottom half of a workman's uniform.

"Ask him if he saw her when he left for work Tuesday morning," Max said. He didn't care what the answer was. He just wanted Tibor to lift his head. He wanted to watch the man's eyes move, hear the timbre of his voice as he spoke about his daughter.

"He says no, he did not see her," Sonja said. "He must leave before seven."

Max wanted to hear more. "Ask him if they spoke the night before."

She put the question to her husband; his answer came back in a rasp. Tears ran from his eyes and choked his voice. Her own eyes welled up as she translated: "He says yes, they spoke about Nadja. She is the younger daughter and she and Irene had a fight on Monday and Irene slapped her. He told her she must not to do this, even when Nadja is starting the fight, because she is older and stronger."

Max had seen and heard enough. In his mind the father was clean. "Please show me where she sleeps." He'd almost said where she *slept*, but had caught himself just in time.

The two girls, Irene and Nadja, shared a small room at the rear of the flat, behind the kitchen. "This is maybe why they fighting sometimes," Sonja said. "Our boy Paul gets a room for himself, but the girls must share."

He stood in the room between two narrow beds, both with white chenille spreads, his hands in his pockets. On the wall above the beds was a cross to which Christ was nailed, his back arched in pain.

"Our other children were born here in Montreal," Sonja said. "But my husband and Irene and me, we lived in Budapest during the war. Irene is maybe too young to remember how hard this was, but I remember. I remember how small she was, how little food we had, how much she cried. Before the war we lived with my parents, but my father was against collaborating with the Nazis, against withdrawing from the League of Nations. His contrary positions, they cost us everything. And when the Soviets invaded, were we rewarded? Of course not. We lost even more."

She put a hand on her chest and shuddered. "Why I am telling you this, Mr. Handler, is because my little girl had a hard beginning to her life. I just didn't want the end to be hard too."

"Tell me about the man you saw," Max said. "Where exactly was he?"

"Across the street, in front of 4120," said Mrs. Peletz, the neighbor two buildings to the north, who spoke in a thick Yiddish accent. She was about fifty, with thick legs and gray hair pulled into a bun.

"Was he coming or going?"

"Just standing with his back against the telephone pole, smoking."

"How long was he there?"

"I don't know. I went to get the mail and he was there. That was maybe eleven. I went out again ten, fifteen minutes later to shake out a rug, and he was still there, still against the pole, smoking."

"Looking at your side of the street or the houses behind him?"

"My side."

"What made you notice him?" Max asked.

"Who just stands there? He doesn't live on the street, he's not talking to no one, there's no bus that comes. Not even looking at a watch. Just smoking. Who does such a thing?"

"And that's why you noticed him?"

"That, and because he was so pale. Most people, it's summer, they have a little color. But not him. Like a ghost he was. I said to my husband, maybe he's been someplace where there's no sun. Maybe he just came from jail."

Max made a mental note to check with Bordeaux Prison and Saint-Vincent-de-Paul Penitentiary, see if they had released anyone in the last month or two with a record of offenses against children.

"How old a man was he, Mrs. Peletz?"

"Younger than you," she said, "but not a boy. Maybe thirty?"

"You get a good look at his face? The color of his hair?"

"A hat he wore, with the brim pulled down," she said. "I just know his face and arms were white."

"He didn't wear a jacket?"

"If he wore a jacket, would I have seen his arms?"

Max smiled. "I guess not."

"Like china they were," Mrs. Peletz said. "The kind they make from bone."

* * *

Max squatted at the base of the light pole in front of 4120 Hô-tel de Ville, which was the ground-floor flat in a brick building with silver-coated staircases winding up to the second and third floors. There were half a dozen cigarette butts on the ground, Player's Plain and du Mauriers with filter tips.

He had just started up the walk to ring the bell when he saw a man in a second-floor window. Tall enough to fill the entire frame, gaunt looking, his neck and head bent at an odd angle. An unmistakable figure.

Max rang the bell to the flat. The lock disengaged and he went up a dark staircase that curved to the right. Waiting there was Jan Albrecht, better known to a generation of Montreal wrestling fans as Baron von Bismarck, the Killer Kraut. In a city that adored its hockey players, boxers, strippers, and singers, wrestlers were among the biggest stars. Even though the Baron was the most hated villain in town—a character who would cut, choke, stomp, and gouge his opponents, brushing aside referees to inflict maximum damage—Jan Albrecht was known as a gentleman outside the ring.

"Hello, sergeant," Albrecht said, extending a massive hand. He was half a foot taller than Max, who stood six feet. His head was huge, with a jutting chin that ended in a bulb split by a cleft. "How are you?"

"I'm good, Jan. How about you?"

"I suppose I could complain," the big man said, pointing at his bent neck with his left hand, "but I will spare you."

"How long you been living here?"

"Since the accident. Rents downtown are high and my earnings are not what they used to be. It's all right. I'm content here. What about you, sergeant? Do you still moonlight at the Forum? You were good security."

"Too busy these days."

To Max's eyes, Albrecht didn't look like he got much sun. But his skin was more gray than white, the color of a dead mouse. And his height and crooked figure would make him familiar to a neighbor.

"You're here about the little girl?" Albrecht said.

"Yes."

"She is dead then?"

"Yes."

"A terrible thing." Albrecht moved stiffly to one side and waved Max into a dim parlor. There was a faded chesterfield with gold and brown stripes and white antimacassars over the rear. A couple of wooden chairs on either side of a chipped wooden table. "You will take a coffee?"

"No thanks. I saw you in the window and wanted to ask if you noticed anyone hanging around the street the day the girl disappeared."

"A constable already came by to ask. Regrettably, I saw no one." Albrecht rubbed the side of his neck, pushing it even farther off center before releasing it with a snapping sound. He had broken it two years back in a bout against the great wrestler Yvon Robert. Albrecht had knocked Robert down, stunned him with a forearm to the throat, and then climbed onto the top rope for his signature finish, a thunderous elbow smash known as the Hammer of Hell. But as he jumped, the toe of his boot had gotten caught under the top rope and he landed on his head, shivered in a violent spasm, and didn't move again for weeks.

"One of the neighbors saw a guy hanging out front that morning, smoking. Very pale," Max said.

"I'm sorry, sergeant, I don't think I saw any such fellow."

"Well, if you remember anything, give me a call."

"Of course. You sure you will not take a coffee?"

"No, thanks anyway."

He heard a door slam at the rear of the flat. Then footsteps, and another door opening and closing.

"Someone else here I can ask?"

"Oh," Albrecht said, "that's just Billy."

"Wild Billy?"

"Yes."

"He lives with you?"

"We have both recently endured somewhat hard times," Albrecht said.

"Call him out here," Max said. "Maybe he saw something."

Albrecht smiled. "Billy hardly looks out the window, as you might imagine."

"Call him out anyway."

"Of course." He walked through the parlor to the corridor that led to the back of the flat and called, "Billy?"

He got no answer. He called again, louder.

A door opened and a voice that was both high-pitched and raspy shouted: "What! I'm drying myself off, for Christ's sake."

"We have company, Billy. Come out here a moment."

"I'm bare-assed."

"Put a robe on and come out. It's Max Handler."

"Who?"

"Sergeant Handler. He used to work security at the Forum."

There was a pause and then Billy said, "Gimme a sec."

Wild Billy Weaver emerged a moment later, all three and a half feet of him, waddling down the hall in a white satin robe with his name stitched over the breast in royal blue. He was rubbing his dark hair dry with a towel.

"Yeah, yeah, I remember you now. How's it hanging, sarge?" Billy reached a hand up to where Max could shake it and squeezed harder than he needed to.

"Okay, Billy. You?"

"Just perfect, only I can't get a decent payday and I can't get laid unless I pay for it, even though I'm hung like a normal guy. Bigger, even. Plus I gotta live with this sad sack." Billy stuck his head to one side, at the same sick angle as Albrecht's, and gave Max a big grin. Max didn't return it.

"I thought midget wrestling was catching on," Max said.

"It's starting to. But Sky Low Low and Little Beaver get the headline fights. I'm stuck on the undercards with Tiny Roe and Pee Wee James. If things don't get better, I'll have to take a job at the Midgets Palace, showing the tourists how us little-halves live."

"At least you can still fight," Albrecht said.

"Yeah, I still got that. So what brings you here, sarge? Who got killed?"

"Shush," Albrecht said. "It's about the little girl across the street."

Billy put the towel down on the sofa. "They found her?"

Albrecht picked up the towel and shook his head at the dark wet spot it had left.

"This morning," Max said. "We're trying to pin down a guy seen around here the day she went missing. Pale guy standing out in the street smoking."

Billy rubbed his chin like he was thinking deep. "Real pale? Like almost pink?"

"The neighbor said white."

"'Cause I saw this one guy who's beyond pale. He's one of those guys that's got no color at all. What do you call them, with the pink eyes and white hair?"

"Albino?"

"Right. Albino."

"You never told me this," Albrecht said.

"Do I tell you every damn thing? Anyway, that's what this guy is. Albino. You see him in a club at night, he looks like a goddamn vampire."

"What do you mean, club?" Max said. "You know him?"

"Sure, I know him. He's a drummer, plays with Kenny Piper's quintet."

"What's his name?"

"Eddie. Eddie Whelan."

"You sure it was him?"

"I saw him, didn't I?"

"The neighbor said he had a hat. She couldn't see his face. How is it you saw him?"

"I just did. Maybe the hat was off for a minute."

"When did you see him?"

"The day she disappeared, like you said."

"What time?"

"In the morning."

"What time in the morning?"

"I don't know, I didn't have my watch on."

"What was he doing?" Max asked.

"Nothing. Just hanging around."

"Why would he just hang around here?"

"The hell should I know? Maybe he was looking to buy a little tea."

"From who?"

"I don't know, I never touch the stuff."

"Then why did you say—"

"'Cause he's a smoke hound."

"Someone around here sells it?"

"I don't know. I only been staying here a few weeks. Right, Baron?"

"Yes," Albrecht said. "A few weeks."

"You sure it was Eddie Whelan you saw?"

"I guess so. He's the only albino I know."

"Guessing isn't good enough, Billy," Max said harshly. "Snatching and killing a nine-year-old girl is the most serious charge there is."

"Then I'm sure, okay? It was Eddie Whelan, 110 percent."

"He ever had this kind of trouble before?"

"How would I know? I never talk to the guy. I just know him because he looks so different."

"You're one to talk," Albrecht said.

The Albatross Club was on Sainte-Catherine, the great glittering strip that cut across the heart of downtown Montreal. It wasn't in the top rank of clubs; Sammy Davis Jr. and Oscar Peterson were never going to play there. But it was no dive. Kenny Piper's quintet pumped out quality tunes, and if the drinks were watered down, it wasn't with a hose.

A clutch of uniformed constables went around back and huddled by the door that opened onto the laneway. Max went in the front with Marois and two other plainclothes detectives. The band was on a raised stage in the back, playing "Cool Breeze," Kenny Piper doing his best to imitate Dizzy Gillespie's trumpet part. Max brushed aside the maître d', and walked past the long bar and through the tables on the dance floor, focusing in on the drummer, whose pallor was pronounced, even by nightclub standards. Marois was at his heels, the other detectives right behind him.

The albino, Eddie Whelan, looked like he had his eyes closed as he worked his snare and high hat. But as the four men approached the bandstand with their hats still on, no drinks in their hands, he leaped from his stool and ran through a slit in the black curtains behind him. Kenny Piper kept playing his horn a few measures but gave it up as the cops jumped onto the stage and followed the drummer through the dark passage.

They ran through a kitchen where pots steamed on gas burners and men in white aprons turned chops and steaks on a flame grill. Whelan knew his way better than they did and had a good ten steps on them when he hit the back door. Max lost sight of him, and then heard shouts from the alley.

Then a gunshot. Then another. Max pulled his Cobra .38 and had it up by his ear as he got to the door. He stopped, not wanting to run out into the middle of a firefight. He leaned slowly out and saw a trash can overturned outside the door. Just beyond the trash can lay Eddie Whelan, blood staining his bright yellow shirt. One round had hit him in the chest, the other in the throat. He had something in his outstretched hand.

"I thought he was pulling a gun," a constable said. He looked almost as pale as Whelan and his forehead was shiny with sweat.

"You shot him?" Max asked.

"Yes sir."

Max took a closer look at the object in Whelan's hand. A syringe. He kneeled down by the body and slipped his hand into Whelan's right pants pocket. Found a couple of singles and a book of matches. In the left was a folded square of paper. Max opened it and saw fine white powder nestled at the bottom.

Forget tea. Whelan was a junkie, not a smoke hound.

Old Vaillancourt had wanted whoever had killed the girl to taste some pain when Max caught him. If Whelan was the one, he hadn't tasted enough.

Even in the best of times, Max struggled to sleep. Too often he'd lie awake missing Naomi and David, his dead wife and child. When he did fall asleep he dreamed of smoke and fire, of burning woods, of charred meat left on a forgotten stove.

At dawn he was walking the lane behind the house where Irene's body had been found. No one else was out except an old woman tending to tomato plants staked in a small patch of earth. When she saw Max, she clutched her robe and moved quickly back into her kitchen.

He didn't know why he was there. The crime scene had been processed. Irene's autopsy was complete. Reports were waiting on his desk. He just didn't want to be at the office yet. He wanted—needed—to be here where Irene had been dumped. Whelan's miserable room on Rue Craig had been searched, but no trace of Irene had been found. She clearly hadn't been killed there.

And who was to say Whelan was guilty of anything other than standing across the street from Irene's house? Since when did junkies abduct and kill little girls? Max had known plenty of them when he worked for vice before the war. Most were only interested in finding heroin or finding money to buy heroin or finding a safe place to shoot up their heroin and ride out the nod.

Up and down the lane he walked, to the south end at Duluth, then past the crime scene up to Rachel. He walked two blocks to Saint-Christophe, where a girl who looked like Irene had been seen walking with a boy in a checked cap. Irene's age or younger, according to the witness. But no boy could have had the strength to do this. Or the hatred of women, which was what usually fueled these crimes.

He walked back east along Rachel. One more time down the lane, he thought, and then he'd go to the office and start looking through the results of Marois's canvass.

Then he stopped to stare at a three-story gray stone building on the north side of the street. It had double doors with etching in the glass. A worm started to crawl through his gut, one he had felt many times before. He stood motionless, hands at his sides, breathing deeply, the way he breathed when he needed to snatch a fleeting thought, hold it, force it into words. When the words came to him, words about the curly haired boy walking Irene through the neighborhood, he ran to his car, shot through the alley, and drove eleven blocks west without touching the brakes.

Jan Albrecht opened the door after three rings, wearing a long gray robe. His eyes were red and his long feet were bare and he was massaging his neck; it seemed more crooked than the day before.

"Sergeant, what's wrong? It's not even seven o'clock."

"Something I need to ask you, Jan. Fast. When Billy goes out, does he ever wear a cap?"

"We all do," Albrecht said—he pointed to a row of hooks behind him where a couple of fedoras hung at eye level.

"Not a hat," Max said. "A cap."

"I think he has one. Yes. A cap with a brim that snaps in the front."

"What color?"

"I'm not sure. Brown, I think."

"All brown? Or brown and white."

"Brown and white, now that you mention it. In a checkered pattern."

Max took out his Cobra and held it at his side. He looked Albrecht in the eye and said quietly, "Tell me you didn't know."

"Know what? I don't—"

"About the girl. About Billy."

"What are you saying? That Billy had something to do with that . . . that horrible thing?"

Max raised the gun and pointed it at Albrecht's chest. It only had a two-inch barrel so if he was going to use it, he had to be close. "Say you didn't know, Jan."

"Of course I didn't. I don't. Billy wouldn't—"

"He would, Jan. He did. Where is he?"

"Asleep."

"Which room?"

"All the way at the back, behind the kitchen."

Max lowered the gun and said, "All right. Take off."

Albrecht swallowed hard. "Why don't I stay? I can help you."

"I don't want help."

"You want to kill him?"

"Get out of here, Jan. Now."

"All right. Let me get my shoes."

"The hell with your shoes. It's not cold out."

"Please don't hurt him," Albrecht said. "He's so small."

So small.

Small like a nine-year-old boy. Small like Irene. Shorter even. His hair had looked almost black the day before when it was wet, but now, asleep in his bed, it was brown and curly.

Max looked around the small room. Billy's white robe hung on a hook screwed into the closet door. On another hook hung a brown-and-white newsboy's cap. He stood at the side of the single bed and pressed the muzzle of the Cobra against Billy's forehead and cocked the hammer. The sound of the rotating chamber woke the little man and he sat up, eyes wild. Max pushed his head back down with the gun.

"Ask me," he said.

Billy licked his lips. "Ask you what?"

"Ask me what I'm doing here."

"Okay," Billy said. "What are you—"

Max drew the gun back and drove his left fist into Billy's face. Billy's head snapped back as blood spurted out of his broken nose. "Ask me again," Max said.

Billy was gasping and swallowing like a landed fish. "I don't—"

Max grabbed his hair and put the gun back against Billy's head. "I said, ask me."

"I'm choking!"

"Are you going to ask me?"

"Yes!" he gulped, blood dribbling over his lips and down his chin. "Please. Tell me why you're here."

"For Irene," Max said. "I'm here for her."

"Irene who?"

Max ground the gun barrel harder against the bony fore-head. "Don't you dare say that," he whispered. "Don't you fucking dare deny her fucking name."

Billy looked down at his sheets. "The girl across the street?"

"I know this isn't where you killed her. But it's where you first saw her. Isn't it?"

"Me? No."

"You saying you never saw her? You lie to me, you twisted shit, I'll kill you."

"Don't I have a right to a phone call?"

A small body wedged under a crawl space. An autopsy report that ran to two pages. Broken milk teeth.

"You have the right to get shot in your lying mouth. Now tell me what happened, Billy. You saw her out there on the street?"

Billy's eyes tried to focus on Max but kept coming back to

the gun. "Okay, sure. I saw her. We were neighbors for three weeks."

"You go for a walk with her?"

"Never!"

"Someone saw you, Billy. Saw you walking with her in your brown-and-white cap. You know where?"

"It wasn't me!"

"You're lying again. Like you lied about Eddie Whelan. Spun us a bullshit story about him hanging around to take the heat off yourself. You know he's dead, don't you?"

"Whelan?"

"We went to bring him in and he tried to dump his needle and his junk and a nervous cop thought he was pulling a gun and put two rounds into him. Know what it sounded like?"

"No," Billy said.

Max put his gun against Billy's pillow, inches from his ear, and fired.

"Jesus!" Billy cried. He tried to get up but Max put his hand on his chest and kept him where he was. Feathers flew up in the air then settled back on the bed and floor.

"She saw you on Rachel," Max said, "walking with Irene, heading east past Saint-Christophe. You know what's there, don't you?"

"What?"

"On the north side of Rachel, between Mentana and Boyer. Number 961."

"961 Rachel?" Billy said softly. "The Midgets Palace?"

"Say it again."

"The Midgets Palace."

"You offered to take her there, didn't you?"

"No."

"What kid wouldn't want to go? All that tiny furniture.

Everything cut down to size. What did you say yesterday? They can see how the little-halves live?"

"I didn't take her there!"

"I'm going to show your lying face to this witness," Max said, "and she's going to say, *Yes, sergeant, that's him, that's the one who walked with her in the checkered cap.* And I am going to take you into the basement of headquarters—no, into a dark laneway—and beat you to death the way you beat her. I'm going to break every bone and crack every tooth in your head. Slowly, Billy."

"You can't."

"I'm six feet tall and almost two hundred pounds. Tell me again that I can't."

"But the law—"

"You think anyone will care about the law once they find out about you and Irene? They all loved that girl, Billy. The whole city has been following the story, searching for her, praying we'd find her alive. Your only hope is to tell me what happened and do it fast, before I get the urge to pull this trigger again. But not into the pillow. Into your knees. Or maybe that big shlong of yours. Isn't it big, Billy? You told me yesterday, it's bigger than other guys."

"I was joking."

"Only women don't go for you. Just streetwalkers, that's what you said. That's why you hate them all."

"I don't hate anyone."

"You wouldn't have to pay Irene, would you? You could take her for free."

Billy didn't answer.

"I bet she thought you were cute," Max said. "A grown man her size? I bet she thought you were harmless. But you're not, are you?"

Nothing.

"I said, you're not harmless, are you?" Max leaned in so close that his words left bits of spittle on the man's cheeks.

"No," Billy whispered.

"You're strong. Strong as hell for a little guy. You can lift your own weight over your head. I've seen it. You picked up that wrestler, what's his name—Tiny Roe?—you picked him up like nothing and spun him around and threw him right out of the ring. Didn't you?"

"Yes."

"So a girl like Irene, you could have done anything you wanted."

"But I didn't want to."

"Maybe not at first. You were nice to her at first, weren't you?"

"Yes."

Hear that? He said yes, the little bastard.

"A pretty little girl like that. I saw her picture in her house. I saw how pretty she was. I bet she smelled good. Did she smell good, Billy? Did she?"

"I guess."

I've got you now, you lying piece of shit.

"You *guess*? You'd only know if you got real close. How close did you get? This close?" Max put his mouth against Billy's bloody nose and bared his teeth, breathed out as if trying to fog a mirror.

"Please," Billy said.

"Please what?"

"Let me up. Let me out of this bed."

"Why? Am I too close?"

"Yes."

"Were you this close to Irene?"

"I have to piss."

"Tell me first how close you were, then I'll let you up."

"I need to piss."

"Piss in your bed, it doesn't matter. You're never going to sleep in it again. You're going to be dead or in jail by lunchtime."

"Okay. If I tell you what happened, you gotta understand . . ."

"Understand what?"

"I just wanted . . ."

"What! Spit it out, Billy."

"It's like you said! After I moved in here, I saw her from the window sometimes. Saw her on the street. Once or twice I said hello to her and she said hello back. That's all, nothing to it. But you could tell she was sweet. Some of the other kids made fun of me, but not her. And I guess she was curious about me. The other day . . ."

"The day she went missing?"

"Yeah. That day. She was walking home and I was walking home and we got to talking and she asked me—straight out, not mean—why I was the size I was. So we talked about it. I told her what it was like to be small and she asked me about the Midgets Palace. Got that? She asked me. She'd walked past there on her way to the park and she was curious about it, I didn't offer to take her there or anywhere else."

"But she asked and you said yes."

"I had nothing else to do. No fights lined up, no social life to attend to. Jan just sits and reads most of the time. I'm going fucking nuts here. So we're walking and she asks if everything is the right size for me where I live. I say no, everything at Jan's is normal size. And she takes my hand and says she's sorry. Okay? She takes my hand. This is important because I've never gone after kids, ever. Never even thought about sex with them, I swear. But there we are, walking together, holding hands, and for the first time in my life, I feel—Christ, I don't know what I felt. But I wasn't with a prostie. She wasn't looking at me like a freak. It was like having a girlfriend. For once in my life, I was walking down the street with a normal girl."

"A girl your size."

"That's right. A girl my size. So maybe I started to feel something I shouldn't have. We stopped at Mentana, waiting to cross, and suddenly I wanted to kiss her. Just kiss her and hold her. I didn't even want to fuck her, I don't think. I mean, I had a hard-on, but I don't think I would have done it to her. I just wanted to stand against her and hold her tight. Maybe just cum in my pants."

Max felt his hand tighten around the grip of his .38.

"I told her we should go down the laneway for a minute. Told her there was a guy who kept rabbits in a hutch in his yard. Told her maybe the guy would let her take one home. And she got this beautiful look on her face, this big smile. Because what kid doesn't love rabbits?"

Later that day, Max sat in the office of his commander, his hands trembling in his lap. He told Bellechasse everything that Billy had told him: how he had walked Irene down the lane and into a shed whose door was unlocked; how he had tried to kiss her and how she had pushed him away and spit on the ground; how he had hit her and kept hitting her long after her body had slumped to the concrete floor, pounding her with his powerful fists and kicking her until his volcanic rage had subsided.

When he was done, Max took a cigarette from a pack on Bellechasse's desk. The commander slid a lighter across the surface. Max needed both hands to work it.

"The pathologist thinks she was probably unconscious after the first blow. I doubt she felt much pain," Bellechasse said.

Max thought of Irene walking down the lane to find a rabbit to take home. "Tell me another one."

OTHER PEOPLE'S SECRETS

BY TESS FRAGOULIS

Sherbrooke Street

A s Catalina Thwaite stood before the black wooden
doors of the stately town house on Sherbrooke Street,
she decided her past and future would never meet.
She pressed the button on the brass doorbell and ran her finger over Dr. Schmidt's nameplate, wiping the print she'd left
with the sleeve of her jacket. Her name would replace it soon
enough. The stone lion's head looming above the doorway
seemed indifferent to such vicissitudes; it stared at its coun-
terpart across the street—a frowning satyr with curled horns
and a face sooted by the elements. The satyr was much more
fearsome and discouraging than the empty-eyed lion. *Just as
well*, thought Catalina. People seeking therapy had enough
anxieties and neuroses without the added pressure of the
devil snarling at them at the gate.

She rang the bell a second time, irritated that her lawyer's
office had yet to forward her a set of keys. She took a mental
note of the first offense committed by Dr. Schmidt's secretary,
Mrs. Dubois, who had been given some time off after her employer's sudden exit. During this time, Catalina had sorted
out the paperwork and prepared for the transition into his
practice. She'd left a message on Friday, asking Mrs. Dubois to
come in on Monday morning at 9 a.m. sharp to begin sorting
and reviving the temporarily dormant files. The old secretary
was either late for their meeting—an intolerable quality to

Catalina, who was pathologically punctual—or had not shown up at all, perhaps unable to digest the fact that the man she had assisted for thirty years was dead. This would surely have given the secretary intimations of her own mortality, or at least of the unlikelihood of her continued employment. Catalina considered dismissing Mrs. Dubois right away, but she had enough to do in the next few weeks without worrying about hiring a new secretary. No, it was better to keep the old dog around until things were settled and she was no longer of use. Then she could be put gently out of her misery.

As Catalina searched for her cell phone in her red leather briefcase—purchased the day before at Holt's for too much money—Mrs. Dubois's woeful voice crackled through the intercom.

"*Dr. Schmidt's office,*" she said, then cleared her throat and tried again, her words wet, unsure: "*I mean doctor's office. I'm sorry. May I help you?*"

Catalina rolled her eyes at the apathetic lion but swallowed her annoyance and assumed a professional if slightly imperious tone: "It's Dr. Thwaite. Can you let me in, please?" she said, her *t*'s sharp as stickpins. She gripped the brass handle, and after a moment of silence, a long, deep buzz unlocked the door.

The first thing Catalina encountered in the sun-drenched entry hall was a Venetian mirror that framed her reflection with an orgy of gilded cherubs and rosettes. She smiled and smoothed away a strand of her otherwise meticulously styled hair. She had seen a hairdresser that morning for a cut and color, even though he had balked at the seven a.m. request. Catalina was not fond of the word *no*, and she knew that, for enough money, the hairdresser would have come to her room at the Ritz-Carlton at four a.m. if she'd so desired. She'd been up, after all, planning every detail of the day ahead. The deep chestnut shade suited her better than the various blonds and reds she'd favored for so many years, and along with the classic Vidal Sassoon inverted bob, she looked dignified and slightly untouchable. She cut quite the figure in her black-and-white houndstooth suit—both the trousers and jacket made for her by a London tailor the week before—and the aquamarine silk scarf tied loosely around her neck. The four-inch undulating heels of her Louboutins made her nearly six-three.

"Worth every penny," she said to her reflection, pulling her shoulders back and jutting her chin forward with the air of someone mildly offended. Catalina knew that three-quarters of success depended on looking the part, on making an impression that inspired confidence and a bit of fear. But Mrs. Dubois was already afraid.

As her aquamarine heels clicked against the red marble tiles, adrenaline surged though her body. It was similar to what she felt when she ran along the trails of Mount Royal, pretending she was being hunted before turning into the hunter. Now she stopped herself from running up the staircase to the second floor, not wanting to spoil the moment she'd so thoroughly rehearsed in her imagination. She ascended slowly, solemnly, holding onto the polished wooden banister, primed for her grand entrance into the new and enviable life which had begun when Dr. Schmidt's ended.

As Catalina walked into the office, Mrs. Dubois was slouched at her small desk, staring at her computer screen, which was playing an electronic-greeting-card version of Bach's "Chorale." It was the background music for the online condolence book of Paperman's, the funeral home that had taken care of Dr. Schmidt's remains. Mrs. Dubois was so absorbed in scrolling through the entries left by grieving friends and clients that she did not notice her new employer's arrival, even though she'd just buzzed her in. The guest book was likely the reason it had taken so long. Catalina had consulted the wretched site several times in preparation for meeting Dr. Schmidt's clients—the ones who had not already moved on to a new therapist, and the ones who would be encouraged to do so. She had not gone to the funeral, nor had she left a comment. Perhaps that was what Mrs. Dubois was looking for.

Catalina grimaced inwardly as she studied the woman in her brown loafers and matching slacks, topped with a pale-blue sweater set that Mrs. Dubois had either bought in a thrift shop or saved from her youth—she wasn't sure which was worse. Her blond hair had the brassy and dried-out quality of box dye, and was teased into a rounded helmet and sprayed into place. She wore glasses too large for her face, with rectangular gold frames and thick lenses divided by the horizontal line of bifocals. A small gold crucifix hung around her neck and was her only piece of jewelry other than a wristwatch and plain wedding band. Catalina knew Mrs. Dubois had been widowed several years before, and imagined that coming to work and keeping the also-widowed Dr. Schmidt and his clients' lives in order had become the woman's raison d'être. Perhaps Mrs. Dubois had hoped that becoming indispensible in the office would get her promoted to something more meaningful than secretary. But despite being only a few years younger than Dr. Schmidt, she was not young enough to satisfy his tastes, neither while Mrs. Schmidt was alive nor after she had died. Mrs. Dubois's sartorial choices had obviously not helped her case.

The waiting room was a decent size, with its twelve-foot ceilings and bay windows common to the older town houses in the neighborhod. But unlike the hallway with its art deco sconces, mermaid chandelier, and parquet de Versailles floor smelling faintly of lemon polish, it had a musty odor and was as drab as Mrs. Dubois. The walls were yellowed and grayed with age, stained by cigarette smoke from the years the vile habit was still permitted indoors. Neurotics and schizophrenics surely filled the now absent ashtray on the coffee table with du Mauriers smoked down to the filter; the burns in its wood veneer betrayed its former location. In its place was a metal bowl filled with wrapped candies that looked shriveled and unappealing. An assortment of outdated magazines littered the rest of the table's surface: *Paris Match*, *Chatelaine*, and a tattered issue of *Police Extra* with a picture of a smug cop on the cover, the headline blaring, "Payé par les Hells!" Catalina thought she could smell stale smoke trapped in the brown fabric of the couch, though perhaps it was carried in Mrs. Dubois's bouffant.

When the door clicked shut, the old woman finally looked up, her eyes glazed as a sleepwalker's. She gave Catalina a wan smile, then burst into tears. "I'm so sorry," she blubbered, and hunched over to dig through her brown bag for a tissue, though there was a box for clients sitting at the front edge of her desk. "I know it's been a week, but until you walked in . . ."

Catalina moved toward the crying woman, towering over her as she laid her briefcase on the desk. With her fingernails, she extracted a tissue from the box and handed it to Mrs. Dubois, who dabbed at the dribbles of mascara that were pooling in her wrinkles. "There, there," she whispered, hoping her voice conveyed sympathy. She stopped short of patting the woman's hand, which looked greasy and was mottled with brown spots. "It must be very hard to move from denial to acceptance so quickly. You've skipped a few very important steps." Mrs. Dubois tried to smile, though she was still leaking blackened tears. "Thank you for coming in on such short notice, Joan." She bent over the secretary's desk and gazed at her so intensely that Mrs. Dubois was compelled to lean back in her chair. "Dr. Schmidt said you were as dependable as an atomic clock."

Mrs. Dubois winced when she heard his name, though Catalina pretended not to notice. She was not the woman's therapist, after all, and was eager to avoid the questions that were swimming behind the woman's watery eyes: Why did Dr. Schmidt do it when his prostrate treatments were going so well? How could she, who saw him daily—more than anyone else—not have noticed his depression? And how did Catalina, who she had never heard of until after his death, come to be named a curator in his professional will? Dr. Weintraub was listed as his first choice, but he had retired to the Cayman Islands years ago and was unlikely to come back to Montreal to settle his old friend's affairs. Catalina knew this because Forrest had mentioned that he hoped to follow Dr. Weintraub's example, though he preferred Bermuda, which he visited every other year during Christmas break.

Catalina's answers were prepared, of course. Yes, Bermuda would have been a more fitting and gentler denouement to his long career, but neither lifespan nor will to live came with a guaranteed end date—something, perhaps, for Mrs. Dubois to mull over as well? And men manifested depression in different ways than women: irritability, violence, impulsivity. These were things she might not have readily noticed in the sterile environment of the office, no matter how well she thought she knew him. Not to mention there was an increased incidence, statistically speaking, of suicidal ideation among psychotherapists. But since Mrs. Dubois wouldn't be around long enough for this first encounter to matter, Catalina didn't bother comforting her with facts or philosophical musings, nor did she explain how she had come to fill Dr. Schmidt's orthopedic shoes, which as she recalled were not that big. For the moment, she would just empathize and validate the woman's feelings—it was what all the literature recommended.

"I can see how hard this has been on you, Joan," Catalina said in her most compassionate tone. She handed the woman another tissue, and Mrs. Dubois wiped her tears, smudging mascara into her crow's feet, then blowing her nose like a rusty trumpet.

"I'm so sorry," the woman replied, trying to smile. "I didn't expect to have such a reaction. I didn't even cry at the memorial service. I guess there was no time to process it—he was at work one day and buried the next." She waved her frail hands in a gesture of helplessness, then lifted her handbag onto her lap and retrieved a dented compact. "Look at me, I'm such a mess." She worked haphazardly on the smudges around her eyes with the soggy tissue. "It's a good thing that no clients are coming in today. There are dozens of messages and just as many referrals that were made before he . . . left us." Her face began to collapse again; she managed to catch it, but not the quaver in her voice. From a drawer she retrieved two folders, which she handed to Catalina: the first was full of little pink callback slips, the second contained almost a dozen intake sheets, which provided basic information about each potential client—name, age, address, as well as a few lines summarizing the reason for the referral. Catalina placed the folder with the pink slips back onto the desk and slipped the second folder into her briefcase. Mrs. Dubois gave her a puzzled look.

"It will be at least a few more weeks before I can return any of these calls," she explained, trying to sound matter-of-fact. "I'd like to spruce up the waiting room, give it a fresh start, and probably the rest of the office too."

A mild panic flitted across the secretary's face as she glanced at the sagging furniture and the fading posters hung with no apparent design on the walls. They illustrated Freud's defense mechanisms—projection, sublimation, denial, reaction formation—with large-headed and frightened-looking characters who were sure to make clients uneasy.

"Feel free to take anything that holds sentimental value for you. I'm sure Dr. Schmidt would have wanted it that way." This statement seemed to placate the secretary, as her only response was a quiet, "Thank you."

"Now, if it's not too much trouble, can you make a list of all the clients with active files? I'd like you to note who should be contacted by phone as well as who should receive the lawyer's letter explaining what has occurred and what will happen next." It was protocol to reach out to each client individually, and Catalina believed that you could get away with almost anything if you kept on top of the smaller tasks. From her briefcase she extracted a flash drive containing the lawyer's letter and placed it before Mrs. Dubois. "Make sure everyone on the list gets a copy of the file labeled, *Schmidt-death-notice.*"

Mrs. Dubois plugged the flash drive into her computer and pulled up the document, which bore the letterhead of Dr. Schmidt's attorney, Anthony Curtiss, and was signed by him as well, though Catalina had composed the message herself for expediency. The secretary pushed her glasses onto the bridge of her nose and silently read the letter.

Dear———,

It is with deep regret that I write to inform you of Dr. Forrest Schmidt's passing. Many of you have known him and counted upon his support for years, and no doubt this news comes as a shock. It is understandable if you have questions about his death, but Dr. Schmidt's primary concern in his professional relationship with you was to keep the focus on your needs and emotions. Although he did not have the time to generate personal referrals for each of you, rest assured that in the coming weeks you will be contacted by his curator, Dr. Catalina Thwaite, who will also be assuming much of his practice. She will confirm any referrals, as well as inform you when appointments will resume at the Sherbrooke Street location. In the interim, should you experience overwhelming distress as a result of Dr. Schmidt's passing and the concomitant halt of your therapy, please do not hesitate to present yourself at the nearest emergency room or call one of the help lines provided with this letter. In closing, I would like to express my deepest condolences for your loss.

Oddly, the letter perked Mrs. Dubois up a bit, though it might have been the prospect of filling the role of next-of-kin by informing the clients of the doctor's passing. The office's voice mail had announced that all sessions were cancelled until further notice, and a statement of Dr. Schmidt's death had appeared in the *Gazette* and *Le Devoir*. There had been no reference to the cause of death, which was certain to be the first question everyone would ask, had Mrs. Dubois not already spilled the beans when she called to cancel their appointments.

"Would you like me to phone them since I already know them all?"

"No," Catalina said firmly, "it would be better if they heard it from someone—" she paused as if to select her words, "—less involved."

Mrs. Dubois looked somewhat sheepish as she nodded,

but she picked up a pen and legal pad, eager to prove she was something more than a quivering sack of grief. "And by what criteria would you like me to select who gets called, Dr. Thwaite?"

"By who is most likely to become hysterical, naturally."

Catalina did not indicate which clients would receive the phone call in addition to the letter. She had yet to decide what would be most interesting.

It took Mrs. Dubois all morning to compile the patient list and personalize and print the letters. Meanwhile, Catalina sequestered herself behind the dark wooden door that led to both Dr. Schmidt's consultation room and study. Like the waiting area, the rooms were spacious, with large windows looking onto the street. The consultation room had the dark wainscoting of what was once a dining room or parlor before the town house had been cut up into office space—two other doctors had offices on the second floor. There was also a fireplace that no longer functioned; a fake log in need of dusting sat on its grate. The mantelpiece was made of the same dark walnut as the doors of the waiting room and study. A porcelain Ming reproduction vase holding dried flowers sat before a wood-framed mirror, and a green corduroy sofa was pushed up against the wall by the windows. This kept the distractions of the outside world away from clients, but afforded them to Dr. Schmidt. Catalina had to admit this was good planning—it went without saying that most of his long-term patients were going to be unbearably dull. (The hysterics would be called, she all at once decided.) A matching armchair sat facing the sofa with an end table next to it, an obvious cousin to the coffee table in the waiting room. A few files still lay upon it instead of being locked away in a file cabinet as professional standards and bylaws required. She wasn't sure who was at fault for the lapse: Dr. Schmidt or Mrs. Dubois. She chose to condemn them both. She sat on neither the sofa nor chair; both looked lumpy and likely to shed a powder of grass-stain green on her lovely new suit. With amused contempt, she imagined the sofa being carried out with Mrs. Dubois stretched across it, complaining to the ghost of Dr. Schmidt about his successor.

Catalina picked up the wayward files and carried them into the adjoining study, tossing them onto Dr. Schmidt's gray metal desk. She would instruct Mrs. Dubois to file them in the matching metal cabinet tucked away in a closet that also contained one of the doctor's old hats and trench coats. All of his belongings looked utilitarian and tired. Perhaps they had all been new once, but their time had clearly passed. More likely they were hand-me-downs, just like the furniture in his apartment on Wood Avenue, which had been left untouched after his mother's death—a dusty shrine of 1940s chinoiserie. Catalina had no such sympathies. The metal desk, the lugubrious sofa, and the faded brown rug would be thrown out immediately; she wouldn't even bother donating them to charity. This would be her favor to whatever down-on-their-luck family might acquire them, giving them a chance to wait for something better to come along, something free of the accumulated dander and burdens of others.

She hesitated at the bathroom door, sniffing the air like a disdainful cat, but was pleasantly surprised to see a spotless claw-foot tub resting on a black-and-white tile floor, as well as a large pedestal sink with a shiny chrome faucet, and a modern toilet paired with a bidet. The bathroom was the only room that looked like it belonged to the town house, probably because someone other than Dr. Schmidt had chosen its fixtures. It smelled of flowery ammonia, evidence of a recent visit by the cleaning staff, who obviously took pride in buffing and polishing the one room in the office that showed the fruits of their labor. A striped bathrobe drooped on a hook behind the door, and the medicine cabinet contained Dr. Schmidt's old razor, shaving brush, and an open canister of shaving soap that had specks of stubble trapped in its melted waves. There were also a few pill bottles: painkillers and vitamins, immunotherapy drugs for his cancer, along with a full bottle of the same sedatives that had dispatched him, which she slipped into her pocket. She would ask the cleaning staff to dispose of his remaining personal effects during their next rounds. From her inner pocket she extracted a yellow cotton handkerchief bearing the initials *FS* and, out of habit, wiped her fingerprints from the medicine cabinet.

While she was removing the traces of her inspection, she heard Mrs. Dubois's feeble voice: "Hello? Sorry to disturb."

The constant apologizing was starting to get on Catalina's nerves—had she been truly sorry, she would not have come into the study without an invitation. No doubt the secretary's territoriality, along with her grief and routine, meant she would be crossing boundaries all the time, which would not do. New locks would be the first order of business, this afternoon if possible: one for the main entrance, another for the door between the consultation room and the waiting room, and one for her study. This would not only prevent Mrs. Dubois and whoever replaced her from barging in, it would keep the crazies contained.

"Not a problem," Catalina called out, stuffing the handkerchief into her pocket as she stepped out of the bathroom. The secretary was looking through the files on the desk, where Catalina's briefcase lay perilously open.

"I'll put these away for you." Mrs. Dubois located the key

to the file cabinet on her key ring, but didn't apologize for leaving the files laying about. Catalina saved her reproach for a more profitable moment. "These are the clients he would have met with . . ." The woman sniffled and hugged the files to her bosom like a picture of a loved one, then quickly turned toward the closet to hide her latest wave of tears. She jiggled the lock on the file cabinet until it opened.

"I've yet to receive a set of keys from the lawyer's office, Joan. Do you think you might leave me yours?"

Mrs. Dubois stopped what she was doing and gave Catalina a begrudging look.

"They'll likely arrive sometime this afternoon, but I can't be asked to wait around for them after you've gone for the day." None of this was true. She'd arranged for the keys to be couriered to the hotel, and they were probably already waiting for her there, but this would take care of the invading secretary and free up her afternoon for something more pleasant than waiting for a locksmith. After tardiness, waiting was a close second on her list of dislikes, and when they coalesced, she could not be held responsible for her actions.

"Oh, that won't be necessary. I have an extra set in my desk." Mrs. Dubois scurried out of the study to get them, and Catalina picked up her briefcase and followed, closing the door behind her.

As Mrs. Dubois rifled through her desk, Catalina looked out the bay windows at the street below. The few people coming and going were well dressed, though not fashionable, and generally older. Women in skirt suits and designer dowager dresses were walking small, fluffy dogs or carrying large colorful bags with the names and emblems of stores frequented by the privileged class. A town car idled before a silver-haired man in a deep-blue suit—it would deliver him to his office or more likely to his mistress's apartment, Catalina imagined. The man checked his cell phone several times, then handed the uniformed driver a small jewelry bag from Birks, which he placed on the front seat. No one seemed to be in any kind of hurry, which was unusual for Montreal. Catalina supposed men like him had enough money to hire others to hurry for them. Mrs. Dubois, on the other hand, was starting to seem frantic as she pulled out file folders, notebooks, and crumpled plastic bags from her desk drawers, desperate to find her extra set of keys so she would not have to hand over her own.

Then, as if finding a lost lottery ticket with the winning number, Mrs. Dubois held up the keys in triumph and gave a little cheer. "Here they are!" She jangled them in the air and huffed a sigh of relief.

"Brilliant," Catalina said, taking them from the secretary and dropping them into her briefcase. "And the list?"

Mrs. Dubois handed over a few sheets of paper with names and phone numbers typed in columns, and the letter *P* handwritten next to the clients who would have to be called. As Catalina flipped through the list, mentally counting how many phone calls she'd have to make, she remembered a joke that she'd heard at a conference: *How many hysterics does it take to screw in a lightbulb? None, because they're all afraid of the dark.* She couldn't recall who had told it, but she refrained from sharing it with Mrs. Dubois.

"I've also printed out copies of the letter and addressed the envelopes," the woman said brightly. "Our regular courier is on his way—I could wait for him if you'd like to go for lunch."

"That won't be necessary." From her briefcase, Catalina extracted a red leather card wallet and handed one of her newly minted business cards to the secretary. *Dr. Catalina*

Thwaite was printed in raised, elegant black longhand on a thick and crisp white bond. The phone number beneath it belonged to an answering service she'd hired to create a barrier between herself and her clients. She knew that other therapists provided their clients with their cell phone numbers, or—God forbid—their home numbers. But Catalina had no interest in granting such unfettered access to anyone.

"Why don't you take the rest of the day off and do something nice for yourself, Joan? And if you don't hear from me in the next few days, give me a ring and I'll tell you how I'm faring here. We can then discuss setting up some appointments— first with the referrals, then with the transfers who have not yet jumped ship." *Or off a building or bridge,* she thought, but kept to herself, since she was sure the old woman wouldn't find it funny. She would laugh about it after Mrs. Dubois left.

The secretary's brow lifted, her eyes narrowed, and Catalina could tell she was displeased but knew enough to keep her tone neutral, her words measured. "Might it be a better idea to resume with old clients first? They have so much to process—losing Dr. Schmidt under such tragic circumstances, having their therapy cut off so abruptly." This time her voice didn't crack. She had been handling Dr. Schmidt's clients for a long time, and in this she felt confident, perhaps even superior, in her judgment. She wore a self-possessed, almost smug expression as she awaited a reply.

"No," Catalina said with no further explanation, and watched the old woman's confidence slowly deflate. After a moment, Mrs. Dubois began to sweep the papers and other detritus on her desk back into the drawers with no thought of order. *Slovenly,* thought Catalina, though her face showed no distaste. Mrs. Dubois would soon cease to offend her senses altogether.

"If you're sure there's nothing else I can do . . ." She picked up her brown handbag and threw her keys in it.

"Nothing, nothing at all," Catalina replied pleasantly, and escorted her to the door.

Through the bay windows she watched the old secretary shuffle up the street. Every few steps she looked over her shoulder, as if desperate for a last glimpse at her world before it disappeared.

"*And to die is different from what anyone supposed, and luckier,*" Catalina recited in the empty office, grinning. Her favorite line from Whitman never failed to infuse her with equanimity and resolve. Death had always been lucky for her. She was not certain Dr. Schmidt felt the same when his time came, though Mrs. Dubois might feel fortunate to finally join him. She looked through the secretary's desk, searching for an address. Tomorrow or the next day she would drop by her flat to settle the matter of her future at the practice once and for all, the bottle of Dr. Schmidt's sedatives resting in her pocket like a love potion, like a sleeping snake.

SUITCASE MAN
BY MARTIN MICHAUD
Notre-Dame-des-Neiges Cemetery

Translated from French by Katie Shireen Assef

Montreal, January 1993

An old man bows against the wind, making his way among the frozen headstones of the Notre-Dame-des-Neiges Cemetery. A heavy suitcase dangles from his fist, leaves a trail of blood on the snow. The man's eyebrows are white with frost, and his eyes shine with the conviction that drives those who have made grave decisions, carried out irreversible acts. When he finally reaches Florence's headstone, he knows he's come to the end of his journey, and he's determined to watch his life leave him like a dark ship disappearing into the horizon.

Under the weight of his years, but especially his suffering, the old man's knees buckle and cease to carry him. When he staggers and slumps forward, arms open, he looks as if he's trying to grab ahold of the clouds rolling across the sky.

Then his body collapses, shooting crystalline snowflakes up into the air. The old man is named Arthur Zourek, but it's been years since anyone has heard his name.

The smell of fast food filled the front seat of the patrol car, its windows frosted over. One of the policemen, whose name tag read *Robitaille*, shoved a handful of fries into his mouth and, chewing, said, "It's terrible. You'd think my daughter walks around the house in lead boots! She had an exam at the university this morning. When I got up in the middle of the night to take a piss, she was still studying. Can you believe it? Every damn light in the apartment was on. Just like her mother. I spend my whole life turning off those friggin' lights!"

Robitaille burst out laughing, shaking his head while his fingers closed down on his dripping hamburger. With his mouth full, he continued: "Me and Michèle, we haven't fucked for weeks. The kids' rooms are practically on top of ours. I think we'll have to move. Now that Justine and her brother are older, we've got zero privacy. We need some more space or we're gonna go crazy . . ." His greasy fingers stroked the ends of his graying mustache. "How 'bout your son? How old is he now, your little guy?"

The man who'd been absently listening to Robitaille's grievances raised his head, worked his jaw for a moment, and fixed his green eyes on his partner. "Martin? Six months."

Robitaille slurped up the last of his Coca-Cola through a straw. "And? How's it going?"

"He's so little, so fragile—it's a miracle, life." The young policeman looked out the window into the deserted Saint Joseph's Oratory parking lot. The patrol car was parked in front of the lot, on Chemin Queen Mary. "You don't want anything to happen to them. You want to protect them from anything that could harm them. From . . ." The cop's eyes gleamed as he choked back tears.

Robitaille, who'd seen a thing or two in his day, suspected his partner was a tormented man, that an immense rift had torn through his childhood like a long and painful scar burned into flesh.

"You want to protect them from others. And from yourself."

Robitaille noticed the rectangular plastic box his colleague held on his knees, containing a sandwich, carrots and celery sticks, a piece of cheese. He ate slowly, chewing each bite carefully as if he were savoring every flavor.

"Your wife packs your lunches, eh?" said Robitaille. "Enjoy it, son. It won't last. Pretty soon she'll start nagging you for not talking enough about your emotions, if she hasn't already."

The young policeman lowered his head, embarrassed at suddenly being the center of attention. Robitaille crumpled up the wax paper that had covered his hamburger, chewing the last bite. "Besides, it's not as if you were much of a chatterbox to begin with."

On the radio, they listened to a hockey match between the Canadiens and the Bruins. When the sportscaster announced a Boston goal, Robitaille banged his fist on the dashboard. "Goddamnit, Roy! Another fast one! Better trade him while he's still worth something. We'll never win the Cup with that moron in the net." He turned the heat up all the way and sighed. "Thirty-three below. Shit, it's freezing—"

He was interrupted by a crackling noise as the dispatcher's voice came over the patrol radio: "Calling all units: Code 063 at 4565 Côte-des-Neiges."

Robitaille turned to his partner. They were only a few blocks away. Without a moment's hesitation, the green-eyed policeman grabbed the transmitter.

"Eleven three. We're on our way."

Robitaille started the engine and shot off at full speed, making the tires spin out on the ice. His partner turned on the siren and revolving lights. The two were silent as the patrol car hurtled through the night. Then Robitaille winced and said between his teeth, "An abused kid. Jesus. We've got a fucking shitty job, son."

Victor Lessard said nothing, but his jaw tightened and his gaze hardened. Sinister phantoms danced before him.

The woman who'd made the call to 911—a gray-haired, wrinkled twig wearing a floral dress—waited for the officers on her apartment's second-floor landing.

Since Robitaille was breathless from climbing the stairs, it was Victor who asked, "What's happened, madame?"

"I heard screams coming from the apartment upstairs," she responded. "A child's screams. I went out into the hallway, and that's where I saw him. The upstairs neighbor, I mean. Coming down the stairs with his big suitcase, the one he's always dragging around with him."

"He lives alone?"

She nodded her small white head. "I've lived here fifteen years. He was here when I moved in. I've never seen anyone else go up those stairs. Except once." Her wrinkled mouth puckered in a sneer of disgust. "A *whore* . . ."

Without reacting to her remark, Victor asked, "Do you know his name?"

She shook her head no. "But everyone on the block calls him Suitcase Man. He's a scary one, that's for sure."

Robitaille, who had finally caught his breath, cut in: "And what exactly is the problem, madame?"

"Besides the screaming?" She fixed her owl's eyes on the cop. "There was blood dripping from his suitcase."

Victor walked up to the staircase, crouched in front of the first few steps, and brushed them with his fingertips. He stood, his index finger covered with blood, and followed the trail of drops up the stairs.

Breathless, his chest heaving, Arthur Zourek sits down in the snow and leans against Florence's headstone. Reaching out his arm, he grabs the handle of his suitcase and pulls it to his chest, cradling it gently as the wind blows and blood spreads dark over the snow.

A melancholy smile crosses the old man's face.

"My little princess suffered too much, Flo. I had to take her with me, I had no choice. You see, Flo—*together for eternity*. I'm coming to join you."

He digs in the pocket of his jacket and takes out a half-empty bottle of pills. Twisting the top off, he brings it to his lips and swallows the remaining tablets. Then he hears shuffling behind him. He raises his eyes and makes out the silhouette of a young man leaning over him. Behind him, gnarled branches blown by the wind seem to reach out to grab him.

"*Bonjour,* Arthur. How are you today?"

The old man nods in greeting to the visitor, a man of around thirty, whose long black hair is flecked with snowflakes and blowing in the wind. "*Salut,* Jérôme. You should put on some clothes, you'll catch a cold."

The young man pulls the lapels of his jean jacket closed, a contemptuous smile curving his lips. "Perhaps you have a coat for me in there?"

Arthur Zourek hugs his suitcase even more tightly. "There's nothing of interest to you in here," he says in a sharp voice. "Nothing, you hear?"

Jérôme shrugs his shoulders and pulls a flask from his jacket pocket. He throws his head back and takes a long swig. "I have what I need to keep warm. You want some?"

Zourek shoots a disdainful look at the flask. "No. I don't drink alcohol."

* * *

The half-open door squeaked loudly as Robitaille gave it a push. The two policemen cautiously entered the Suitcase Man's dark apartment.

"Police!" Victor called out.

Flashlights in one hand, pistols in the other, the men moved silently, each covering the other. Robitaille buried his nose in his forearm. A fetid odor of decaying matter and cat urine filled the room. "Oh god, it reeks in here."

He turned on the living room light, and a mountain of random filth appeared: a soiled mattress, a lamp with a ratty shade, a cooler, a TV in a solid wood case, a teddy bear's head on a stand, suitcases, dirty clothes, a turntable, records, an overturned sofa, dusty picture frames, and many stacks of newspapers.

Victor headed for the kitchen, where a pan of dried spaghetti sauce congealed on the stove. On the counter, fruit flies swarmed around rotten fruit and cartons of Chinese food. Garbage bags full of empty cans were piled in a corner, and bundles of old lottery tickets lay on the table.

A corkboard was fixed to the door of the pantry. Amid a jumble of papers, a few black-and-white photographs stood out. Victor examined them for a moment. In one of them, a little girl of six or seven wore a polka-dotted dress. Barefoot in the grass, she smiled timidly at the camera. In another, which looked to be from the same period, a man of around thirty stood with a young blond woman. An uneasy feeling came over Victor. The couple wore a look that was almost frightening.

Leaving the pantry to take a look around, Victor made his way down the hallway. Suddenly he recoiled, his heartbeat quickening. Bloody footprints were still wet on the wood floor. He thought he should alert Robitaille, who was inspecting the dining room, but he was unable to move, rooted to the spot by the force of his imagination.

What would he find at the end of this hallway?

Not a dead child. He wouldn't be able to bear it.

After shaking off the thought, he followed the trail of footprints and traced them back to another room. The door was ajar. The hallway was dark, and for a moment everything seemed to sway before him. An irresistible force drew him forward. His eyes were glued to the strip of light showing under the doorframe, and his heart pounded wildly in his chest. He stepped up to the door and knocked loudly.

"Police!"

Not a sound. Victor lunged at the door and pushed his torso through the opening, pointing his pistol into the room, ready to fire at the slightest provocation. For a moment, he thought the room was empty—until he saw what was there on the floor.

It took a moment for the nausea to come over him. His gallery of phantoms had just come alive again, the one that had haunted him since that July day in 1976 when his father had savagely murdered his mother and his brother Raymond, before turning the gun on himself.

Victor swallowed. He felt an immense pressure in his chest. At his back, his partner's voice startled him.

"Oh fuck. We'd better call backup."

Robitaille's eyes widened in horror as he saw what Victor had been staring at: on the ground, a kitchen knife bathed in a pool of blood, strewn with short hairs.

A message had been traced with fingers on the floor: *Together for eternity.*

Defying the cold, the howling wind and snow gusts bending the cemetery trees, the young man in the denim jacket slowly approaches Zourek, whose face is now livid.

"There was another disappearance, Arthur. Right next door to you. What a coincidence, eh?"

"Why are you telling me this, Jérôme? What are you trying to insinuate?"

The young man stares at him with eyes full of reproach. "You know very well why I'm telling you this. There were others after—"

"Nasty little liar! You think you can mess with me?"

"Why so aggressive? After all these years . . ."

Arthur Zourek's vision begins to blur. "You took her from me . . . She was my life . . ."

Jérôme shakes his head. "You've never accepted the truth. *I'm* the one who should be angry."

Zourek's eyes open wide as he murmurs, "The bloodshed did me good. It calmed me."

The young man clenches his fists. "What are you hiding in that suitcase, Arthur? Let me see." Jérôme steps forward and fixes the old man with his sullen eyes. Before Zourek can react, the young man grabs the handle of the suitcase and yanks at it with all his strength. The old man clings to it with the force of his despair.

Suddenly the buckles give way and the lid of the suitcase opens, sending its contents flying through the air before falling silently on the snow, near the front of the headstone. Struggling against his fatigue, the old man crawls forward and retrieves a small, blood-soaked corpse. He hugs it to his chest, murmuring words of comfort.

As they continued to search the apartment, the policemen discovered another room, meticulously clean. A little girl's room frozen in the 1950s. They'd also found, near the pool of blood, a photo album with a warped cover.

After donning latex gloves, Victor examined the photos. The album contained carefully organized newspaper clippings spanning four decades. The oldest one was from 1951, the most recent from December 1992. Victor skimmed through the clippings and quickly found a common theme: they were all related to the disappearances and murders of children in Montreal.

A stack of utility bills and invoices landed on the table. Victor looked up at his partner.

"I found those on the corkboard. Apparently, the tenant's name is Arthur Zourek."

"You checked with Central to see if he has a record?"

Robitaille nodded. "No record, but he was interrogated in relation to a murder in 1959. No charges made, though."

Victor frowned. "You have any more details?"

"Files from before 1980 haven't been computerized. They're digging through the archives."

Robitaille came up behind his partner and started to read over his shoulder.

The most recent newspaper clipping cited the disappearance of an eight-year-old girl in a park in Côte-des-Neiges.

"The last disappearance happened three weeks ago," Victor said softly. "Are you thinking what I'm thinking?"

"That we're just around the corner from Jean-Brillant Park?"

The two policemen looked at each other.

"We should call major crimes," said Robitaille.

Even though his partner had more seniority, Victor had gained a kind of authority over him. So Robitaille did not take offense when Victor said, "Call Ted Rutherford. Tell him you're my partner and that we need his help."

"You know Ted Rutherford? He's a legend."

Victor almost explained that Rutherford was the first officer to arrive at the scene of his family's massacre, that the star investigator had been his inspiration to pursue police work. But instead, he bit his lip.

As Robitaille headed for the wall phone, Victor continued examining the newspaper clippings. He found the oldest ones and read them carefully, wondering what it all meant. Then his gaze fell on one of the bills that Robitaille had left on the table. An idea crossed his mind. And then it clicked.

Victor shot out of his chair and headed for the door. Robitaille, who'd been on hold the past few minutes, asked where he was going.

"Hang up. We're leaving."

Robitaille cupped his hand over the phone. "Why? Where are we going?"

Moving quickly, Victor answered without turning around: "Notre-Dame-des-Neiges Cemetery."

The old man cradles the body against his coat, and screams over the roar of the wind. Flurries of snow swirl around the headstone. "You see what you've done, you little bastard? Leave us, now!"

Jérôme opens his mouth to reply, then thinks better of it. The two stare at each other for a long moment. The young man eventually winces, turns on his heels, and walks away. Before he vanishes into the snowdrift, the old man notices that the back of Jérôme's head is covered in blood. And through his shattered cranium, brain matter glistens.

Arthur Zourek closes his eyes.

Bathed in the glare of revolving headlights, the policemen sat motionless in a contemplative silence. They'd easily found the spot and parked the patrol car a block away.

When they arrived at the cemetery, the snow on the ground was perfectly smooth; the wind had swept away any footprints around the headstone. An open suitcase lay a few meters from the grave. An empty bottle of pills, a girl's clothing, and toys stained with blood were scattered in the snow like bizarre offerings.

Robitaille spoke after a long moment: "How'd you know about the cemetery?"

Lost in his thoughts, Victor took a moment to reply. "One of the bills you found was a statement from the cemetery, for the maintenance of Florence and Rosalie Zourek's graves."

Robitaille shook his head. "I mean, how'd you know he would come here?"

"I read the oldest newspaper clippings, the ones about the unsolved murder of little Rosalie Zourek, six years old."

"The daughter of Arthur and Florence Zourek . . ."

Staring into the distance, Victor nodded. "Then I remembered the words *together for eternity* written next to the pool of blood. It made sense when I saw the bill. It was intuition, really."

"And the pedophile who had his skull bashed in by a hammer in 1959? You think the old man killed him? Zourek was the only witness interrogated by the investigators."

On their way to the cemetery, Central had given them the information from the archives about the murder of Jérôme Gaudreau, a thirty-five-year-old repeat offender convicted of sexual violence against minors. At the beginning of 1953, Gaudreau had been suspected of committing a series of child abductions. But he'd been released a few days later, after he was cleared due to insufficient evidence.

Victor shrugged his shoulders. "The abductions apparently continued after Gaudreau's death."

"Poor old man. To end like that . . ."

Victor nodded, choked up with emotion. His head was full of grisly images, disfigured by time, and he stared at Arthur Zourek's frozen body, partially covering the headstone.

ROSALIE ZOUREK
1945–1951
FLORENCE ZOUREK
1922–1963
ARTHUR ZOUREK
1918–

In his arms, the old man clutched a disemboweled cat. He held it as one holds a child. As he would have held his little Rosalie more than forty years earlier.

ABOUT THE CONTRIBUTORS

Frederick Duchesne

SAMUEL ARCHIBALD is the author of the short story collection *Arvida*, which was short-listed for the Scotiabank Giller Prize and the Best Translated Book Award. He lives, writes, and teaches genre fiction and creative writing in Montreal. He is also a playwright, screenwriter, baseball coach, and avid fly fisherman.

Jean Estevez

KATIE SHIREEN ASSEF is a writer and translator of French. Her first book-length translation was Akashic's *Brussels Noir*, and her translation of Valérie Mréjen's novel *Black Forest* is forthcoming from Phoneme Media. Her work has been featured in journals such as *Drunken Boat*, *FENCE*, *Epiphany*, *Joyland*, *PANK*, and *Sakura Review*. She lives in Los Angeles.

Olivier Basilières

MICHEL BASILIÈRES was born and raised in Montreal's Milton Park neighborhood. His first novel, *Black Bird*, won the Amazon.ca/Books in Canada First Novel Award and was short-listed for the Stephen Leacock Memorial Medal for Humour. His second novel is *A Free Man*, and he currently teaches creative writing at the University of Toronto's School of Continuing Studies.

Jane Heller

ARJUN BASU is the author of *Squishy*, a collection of short stories short-listed for Canada's ReLit Award. *Waiting for the Man*, a novel, was long-listed for the Scotiabank Giller Prize in 2014. Born and raised in Montreal, he lives in the Mile End neighborhood, where he has never seen a single horse. He is currently at work on his next novel, and the one after that.

Jacques Filippi

JACQUES FILIPPI started his career as a journalist and has now been a bookseller, translator, sales representative, and editor for almost twenty years. He started his blog, *The House of Crime and Mystery*, in 2011, and cofounded the QuébeCrime Writers Festival a few years later. His blog is now a website where you can read his reviews, interviews, and other views. He is also hard at work on a trilogy of crime novels.

TESS FRAGOULIS's first book, *Stories to Hide from Your Mother*, was nominated for the Quebec Writers' Federation Best First Book Award. In 2003, her novel *Ariadne's Dream* was long-listed for the International IMPAC Dublin Literary Award, and received an honorable mention for the Amazon.ca/Books in Canada First Novel Award. Her latest novel, *The Goodtime Girl*, was published in 2012. Fragoulis lives, writes, and teaches in Montreal.

PETER KIRBY was born in Ireland, grew up in Brixton, and spent years as an itinerant cook in the US before settling down to study law in Montreal. He is the author of the Inspector Luc Vanier series, and his latest novel, *Open Season*, won the 2016 Arthur Ellis Award for Best Novel. He practices international law and has been recognized by *Benchmark Litigation* as a star in international arbitration; the magazine *American Lawyer* has named him as one of Canada's leading 500 lawyers.

GENEVIÈVE LEFEBVRE is a scriptwriter, translator of plays, novelist, speechwriter, columnist, and regular contributor to online and print publications like *Châtelaine, Elle Québec, Clin d'oeil,* and the *Journal de Montréal*. Her most recent novel, *All the Times I Never Died,* was published in early 2017. When she's not writing, Lefebvre runs with Maggie, her canine sprinter.

JOHN MCFETRIDGE was born and raised in Greenfield Park (now part of Longueuil) on the South Shore of Montreal. He is a graduate of Concordia University, and the author of the Eddie Dougherty series (*Black Rock, A Little More Free, One or the Other, Another Brick in the Wall*). McFetridge has also written for film and television, and is the coeditor of the anthology *2113: Stories Inspired by the Music of Rush.*

CATHERINE MCKENZIE is the best-selling author of six novels, the latest of which is *Fractured*, named one of the 25 Big Books of Fall 2016 by Goodreads. She is also the author of the legal thriller *The Murder Game*, written under her pen name, Julie Apple. She writes and lives in Montreal, where she attended McGill Law School, and works as a lawyer.

MARTIN MICHAUD has been hailed by critics as the "thriller master of Quebec." His seven crime novels are best sellers in Quebec and Europe, and he has received the Arthur Ellis Award, the Prix Saint-Pacôme, and the Tenebris Prize. His Victor Lessard series is now adapted for television, and the movie rights for his stand-alone thriller *Beneath the Surface* have been optioned in the US.

ROBERT POBI is a best-selling novelist whose work has been published in more than fifteen countries. He divides his time between Montreal, Florida, Northern California, and a cabin on a lake in the mountains somewhere. His first short story (written when he was twelve) earned him an expulsion from school. He has given up collecting speeding tickets and spends his spare time avoiding social media.

PATRICK SENÉCAL was born in Drummondville and published his first novel in 1994. Four years later he published the best-selling novel *On the Threshold*. His books have been translated into many languages, and a few have been adapted into successful movies. Well known for his horror novels, he nonetheless lives a quiet life with his wife and two kids.

JOHANNE SEYMOUR worked as a screenwriter and a TV director before she started writing the Kate McDougall novels in 2015. The five volumes are now published in Europe and *The Scream of the Deer,* the first in the series, has been adapted for TV. Seymour was also the founder of Les Printemps meurtriers, which was a popular crime festival in her town of Knowlton, Quebec.

HOWARD SHRIER is a two-time winner of the Arthur Ellis Award. His acclaimed novels include *Buffalo Jump, High Chicago, Boston Cream,* and *Miss Montreal.* Born and raised in Montreal, Shrier started out as a crime reporter at the *Montreal Star,* and has since worked in theater, television, sketch comedy, improv, and corporate and government communications. He lives in Toronto with his wife and sons, and teaches writing at University of Toronto's School of Continuing Studies.

Lorraine Sommerfield

BRAD SMITH is a novelist and screenwriter who was born and raised in the hamlet of Canfield, in southern Ontario. He has lived in South Africa, Alberta, British Columbia, Texas, and has worked a variety of jobs—farmer, signalman, insulator, truck driver, bartender, schoolteacher, maintenance mechanic, roofer, and carpenter. Smith has published nine novels and adapted his 2003 book *All Hat* for the screen. It premiered at the Toronto International Film Festival in 2007.

Mary Lee Maynard

IAN TRUMAN is a novelist, poet, and visual artist from the East End of Montreal. He is a fan of dirty realism, noir, satire, punk, and hardcore, and hopes to mix these genres in all of his work. A graduate of Concordia University's creative writing program, he won the 2013 Expozine Alternative Press Award for Best English Book.

Yves Renaud

DONALD WINKLER is a three-time winner of the Governor General's Literary Award for Translation (French to English).

Jordan Matter

MELISSA YI is an emergency physician who writes mystery novels. CBC Radio's *The Next Chapter* selected *Stockholm Syndrome*, her medical thriller about a Montreal hostage situation, as one of the best crime novels of summer 2016. Yi's short fiction has appeared in *Sleuth Magazine*, *Indian Country Noir*, and *Fiction River Special Edition: Crime*, which was nominated for the Derringer Award. In her spare time, she chases after two small children and one large rottweiler.